Praise for *Promise Me Something*

"Kocek's hard-hitting first novel offers smart dialogue, sharp descriptions, and a plot that unfolds in unexpected ways, as she explores the destructive power of casual, everyday homophobia."—*Publishers Weekly*

★"High school as crucible of character is a mainstay of teen fiction, but seldom have its dilemmas and dramas been so precisely re-created in all their brutal, claustrophobic intensity as in this debut: part morality play, part suspense tale... Compelling, honest storytelling."—*Kirkus Reviews*

"*Promise Me Something* tackles weighty issues of harassment, family dysfunction, suicide, and homophobia within the context of adolescent identity and friendship, while maintaining the focus of the story on characters whose complexity feels real and whose lives may be our own, our next door neighbor's, or our best friend's."—*VOYA*

"The heavy themes are explored as gently as possible without glossing over uncomfortable situations. All of these elements, including a plot twist, make this book a better-than-average problem novel."—*School Library Journal*

"The topics of bullying and LGBT teens are well chosen and provide realistic insights into discrimination of gay teens."—*Booklist*

promise me something

promise me something

sara kocek

ALBERT WHITMAN & COMPANY
CHICAGO, ILLINOIS

Library of Congress Cataloging-in-Publication data
is on file with the publisher.

Text copyright © 2013 Sara Kocek
Hardcover edition published in 2013 by Albert Whitman & Company
Paperback edition published in 2015 by Albert Whitman & Company
ISBN 978-0-8075-6643-5
Printed in the United States of America
10 9 8 7 6 5 4 3 2 1 LB 20 19 18 17 16 15

Design by Ellen Kokontis and Jenna Stempel
Cover images © mitarart/Veer and Shutterstock.com

For more information about Albert Whitman & Company,
visit our web site at www.albertwhitman.com.

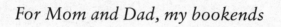
For Mom and Dad, my bookends

"There is a crack in everything. That's how the light gets in."

—Leonard Cohen

The night Olive Barton vanished into the woods at Talmadge Hill, I got my first kiss. I was wearing sticky drugstore lip gloss that smelled like a Creamsicle. Sugar-drunk off cherry soda and peppermint patties, I had no idea that a mile away in the frigid dark, the night was opening its mouth to swallow a girl.

September

We moved en masse like a rain cloud, past the gray lockers and matching gray walls, past the boys' bathrooms by the stairs, past the wads of gum wedged in the hinges of the windows. Everybody coming from Mr. Murphy's history class had their tests in their hands—for me, my first test of high school. The crowd pressed in on us from all sides as we squeezed through the double doors and into the cafeteria. No matter what day of the week, it smelled like Sloppy Joes.

I unrolled my test to look again at the *A+* on the top of the page, and that was when I heard the voice behind me. "Congratulations," it said, barely audible over the cafeteria roar. I turned around and saw the shy, mousy girl who sat behind me in history. Her face was thin and pale, half hidden by a curtain of dull blond hair. She was wearing a button-down yellow blouse and black tights under a plaid skirt. "You must have studied hard," she said, only her voice wasn't mousy at all. It was quiet and razor thin.

The crowd pressed us deeper into the room. We streamed past the vending machines toward the hot lunch station, where three women in hairnets served up the usual globules of organic matter that varied in appearance but not taste from day to day.

"I got a C," said the girl, now beside me. Her two front teeth tilted toward each other like they were afraid of the other teeth. "I'm Olive, by the way."

"Nice to meet you," I said, picking up a tray. It didn't take a genius to tell that Olive wasn't popular. On the totem pole of faces at Belltown High, hers was stacked somewhere just above the girl with the unibrow and the boy who wore sweater-vests every day.

"I don't know if you've noticed," she said, stepping closer to me and scooping corn onto her plate, "but we have two classes together. And homeroom."

I nodded, a flicker of hope in the pit of my stomach. Olive may have been dressed like a Sunday school teacher, but she was the first person all week to notice me. "English and history, right?" I asked, reaching for the slotted spoon. Friends were friends, popular or not.

"Yeah." She tucked a strand of stringy hair behind her ear and moved on to the mashed potatoes. "I've been trying to figure you out. Are you aloof because you're shy? Or are you aloof because you're a snob?"

"Aloof?" The little flame of hope extinguished itself.

"No offense."

"I'm not aloof." I turned around to see whether anybody in the lunch line was listening, but fortunately only a group of boys was standing behind us and they weren't paying attention.

"Then how come I never see you talking to anyone?" Olive asked, plucking a square of pepperoni pizza out of the tray. "It doesn't make sense. You look like a cheerleader."

In the shiny stainless steel pole holding up a rack of milk cartons, I watched my warped eyes blink. What did that even mean?

"My friends go to Ridgeway," I said at last, choosing a slice of pizza and sliding my tray toward the register. Ridgeway was Springdale's other high school, and it was usually referred to as "Richway" because of its special architecture program and carpeted hallways. Finding out that my house had been redistricted to Belltown High was one of my all-time worst memories of eighth grade.

"They *all* go there?" Olive dug around in her pocket while the lunch lady rang up her total. "It must suck not having any other friends."

"It's not like that," I said, looking around for an open spot to sit. Olive was turning out to be weirder than I thought. She wasn't anything like my Ridgeway friends.

"You want to sit together?" Olive asked. "I mean, unless you have other plans?"

"I kind of have to study," I lied, craning my neck to see whether there were any free spots at the homework table, where people sat silently and worked while they ate. No luck.

"Can't you study after school?" Olive asked. "Or will you be too busy hanging out with your Ridgeway friends?"

"We mainly see each other on weekends," I told her, glancing over at the corner of the cafeteria where the band kids sat. No spots there either.

"On weekends," Olive echoed. "I wonder how long that'll last."

We wound up at a table near the far left window, where the

student teachers usually ate. Today it was empty, so Olive spread her stuff across one of the benches. I put my backpack down on the floor next to my feet and resigned myself to sitting with her.

"I've been meaning to ask you," she said, "what do you think of Ms. Mahoney? Did you see how she spelled *controversy* on the blackboard?"

Ms. Mahoney was our English teacher—straight out of college and new to the school. I liked her just fine except for the way she always forgot my name. "I think she's nice," I said.

"Well, I think she's an idiot." Olive took a swig from her Coke bottle. "What kind of English teacher can't spell *controversy*? If she spells it wrong again, I swear to God I'm going to say something." She wiped her mouth with the back of her hand. "What?"

"Nothing."

"No, what is it?" She put down her soda. "Tell me."

"It's nothing," I said again. "It's just—can you not swear to God around me?" I felt stupid as soon as I asked. I knew I shouldn't have phrased it as a question.

She laughed but then stopped at the expression on my face. "Wait, seriously?"

Why did people always think I was joking? I was tired of explaining myself. I put down my slice of pizza and said, "Seriously."

"Sorry." Olive straightened her face. "Are you Mormon?"

"Catholic," I said, taking a sip of chocolate milk. "What are you?"

She laughed. "Recovering Catholic."

Recovering from what? I wanted to ask, but I didn't get a chance. Out of nowhere, something thwacked me in the back. I whipped around, confused.

It was a banana. A banana in the hand of a cute boy in flip-flops, sprawled out on the floor behind me.

"Sorry," we said at the same time. Then I reached down and yanked my backpack out of the middle of the aisle, where he'd tripped over it. As I stuffed it under my seat to hide the evidence, he rose to his feet and brushed off his jeans. "Are you OK?" I asked, staring at his hair. It was coppery, the color of a brand new penny.

"Yeah, my fault," he said, grabbing the bruised banana and shoving it in his pocket, where it stuck out like an odd yellow handle. Only then did I recognize him. We had gym together first period every Monday, Wednesday, and Friday. I was used to seeing him in long nylon shorts.

"Have we met?" he asked. "You look familiar."

"Yeah," I said. "In gym." Around his neck hung a guitar pick on a leather string. It was twisted around, and I had the urge to reach over and turn it in the right direction.

"What's your name?"

"Levi," I said.

He laughed. "No that's *my* name."

Across the table, Olive snickered as I snapped back to life. "Reyna," I corrected myself, wishing she would shut up. "Reyna Fey."

"Rain-uh?" he repeated. "Like the weather?"

5

Olive let out an exaggerated snort.

Levi paid her no attention; he just looked at me like he was trying to figure me out. His eyes were warm and brown with little flecks of gold. After what felt like an eternity, he said, "Well, see you later, Rain-uh," and headed toward the double doors.

Olive pushed her Coke bottle toward me the minute he walked away. "You poor thing," she said. "You're bright red. Have a drink."

"What just happened?" I held the bottle to my forehead.

She laughed. "You acted like a moron and he thought it was cute."

A moron? I felt like crawling under the table and hiding there for the rest of the day. "It was something about his eyes," I said, slouching in my seat. "I just couldn't think."

"That much," she said in a sarcastic drone I would come to know well, "was obvious."

I probably shouldn't have walked with Olive to our next period after lunch since I wasn't sure I wanted to be friends with someone so judgmental. But she just kept talking after the bell rang, and it was hard to cut her off or break away. And when she followed me into the parking lot at the end of seventh period, I didn't stop her. To be honest, it was nice to have company, even if that company was so...Olive-ish.

We sat together on the ledge of the stone wall in the parking lot while we waited for our rides, Olive quizzing me like I was filling out an application to be her friend. "So, you're religious, right?" she asked as soon as we sat down. Her fingers found a few loose pebbles and flicked them over the edge, one by one. "Don't tell me you're a Republican."

"I'm not," I said, wondering why she thought it was OK to say whatever popped into her head, no matter how rude. "But I'm not a Democrat either. I don't care about politics."

She frowned. "You should care."

I watched as an old, beat-up station wagon pulled into the driveway, passed the bus lane, and parked in a handicapped spot.

"At least tell me you're pro-choice," she said, watching me intently. When I shrugged my shoulders, she threw her hands in the air and sighed. "I don't get it."

"What?"

"Connecticut is a liberal state. We have Democratic senators. We have gay marriage. Yet, somehow, everybody in this school is Sarah Freaking Palin."

"I have to go," I said.

"See, that's exactly what I'm talking about. If you just walk away from every political debate without even trying to—"

"No, my dad's here," I said.

"Oh." She turned to look out across the parking lot, but I didn't point out my father's car. I didn't want her to see his face behind the windshield—still purple and bruised from the accident.

I hopped off the wall and as I turned toward Olive to say good-bye, she tossed a pebble that narrowly missed my ear. "Hey!" I blurted.

"Do me a favor and pass me my notebook?"

I stared at her in disbelief. What kind of person throws a pebble at someone's head? But she didn't even blink. Reluctantly I asked, "What notebook?"

Olive grinned. "The one where I write mean things about you."

Not funny. The more time I spent with Olive, the less I wanted to eat lunch with her again tomorrow. Then again, people at Belltown weren't exactly lining up to be my friends. A voice in my head whispered, *beggars can't be choosers*.

I crouched down and unzipped her backpack, fishing around for her notebook. I started to ask if I was looking in the right pocket but stopped when I saw it—a bloodred moleskin journal. The pages were so worn around the edges that I wondered whether she took it to bed with her at night to squeeze like a teddy bear.

"See it?" she asked.

"Yeah." I pulled it out. There was a stack of stapled papers underneath it—her history test, crumpled but visible, in the mouth of the backpack. It wasn't the test itself but the grade that gave me pause. Red marker stared me in the face: *A+*.

"Can you hand me a pen too?"

"Sure." I grabbed one from the front pouch and decided to ignore the grade. If she'd meant for me to see it, I had no idea why.

★ ★ ★

"Hi, kiddo." Dad looked more tired than usual, but his face was less puffy than it had been in weeks. His bruises from the accident had been fading all month from navy blue to purple to raspberry, and today they looked almost yellow. I pulled open the door and slipped into the seat as he turned the ignition. Once I buckled my seat belt, we pulled wordlessly out of the parking lot.

I wouldn't have minded a silent car ride—the stitches made it hard for Dad to speak—but as we turned left onto the main road, he opened his mouth and, with a lot of effort, asked who I'd been sitting with on the wall. "A new friend?" His voice was slurred from the disfiguration around his upper lip.

"Probably not," I answered.

"Come on." Dad was trying hard to enunciate. "Is she nice?"

I surprised myself by laughing. "Not really," I said. "She's weird and bossy."

Dad frowned with just one side of his mouth. "You've got to make new friends sooner or later, Reyna. Give her a chance."

We were driving north on Oakwood Avenue, Springdale's main artery. To our left was Durham Drive, where Abby, Leah, and Madison—my three best friends—lived in identical blue houses side by side; to our right was Hickory Ridge Road, where I'd lived since I was little in a house the color of a strawberry. Two roads, not a mile apart, rezoned for separate high schools that might as well have been on opposite sides of the universe.

"Guess what?" Dad said. "We're having pizza for dinner."

I didn't have the heart to tell him I'd eaten pizza for lunch. Ordering takeout was all he had the energy for these days.

"Is Lucy coming over to eat with us?" I asked. Lucy was the woman Dad was dating.

Dad adjusted the rearview mirror. "She's out of town."

"What?" I stared at him.

9

"She's out of town for a few days."

"No way," I said. "Again?"

"All of this has been hard on her." Dad gestured at the bruises on his face.

"It's been hard on *you*." I felt a lump gathering in my throat, felt the familiar swell. Dad glanced sideways at me and I turned my head quickly toward the window.

★ ★ ★

After dinner I felt sick. Greasy. Bloated. I'd eaten nothing but pizza for days. While Dad got settled on the couch in front of the TV, I headed to my room to "do homework," otherwise known as lying on the floor like a zombie.

Along the back wall of my room, Mom's old stuff lined my bookshelves. There was her tennis trophy, a hairbrush, a teddy bear she'd given me, her sewing machine, and, of course, her photograph. Taken on the day she graduated high school, it was browning in its turquoise frame. Turquoise was her favorite color, and one of my favorite things about the picture was how the frame matched the turquoise necklace she was wearing. I stared at the resemblance between us. I'd inherited her dark, bone-straight hair and deep-set brown eyes.

Next to the photograph was all her Catholic stuff. She had a string of rosary beads, three copies of the Bible, two crosses, and a tall silver chalice that belonged to my great-grandfather Francesco, who had been a priest in Spain. All of it had ended up in my room because Dad didn't like looking at it. After Mom died, he hated anything to do with God.

Everything on Mom's bookshelves had accumulated exactly

seven years of dust. I cleaned the rest of my room every two weeks, vacuuming in the closet and wiping down the surface of my desk. But I never touched her shelves, and the room was dusty as a result. Perpetually cloudy, like living in a place where it always rained.

Thinking of Mom, my eyes grew watery. I didn't really miss her anymore—seven years had blunted the ache—but I missed remembering her. I used to be able to recall the exact color of her lipstick and the sound of her laugh and the names of all the saints she prayed to. Not anymore.

I needed to call Abby to take my mind off things. Still sprawled across my carpet, I pulled out my phone and called Abby's cell, but she didn't answer. I called again and got her voicemail. I went back to staring at the ceiling before hoisting myself up to get on my laptop to see if Madison or Leah were online.

Madison was.

Hey Maddy, I typed.

Hey!!!!! she wrote back almost instantly. *What's up?*

A new instant message popped up. *Reyna!* It was from Abby. She had her status set to invisible, probably trying to hide from another boy with a crush on her.

Where are you? I tried calling you, I replied to Abby.

I'm with Madison. Hold on a sec. My phone was on silent. I'll start a group chat.

I wanted to vent about making a fool of myself in the cafeteria, but not with Madison there. She had a habit of making herself the center of every conversation. Plus, there was something weird about the three of us having a group chat when the two of them were together without me.

Madison wrote, *So, are you sleeping over tomorrow?*

I wish. Lucy's out of town, I replied.

That sucks, Abby typed and added a picture of a sad-looking puppy. *You shouldn't have to baby-sit your dad.*

My fingers hovered over my keyboard trying to think of a reply, but two more IM blips interrupted me. *OH MY GOD!!!!* Madison typed. *One sec.*

What's going on? I wrote back, but there was no answer. Whatever was happening—whatever they were talking about in her room—it was obviously too interesting to waste time typing about. Once again, I was out of the loop.

Finally there was a message from Abby. *Sorry!* she wrote. *Guy drama.*

Who? I wrote.

A sophomore at RHS, Madison answered.

RHS?

Ridgeway High School.

Right. The oasis my unfortunate street address had shut me out of.

Anyway, he's in geometry with us and he says he's going to write a mathematical proof that Abby's the hottest girl in the class. Madison sent me a screenshot of a guy with short black hair and pale blue eyes. He reminded me of a wolf.

I stared at Mom's old textbooks, trying to think of something to say. Then I wrote, *Isn't he a little stupid if he's a year behind in math?*

Whatever, Madison typed. *He's like twenty on a scale of one to ten.*

Apparently that's all the math you need in life, Abby wrote.

I have to go. I stared hard at the screen, fighting back tears, wishing I went to school with my best friends and wishing I could talk to Abby by herself.

Why? Abby asked. *Does your dad need your help?*

Yeah, I lied, *I have to go help him up the stairs.*

She and Madison sent more pictures of sad puppies and we agreed to have a sleepover the next weekend with all four of us, even though high school was turning Leah into a slut, or so Madison said. I signed off and closed my eyes. Relaxed my jaw. Thought about the color turquoise.

Who is this?

I saved your life. Remember?

Not you again.

Aren't you going to thank me?

The answer is still no.

How old are you?

Why do you want to know?

Just curious.

16, but I could be lying.

It's OK if you are.

Do you still want to talk?

2

I could have—should have—done more to shake Olive off. She was like one of those prickly thistles you pick up on your clothes while hiking, and by the end of September she had attached herself to me with a degree of persistence I found both annoying and admirable. No one had ever tried so hard to be my friend.

The point of no return came during history one morning when Mr. Murphy assigned us a project on ancient Mongolia to be completed in groups of two. Instantly, before he'd even finished his sentence, I felt a tap on my shoulder and knew it was Olive.

Ignoring it, I scanned the room, hoping to make eye contact with someone else. It's not that I wasn't grateful for Olive's friendship—she seemed interested in my stories about middle school, and eating lunch with her was less lonely than sitting at the homework table. I even snorted on my milk one day listening to her impersonation of Ms. Mahoney reciting Shakespeare. But none of it changed the fact that she was rude and pushy and wore pleated skirts from the '90s.

This was my chance to meet someone new. But no one was looking at me. The room began to buzz as the popular girls claimed each other. With no other choice, I turned around, expecting Olive to ask me if I wanted to be her partner. But she didn't. She just cocked her head to the side and waited, as though I were the one who tapped her.

"Want to work together?" I asked finally. It was either that or raise my hand to tell the whole class I needed a partner. Olive wasn't *that* bad.

She smiled. "Sure."

"Groups of two," called Mr. Murphy as the buzz in the room evolved into chitchat. Lennie King, a popular Asian girl, was showing somebody her double-jointed thumb, while Timothy Ferguson, a skinny boy wearing ear buds, sang to himself, "Keep your ey-eyes open, keep your ey-eyes open."

"Gaga!" barked Mr. Murphy. "Put away the iPod before I throw it out the window."

Tim turned pink and shoved the ear buds into his pocket.

"Listen up." Mr. Murphy surveyed the room with beady eyes. He had the short, stocky build of a drill sergeant and perpetually tan forearms. "I don't want any flashy business. You're putting together a PowerPoint presentation, not a song and dance. I don't want to see any fairy wings, especially if your name is Timothy Ferguson."

A few people laughed as Tim gave a nervous grin and flapped his arms like wings. Behind me, Olive tapped her feet on the metal bar below my seat, where my books sat.

"Here's the list of acceptable topics," Mr. Murphy finished, passing a short stack of paper down each aisle. "You have until Friday to pick one. Questions?"

While a few people raised their hands, Olive began scribbling notes. I could hear the faint scratch of her mechanical pencil as she applied pressure to the page. So far she hadn't spoken a single word in class all year, and I wondered if anybody else in school even knew her name. Then I realized a handful of people must have known her in elementary and middle school.

When he'd answered all the questions, Mr. Murphy turned on the overhead projector and began his lesson on ancient Chinese warfare. I settled into my chair, felt the brush of a knee across my lower back, and straightened up.

★ ★ ★

At lunch, Olive was waiting for me with her arms crossed over her chest and her chin jutting out. She scrunched her eyes and made her voice gruff. "Okay, listen up. I don't want any flashy business. This is lunch. We have spinach to eat. I don't want to see any fairy wings—"

I laughed and sat down across from her. Olive was definitely weird, but she could be sort of funny. Maybe our project wasn't totally doomed.

"This is not a song and dance," she continued. "Spinach is serious stuff."

"Mr. Murphy is kind of intense," I said, reaching down to slide my backpack under the seat where no one would trip over it.

"I know." Olive frowned, dropping the act. "Poor Tim Ferguson."

"Yeah."

Her face brightened. "I'm glad you and I are working together though."

I gave a halfhearted smile—my best effort.

Her face fell. "Is something wrong?"

"Of course not," I lied.

She sighed. "Look, I know it seems like forever ago, but I think we might have gotten off on the wrong foot on the day we met. I don't think you're aloof. I'm sorry I said that."

I didn't answer. I had a lot of reasons for finding Olive strange, and her insulting me within five seconds of introducing herself was only one of them.

"I think I probably scared you off," she went on, looking down at her tray. "With my honesty and everything. I do that to people—"

"Don't worry about it," I said, wishing she'd change the subject. Anyone else would have, but Olive had no awkward radar whatsoever.

"Well, I take it back. You're just private. That's what I think now. You keep your thoughts close to you. There's nothing wrong with that."

I almost said, *Yeah, you should try it.*

But then she surprised me. "Honestly, sometimes I wish I were more like you, Reyna. I probably wouldn't alienate as many people." Olive looked down at her blob of creamed spinach and poked it with her fork. "I wish certain things didn't come out of my mouth."

For a moment, I saw a glimmer of a girl I actually wanted

18

to be friends with. But then she shook her head and snapped back to her normal self. "In the end, though, I think it's better to be completely honest about what I'm thinking. You can always trust me that way."

"True," I said. On the plus side, it was nice to know she would never lie to me. Whereas I told a hundred lies every day—lies like *I feel fine* and *I don't mind*.

"Anyway, for our history project, how about we do feudalism?" she asked, reaching into her backpack to pull out the list of suggested topics. "It's *so* interesting."

I stared at her. Feudalism?

"I'm kidding!" She laughed. "It's called sarcasm, Reyna."

"OK, I thought you seriously wanted to do our project on feudalism." When I smiled this time, it was real.

"How about Genghis Khan?" She scanned the list of topics. "He was the vicious military guy who conquered half of China."

"Sure."

"Good." Olive grinned. "I'm excited. You want to come over to my house today to start the research?"

"I can't." I swallowed my mouthful. "I have to get home to my dad."

She looked disappointed. "Why? Does he have you on a leash?"

I sighed. There was no point in holding back the truth. "He has four broken bones," I said. "And I have to take care of him because I'm the only one—my mom died when I was seven."

"Shit." Olive put her plastic fork down on her tray. "Really?"

I looked out the window. "Please don't swear." Swearing was one of the things that reminded me of Mom—how she used to slap Dad on the knuckles anytime he did it.

"Well, I'm sorry for bringing it up." She took a swig of milk. "But you know something? I used to wish my mom would die."

She was watching me with a totally blasé expression like she'd just told me it was raining outside. I almost said, *Olive, this is one of those times when you might want to keep your thoughts to yourself,* but she beat me to it.

"Sorry—I guess that's inappropriate," she said. "Or insensitive or whatever."

I wondered if rudeness was something Olive had been born with, like a bad heart or webbed feet. If she didn't seem so clueless, I probably would have gotten up and walked away.

"I guess I wanted people to feel sorry for me," she went on. "I thought that if she died, they'd love me more."

"Look, I don't want to talk about it," I told her, rolling the napkin on my tray into a ball. "Can we change the subject?"

"Don't be offended," she said. "I know it doesn't work like that. One time in seventh grade my mom was late to pick me up from school, so I started thinking she got into a car accident. I walked all the way to the police station and told the cops, and you know what they did? They didn't comfort me. They just said, 'OK, kid, sit over there.'"

I waited for her to finish the story, but she just sat there mashing her fork into the curved surface of a tater tot. "My point is, life's a bitch," she said at last. "My mom wasn't in a car accident. She was getting a pedicure."

That was it—I'd reached my limit. Rising to my feet, I grabbed my backpack and said, "I have to go."

Olive's eyes widened. "What's wrong?"

"I told you. I don't want to talk about my mom."

She looked shocked. "I'm sorry. I didn't mean—"

"Was that story supposed to make me feel better?" I picked up my tray of spinach and potatoes. "Am I supposed to be happy your mom was getting a pedicure?"

"No!" she said. "But at least I'm being honest with you. I bet everybody else just says, 'Oh what a shame. I'm sorry for your loss.'"

It was true. That was exactly what most people said. It was called manners.

"Look, I'm sorry," she said again. "Please don't go. You're the only person in this school who needs a friend as much as I do."

I wanted to say, *Olive, you have a weird idea of friendship.* But I couldn't deny it. She was right.

"Fine." I sat down slowly and poked at the food on my tray. Olive and I might have less in common than a bird and a fish, but we were both alone.

Suddenly she put her hands on the table, leaned forward, and lowered her voice. "Don't look now, but your boyfriend's right behind you." She jerked her head to the left, and I turned around to see Levi, the cute boy in flip-flops, walking toward

21

me with a brown bag lunch. The world shifted. "Hey, Reyna," he said, bobbing his head at me. "What's up?"

"Not much." I scooted slightly on the bench in case he wanted to sit down at our table. But he didn't. He seemed to feel like standing up and swinging a key chain around his thumb.

"So," he said. "A little bird told me you guys have Mr. Murphy for history."

"We do," said Olive, her eyes narrowing. "Why?"

"I'm thinking of switching into his class," said Levi. "My schedule got all messed up when I quit band. What do you think? Is he good?"

"He's nice," I said.

Olive made a face. "You think everyone's nice, Reyna." She turned to Levi. "Mr. Murphy is a chauvinistic wannabe football coach who doesn't know the difference between who and whom."

"Cool," said Levi, meeting my eye. "I'll probably switch in, then. Thanks." Without even looking at Olive, he turned on his heel and headed for the door.

"What does he mean, *cool?*" Olive gaped. "I was trying to dissuade him. I don't want him distracting you from our project."

I shrugged, watching the back of his head as he moved through the crowd.

"No way is he joining our group," she said. "No way. No how."

★ ★ ★

She didn't have anything to worry about. When Levi showed up in history the next day, the first thing Mr. Murphy did was

22

pair him with John Quincy, the only other guy in class without a partner. I couldn't see Olive's face behind me when it happened, but I felt her feet tapping gently against the back legs of my chair.

"Don't think you can slack off just because you're new," Mr. Murphy told Levi, shoving a stack of handouts at him. "You'll have a makeup test this Friday on the material you missed."

Levi's mouth dropped open. "*All* of the material?"

Mr. Murphy gave him an evil smile. "Yes, all of it. Unless you'd prefer to wear this for the rest of the period." He stepped over to his desk, slid open a drawer, and pulled out a giant purple Dr. Seuss hat with the word *Sissy* embroidered on the rim.

Everyone laughed.

Mr. Murphy looked extremely satisfied with himself. "A gift from one of my old students," he told us. "Step out of line and you wear the hat. *Capiche?*"

Levi nodded and took the seat diagonally in front of me to my left. It was one of the only open seats in the room, and for that I felt fortunate—I'd be the one staring at him from behind; not the other way around. Mr. Murphy had barely begun to write on the blackboard when I felt a jab in the middle of my back. I whipped around and saw Olive wearing a poker face, staring straight ahead at the blackboard. I almost turned back around, but then I noticed her hand hovering awkwardly near the back of my chair. She was holding out a note, so I grabbed it and unfolded it.

Pay attention! it said in tiny, neat handwriting. *If your grades start slipping because you're besotted, you're not going to make a very good partner.*

I didn't write back. Who used the word *besotted* anyway?

★　★　★

Lucy came back that night. She parked on the street in front of our house and rang the doorbell as though she didn't own her own copy of the key. When I answered the door, I was expecting a deliveryman with our Chinese food. Lucy's face startled me.

"May I come in?" she asked, so tall and willowy that she had to bend her neck to look average height. I could see right away that something was wrong with her face. Her cheeks were puffy and red from crying.

"Are you OK?" I asked, stepping aside to let her pass. Her "weekend trip" to Michigan had turned into a two-week fiasco, and now that she was back, I wasn't sure what to think. Dad had called her twice yesterday and gotten no response. I was relieved to see she was alive but the sight of her also made me sick.

"I've been better." She gestured at her red eyes and gave me a nervous smile. "Where's Ethan?"

"Getting ready to eat," I said, trying not to breathe in her smell. The perfume reminded me of the day of Dad's accident.

"Thanks." As she swept past me down the hall, I wondered for the millionth time what on earth possessed my father to keep dating the woman who had crashed his car and nearly killed him. Was he a masochist? It just didn't seem right to me. Especially not after what had happened to Mom.

But tonight, after two weeks apart from Lucy, his face broke out in a grin when she walked into the kitchen. "There you are!" he said, knocking his chair as he stood to embrace her. He had to balance on the foot that wasn't in the cast. "Where have you been?"

"Sit." She crossed the room in two long strides and helped him back into his chair. "You'll break your other ankle."

"We thought you'd be back yesterday," said Dad. "Why didn't you answer your phone?"

"I'm so sorry, Ethan. " Lucy had bags under her eyes, and her short, feathery haircut was ruffled, like she hadn't taken a shower in days. "I wanted to call you and fill you in, but I just couldn't find a free moment."

"Is everything OK?"

"In a manner of speaking." She sat down on one of the other kitchen chairs and ran her manicured fingernails through her hair. "Right before I was supposed to drive to the airport, my mother had an episode."

"Episode?" I pulled out a chair and sat down.

Lucy glanced at me, then at Dad.

"Reyna…" Dad looked apologetic. "Could you give us a few minutes alone?"

I opened my mouth to protest, but at the look on Lucy's face, I changed my mind. She pressed her lips together, apparently reliving some terrible memory. So I stood up, gathered my sweatshirt off the kitchen table, and walked out of the room. Then I stopped in the hallway just around the corner and listened.

"Was it the epilepsy again?" asked Dad.

25

I couldn't hear what Lucy said, but I heard a chair scrape against the floor and imagined Dad leaning over to rub her shoulders. It was just like him to offer her a hug, even though he was the one who needed comfort. After all, she walked away from the accident without a scratch. Dad was the one who got pummeled.

Leaning closer toward the kitchen, I tried to hear what had happened to her mom, but I couldn't make out the words. All I could hear were a few phrases: "Epileptic seizure," "emergency room," "insurance policy."

Then Dad said in just above a whisper, "Shit. I'm sorry."

I leaned my forehead against the wall. I hated when Dad swore. Mom would never have tolerated it. It made me feel like he'd forgotten her.

"I know this is a horrible thing to say"—Lucy's voice was quivering—"but between taking care of you and taking care of my mom, I just need a few more days to take care of myself."

"I understand," said Dad.

"I'm a lousy nurse."

"Shhh." Dad was probably hugging her, stroking her hair.

I understood why she was overwhelmed, but it annoyed me all the same. Lucy had been driving the car when the accident happened—*she* was the one who blew the stop sign, and it was *her* fault Dad needed a nurse now. What gave her the right to complain? Retreating to my room, I headed straight for my laptop. Google loaded slowly as I stared at the screen. *How to get your dad to break up with his girlfriend*, I typed.

The doorbell rang again. Like an automatic reflex, I

closed the browser and stared at the turquoise wallpaper on my desktop. Dad and Lucy would get the door. It would be the Chinese food this time, and we would all sit down around the kitchen table to eat dinner together for the first time in days. There would be two portions of mu shu pork, Dad's favorite, and I knew he'd offer all of it to Lucy. At least it wasn't pizza.

I startled when I heard Lucy call from the front door, "Reyna! It's for you!" I stood and walked out of my room, confused. Did she want me to pay the delivery guy?

But as I rounded the corner and looked down the hallway, my heart leapt. Abby, not the delivery guy, stood in the doorway with Tupperware in her hands. Her long cinnamon-brown hair was pulled into a ponytail with little wisps flying around her face. Outside, Mrs. Stewart waited in their minivan, the engine still running.

"Abby!" I called, rushing to the door. "What are you doing here?"

"I can't stay," she said. "But I brought your favorite." She indicated the Tupperware.

"Chocolate toffee bark?" I took the container from her and peered inside. Sure enough, it was filled with slabs of caramelized dark chocolate. Leaning in to squeeze her around the shoulders, I said, "Thank you, thank you, thank you!"

"They're just leftovers," said Abby. But she was grinning, and I had a feeling she'd baked them just for me. I missed her so much right then. I wanted to drag her to my room and never let her leave. We'd talk for hours just like we used to,

27

analyzing our old teachers and naming our future children. Then we'd watch *American Idol* with Dad. He would stick up for all the terrible singers while Abby and I booed them. Lucy would leave, and everything would be back to normal.

But at that moment, the delivery guy pulled into our driveway and honked. Mrs. Stewart was in his way. "I better go," said Abby, leaning in to hug me again. There were strands of golden retriever hair stuck to her fleece jacket from her dog, Gizmo. The familiarity of it made my throat squeeze up.

"Can't you stay for dinner?" I asked. "We're having Chinese food."

Abby turned to face the driveway. From the front seat of her car, Mrs. Stewart held up her wrist and tapped the face of her watch.

"She can wait five minutes. Let's go to your room," Abby said, grabbing my wrist. "I have something to show you."

I followed as she tugged me down the hall. She was already taking out her phone and scrolling through the photo library by the time we got to my room. "You're not going to believe this," she said, holding out her phone so I could see the screen. "Look what Leah got this morning when she was supposed to be in science with me and Madison."

I stared at a photo of someone's ankle with seven pink stars drawn in the shape of the Big Dipper. Then it hit me. "Is that a *tattoo*?"

Abby nodded.

"Oh my God." I felt my mouth drop open. "How—where did she—"

"Micah," said Abby. That was all the explanation I needed. Micah was Leah's older brother, and he had six tattoos of his own. He probably knew just where to take her that didn't require parental permission.

"Wow," I said. "How is Madison taking it?"

"Oh, you know Madison." Abby cracked a smile. "She practically threw a tantrum."

I tried not to laugh. After all, it wasn't funny. Madison and Leah were planning to get matching tattoos when they turned eighteen. For Leah to get one first was unheard of.

"Anyway, I have to go," said Abby. "I just wanted to show you the photo."

"Her mom and dad must be pissed too," I said. I didn't want Abby to leave. I wracked my brain for something else to talk about—some reason she should stay.

"Not as much as Madison." Abby smiled. "But anyway, don't tell them I showed you the picture. Leah wants to show you yourself."

Mrs. Stewart honked in the driveway.

"Gotta go." Abby leaned in to give me another hug. Then, before I could think of another excuse to delay the inevitable, she was gone.

★ ★ ★

On Wednesday, Olive was in a good mood.

"Rarrrrrr," she said as I sat down next to her in homeroom before the first period bell. "I hear you're making a PowerPoint presentation about my conquest of northeast Asia. Rarrrrrr."

I laughed. "What are you, a dinosaur?"

"I am Genghis Khan, the punishment of God. I have come to pillage and plunder your village. You will surrender to my empire. Rarrrrrr."

I laughed again. Olive could be such a dork when she was in a good mood. It was kind of endearing, like how Abby and Madison used to pretend to talk to each other in Parseltongue whenever Abby's mom was nearby.

"Seriously," she said, smiling. "When are we going to work on our project if you have to be with your dad constantly?"

Behind her, a group of girls was whispering loudly. She turned a little farther in her chair to face me, ignoring them.

"We can do it this afternoon," I told her. "My dad's girl-friend is back in town."

Olive started to say, "I live on Cedar Street—" when the girls behind her erupted into giggles. "What?" she gave in, turning around. "What is it?"

More giggling.

"I'm not stupid." She gripped the back of her chair. "I can hear you."

"And we can hear you too," said a tall girl named Gretchen. She crossed her eyes and imitated Olive's growl. "Rarrrrrr."

Olive pursed her lips. "Is that all?"

"No," said Gretchen. "I want to know why you're wearing that uniform. This isn't a private school, Olive Garden." She laughed. "I mean—Olive Barton."

Olive's cheeks flushed, but she didn't back down. "Very funny. My name sounds like an Italian restaurant. You're so original, Gretchen."

"You didn't answer my question."

Olive smoothed her pleated skirt. "It's not a uniform if no one else wears it."

"Whatever," said Gretchen.

Olive stared at them for a second then turned around. "They are so deeply irrelevant," she told me. But the pink in her cheeks betrayed her.

I had the urge to say that the name Gretchen reminded me of a witch—that's what I would have said to Abby to make her feel better. But something told me Olive's good mood had vanished. Instead I blurted, "Why *do* you wear pleated skirts?" What I meant was, *what are you trying to prove?*

"Do me a favor, Reyna." Olive glanced over at the second hand on the clock, which was climbing steadily toward the twelve. I could see her eyeballs following it upward. The bell would ring at any moment.

"OK," I said. "What?"

She grabbed her backpack and stood up. "Follow your better nature."

★ ★ ★

Olive's house was big and clean, with large abstract paintings that resembled parts of the human digestive tract. When I stepped in, I was hit with a blast of air conditioning.

"Walk fast," she instructed. "My room's upstairs."

"Why?" I asked.

She rolled her eyes. "Because it is."

I meant *why are we walking fast?* But I didn't get a chance to say so. Before I could, a door opened at the end of

31

the hallway and a woman in a faux-silk nightgown stepped out. She was wearing hair curlers and carrying a glass of wine.

She was obviously Olive's mom. They looked exactly alike: the thin, angular face, the dull blond hair. Only her smile was different. It was wide and artificially white, like something from a toothpaste commercial. I heard Olive groan, barely audible. "Hi, Mom," she said.

Mrs. Barton was beaming at me. "What do we have here?"

"Hi—" I started to say, but Olive cut me off.

"Mom, this is Reyna. Reyna, this is my mother." She moved a step closer toward the staircase. "We're going upstairs to work on our homework."

"*Pleasure.*" Mrs. Barton stepped forward and extended a thin, bony hand.

"Mom, we have work to do," Olive said, grabbing hold of the railing along the staircase. "We'll be in my room." She stomped up loudly.

"Can I bring you a plate of cookies?" Mrs. Barton called after her, but Olive didn't answer.

"No thanks," I said and followed Olive up the stairs.

Olive was waiting for me at the top, standing in front of one of the bedroom doors. "Welcome to my prison," she said as she pushed open the door.

The room looked expensive and frilly, like it had been decorated years ago when Olive was in kindergarten. Everything was done in shades of white—the lacy bedspread, the curtains, the wicker dresser—except for the carpet and the throw pillows on the bed, which were the pale green color of sea foam. There were no posters on the walls, no books or magazines on the bookshelves, no stuffed animals on the bed—no trace of Olive whatsoever. There was only one book on her bedside table: *Anna Karenina*.

Olive didn't say anything at first. She was closing the door and pulling off her shoes and socks. Once she tossed them in the direction of the hamper, she muttered, "My mom's such a fake. Do we want a plate of cookies? Who does she think she is? Betty Crocker?"

"She seems nice enough," I said, sitting down on her bed. It was softer than mine; the kind that swallows you up.

"Of course she does," said Olive. "To you."

While I took off my shoes and set them neatly on the carpet, Olive walked over to the bedside table and picked up her book. "Tolstoy says that all happy families are alike." She thumbed through the first few pages. "And yet every unhappy family is unhappy in its own way. Doesn't that suck?"

"Why?" I said.

"Life is lonely enough already!" Olive burst out. "You shouldn't have to worry about being the only freak in the world with your particular problems."

The outburst reminded me of the time in fifth grade when Abby got angry at a book just for having the word *crazy* in the title. That was the day I found out she was adopted, and that her birth mother was mentally ill. Abby had been sitting on that secret for years just because she thought people would tease her for it. "You're not the only freak with your particular problems," I said to Olive. "Someone out there is going through it too. Trust me."

"Thanks." As she gave me a small smile, my mind jumped forward to the idea of inviting her to a sleepover with Abby and me. We'd have a lot to talk about when it came to our mothers.

But her face hardened quickly into a mask, the smile vanishing as quickly as it had come. "Anyway, let's not talk about my mom," she said, pulling our history textbook out of her backpack. "It'll only depress you, and you'll never want to come back here."

"It won't depress me." I wanted to tell her about Abby's birth mother, and how I'd heard much worse, but Olive shook her head.

"I don't want to talk about it."

"Whatever it is, you can tell me."

"Tell you what?" she burst out. "That my mom's drunk at three in the afternoon? I would think it was obvious."

"Oh." I felt like an idiot. So that was why Mrs. Barton was acting so friendly.

"Take a look at this." Pulling open the bottom drawer of a bright white filing cabinet, Olive showed me two bottles of whiskey, one bottle of vodka, and half a bottle of coconut rum. "This is what I've confiscated so far this week. And it's only Wednesday."

I hardly knew what to say. "She's an alcoholic?"

"Ding, ding, ding!" Olive clapped, a glint in her eye. "Give the girl a prize!"

"How often does she drink?" I couldn't even remember the last time I saw Dad open a bottle of wine. Alcohol gave him headaches.

"Reyna, it's not really a question of how often. It's how much."

"I know," I said. "But—"

"Look, it's not that complicated," Olive snapped. "She drinks. She gets angry. She says things she regrets. She drinks more. Do you want to start by taking notes on the Genghis Khan chapter? We can share my book."

"Relax!" I said. "I was just asking." So much for the sleepover idea. Olive was like a clam—every time I caught a glimpse of her softer side, she snapped herself shut.

"Sorry." Her eyes looked clouded. "Can we just do our work?"

We lay down side by side on our stomachs, the sea-foam carpet itchy against my elbows, as Olive flipped open her book to the section on ancient Mongolia. "You write down dates and names," she instructed, uncapping a ballpoint pen. "I'll look for the bigger picture stuff."

I almost protested, but the look on her face shut me up. So I read a paragraph summarizing the nomadic tribes of northeast Asia and had just barely gotten to the first mention of Genghis Khan when Olive finished reading the whole spread. "Tell me when I can flip," she said, waiting with her thumb and forefinger on the corner of the page.

"Flip," I sighed. "Whatever."

The clock on her wall ticked quietly above us as we worked, and before I knew it, my dad was honking in the driveway.

I'm glad you didn't...you know...

What, blow my brains out?

Pretty much, yeah.

I'm glad you didn't either.

How have you been since then?

Fine, I guess.

How have you really been?

I swear to God, better.

Then promise me something, and I'll promise the same to you.

I don't even know you.

Never. Lie. To. Me.

October

3

It was Saturday night, and Leah was sitting at the foot of her bed, braiding Madison's hair, while Abby sat cross-legged on the floor behind me, combing my hair with her fingers. We were taking turns giving each other French braids, but as usual, it wasn't about hair. Leah and Madison talked about boys and gossip while Abby tried to psychoanalyze all of us. As for me, I loved falling into rabbit hole conversations—those weird, quasi-philosophical discussions that anybody besides the four of us would have found stupid.

Abby straightened my part with her fingernail. "So, Reyna," she said. "Have you made any new friends yet at Belltown?" Her psychoanalysis had begun.

"Sort of," I answered, hoping to leave it at that. At our last sleepover, we talked about whether colors looked the same to different people, and how it felt lonely to live in a world where you couldn't be sure. I would have rather gone down that rabbit hole again.

But Leah spoke up a little too quickly, giving the conversation a rehearsed feel. "Belltown has super lame people," she said with a furtive glance at Abby. "I wouldn't be surprised if it takes you a while to find your crowd, Reyna. Don't feel bad."

They were obviously worried about me; otherwise they wouldn't have prepared talking points to make me feel better. My cheeks prickled. I didn't need their pity.

"You must have met *some* people," prompted Madison, eyeing me from the bed.

"I have," I sighed. If they were staging an inquisition, there was no avoiding the subject of Olive. "I've been eating lunch with someone. It's just—" I paused to think of the best way to explain it. "Have you ever been friends with someone you don't really *understand*?"

Leah and Madison nodded, pointing at each other. Then they laughed.

Abby asked, "What don't you understand about her?"

I thought of the time Olive threw a pebble at my head, but that seemed too weird to even describe. "Sometimes I like her," I said. "She can be funny when she's in a good mood. But most of the time she's in a bad mood. And then she's rude and bossy."

"Reyna, you have to stand up for yourself." Abby tugged on my hair. "Obnoxious people will take advantage of shy people like you."

"So true," said Leah. "Don't be a doormat."

Madison smiled. "Remember the time in fifth grade you let a boy draw on your pants with a sharpie because you felt bad saying no?"

"Can we talk about something else?" I asked. On Monday, Dad would be going back to work for the first time since his car accident; I would have liked to talk about that—to get the worry off my chest.

39

"Sure," Leah volunteered. "I hooked up with Drew Tubman."

"*What?*" Madison practically fell off the bed.

Leah giggled. "I've been waiting for the right time to tell you guys."

I wasn't sure what was worse—reliving embarrassing memories from elementary school or discussing high school gossip that had nothing to do with me. I decided it wasn't the right time to bring up my dad going back to work. "Who's Drew Tubman?" I asked.

"A sophomore on the varsity soccer team," said Leah, positively glowing. "I cornered him on the field after Thursday's match."

Madison looked meaningfully at Abby as though to say, *I told you this was going to happen.* Then she turned back toward Leah. "What base did you guys—"

"Third."

Madison gasped. "In the middle of a soccer field?"

"On the sidelines."

"Wait a minute, *which* third base?" asked Abby. We all knew it had several possible interpretations ranging from a hand down the pants to full-on oral sex. "A blow job?"

"The other one."

"Are you serious?" Madison's mouth was hanging open.

Leah laughed. "You guys will get there soon!" She sounded like a kindergarten teacher consoling a bunch of kids who failed to make it across the monkey bars.

"I have to go to the bathroom," said Madison, standing abruptly.

"Me too." Abby let go of my hair and stood up, obviously following to talk to Madison.

And that was how I ended up alone in the room with Leah, wondering how long it would be before the four of us didn't know each other at all.

★ ★ ★

On Sunday morning, I got up extra early and had the urge to go to Mass. I hadn't been in ages—not since Dad's accident. Mom used to go every weekend. Once in a while I would go just to feel closer to her, but sometimes being there would bring back too many memories and I'd have to get up and go to the bathroom to wait for my throat to stop feeling so choked.

Dad refused to come with me. ("Church was your mom's thing, not mine," he said.) He dropped me off while Lucy stayed home and cleaned the house. As we pulled into the church's circular driveway, I felt a swell of excitement in the pit of my stomach. But when I glanced over at Dad, his eyes looked distant and clouded.

"Memories?" I asked.

He nodded.

"Are you sure you don't want to come with me?"

"I'm sure," said Dad.

I rolled down the window to let in a gust of crisp autumn wind. The sky was a bright and vivid blue, the color of my old retainer—the one I got to match Abby's braces in sixth grade.

"I just thought it would be nice to go together," I told Dad, unbuckling my seat belt. "We can sit near the back, if you want."

"Reyna, that part of my life is over now," answered Dad, the expression on his face hard to read. "I'm going home to make an omelet."

"Have it your way." I climbed out of the car and closed the door. After seven years, I didn't expect anything different. I just wished he could see what I saw.

Inside, the sanctuary was soaked in light. It poured through the stained glass windows and lit up the hairs on my arms. Mom was everywhere at St. Stephen's—in every Bible, in every pew, in every nook and cranny of the sanctuary. Everywhere my eyes landed, I felt a memory move through me like a ghost. The day she took me to my first confession because I stole a dollar from Dad's wallet. The night she brought me with her to light a memorial candle for my great-grandmother Alma. The morning of my first communion, when she reminded me a million times not to spit out the wafer because I was a picky eater and she knew I wouldn't like the taste.

Dad didn't know what he was missing. In here, she was still alive.

★ ★ ★

In history on Monday, Olive invited me over to her house again after school. "Or we could work in the media center," she said, "but then we'd have to whisper." She didn't blink as she waited for my response, and it was hard to say no to a face that wasn't blinking.

We ended up agreeing to meet in the parking lot at the end of seventh period, and as I waited by the flagpole for her to arrive, I remembered with a jolt that it was Dad's first day back in the office. I pulled out my phone and texted him, *How's it going?*

Busy, he wrote back right away. *I have 900 unread messages!!!*

The exclamation points were a good sign. Dad only used them when he was in a good mood.

"What are you so happy about?"

I jumped. Olive had appeared out of nowhere, ready to walk with me to her house. "Nothing important," I said, slipping the phone into my pocket. "I'm ready if you are."

But she wouldn't drop it. "Exchanging texts with Lover Boy?"

"Lover Boy?"

"Banana Boy, if you prefer."

It took a minute to click, and when it did, I had to remind myself not to get annoyed. In her own way, Olive was just trying to be funny.

"No, I don't have Levi's number," I said. "I wish I did though." If I'd been walking with Abby or Leah or Madison, they would have said, "What are you waiting for? Ask him!" but Olive just made a sound somewhere between a cough and a snort.

"What?" I felt the familiar prickle of annoyance that always seemed to lurk under my skin whenever I was near her. "What's wrong with Levi?"

"Frankly? You want to know what I *really* think of him?"

"What?" I wasn't sure I wanted to know.

"As my Aunt Millie says, I've met more interesting carpet samples."

"At least he's friendly," I said. *Unlike some people.*

"Sure, he's friendly," she conceded. "Like a dog that walks up to another dog and sniffs its butt." Then she laughed at her own joke. "Plus, his hair is stupid. I hate red hair. Yours is so much prettier." Without any warning, she reached up and touched the back of my head. "It's so silky."

"Whatever," I said, stepping away from her hand. Why did she have to be so weird? For every rude thing she said to me, there was another opposite nice thing. The traffic light changed from red to green, and we crossed the street.

The worst thing about walking to Olive's house was crossing the train tracks that ran parallel to her backyard. Ever since Dad's accident, I was afraid of objects that moved quickly. Scratch that—ever since *Mom's* accident. No matter how many times I looked both ways before crossing the tracks, I always held my breath as I stepped over them.

Olive didn't understand, of course. When she saw me pause near the crossing gate, she just laughed, stepped out into the center of the tracks, and stood there with her arms wide open. "Hit me with your best shot!" she called in the direction of Talmadge Hill, where the next train would come from. Then she laughed, hopped off the tracks, and led me across the remaining distance toward the edge of her backyard.

Olive's mom wasn't home that afternoon, so we took a tub of ice cream and a canister of whipped cream to her room. She looked gleeful as we shut the door behind us. "I'm not supposed to eat junk in my room," she explained, handing me a bowl. "I do it all the time, but not usually with a friend over."

"Me too," I said. "Sometimes I eat cereal in bed."

"My mom would kill us if she saw this." Olive sprayed whipped cream directly onto her tongue. "She's opposed to gluttony of any kind, which is why she hates herself so much for being an alcoholic. And me, for being addicted to candy."

I put down my spoon, surprised. "You're addicted to candy?"

Olive scooted away from me on the carpet toward the same oversized filing cabinet where she'd shown me her mother's alcohol. Only this time she opened the middle drawer instead of the bottom one, so I got to my knees and leaned over to see what was inside. Sure enough, it was filled to the brim with candy. There were hundreds of Tootsie Roll Pops, miniature Twix bars, Starbursts, and lollypops. "I have a good metabolism," was all she said.

It might have been a sudden rush of sugar from the ice cream or it might have been the sheer quantity of candy in the drawer, but for some reason, I lost it. I started to laugh.

At first, Olive looked upset. She frowned, popped a Tootsie Roll into her mouth, and waited for me to collect myself. But I couldn't. It was impossible. Laughing, like crying, becomes an automatic reflex capable of sustaining itself, and the more I tried to stop myself, the harder I laughed. "I'm not laughing *at* you—" I tried to say.

Olive chewed her chocolate slowly and stared at me as though trying to figure out what was so funny, but when I finally fell over onto my side, something changed in her face. She covered her mouth with her hands and began to laugh.

We were both embarrassed. Neither of us knew what was so funny. But we just kept laughing, and before I knew it, we were hysterical. Bent over and gasping for breath, Olive took a handful of Tootsie Rolls out of the drawer and threw them at me. They landed in the folds of my blue jeans, so I scooped them up and threw them back at her.

Somewhere in the corner of my mind, I saw us as though from above: the two of us sprawled across her bedroom floor, pegging candy at each other and laughing so hard our sides hurt. We collapsed onto the carpet to catch our breath, Tootsie Rolls littered across the triangular spaces between our arms and legs.

Congratulate me.

For what?

I made a friend.

On the forum?

No, in actual life.

Wow.

I know, right?

What's she like?

Sad.

Ha. Go figure.

No, I don't mean like us.

You mean she doesn't have a
death wish?

**I mean she's sad but she doesn't even know
she's sad.**

How is that possible?

She's profoundly and sweetly sad.

Olive, have you gone off your meds?

I'm not on meds.

Are you OK?

I'm wonderful.

4

October twenty-first, the due date of Mr. Murphy's ancient China project, arrived amid a flurry of Halloween discussions across the school. In homeroom and in the hallways, everyone was talking about their plans for Halloween—even antisocial people like Olive.

"OK, here's the idea," she told me in homeroom on the morning of our Genghis Khan presentation. "I'll be the man with the pitchfork, you'll be the woman with the brooch." She was holding out a photocopy of the famous painting *American Gothic*. "We'll march together in the freshman parade, OK?"

I got the sense I didn't have much of a choice in the matter. Olive thought it would be a hilarious mockery of everyone who took the parade seriously. I thought it would be possibly awesome or possibly a disaster—I wasn't sure which.

Amazingly, Levi liked the idea. While we waited for the second bell to ring in history, he tapped me on the shoulder and asked what I was planning to be for Halloween. Olive was in the back of the room, setting up the overhead projector for our presentation, and Mr. Murphy was busy writing out a hall pass for Timothy Ferguson—or *Nancy* Ferguson, as he'd taken to calling him. So I showed Levi the grainy photocopy of the painting and said, "Olive thought of it."

He looked at it and grinned. "Awesome."

I almost said, *Really?* like an idiot but stopped myself.

Levi smiled. "Maybe I could be the frame around you."

I could've sworn I felt every little vein and capillary in my cheeks erupt, flooding my face with heat. I opened my mouth to say something, but he cut me off.

"Of course, then I'd have to be the frame around Olive too." He twirled his guitar pick necklace between his thumb and forefinger. "Too bad."

I wanted to say something flirtatious, but Olive chose that moment to summon me from the back of the room.

"Coming!" I called, trying hard not to trip over my feet as I stepped away from my desk. Then I turned and smiled at Levi, who was watching me with his head cocked to one side, as though he found me just as perplexing as the painting. "I'll see you later," I told him. And then, before I lost my nerve, "Maybe you can be the frame anyway."

In the back of the room, Olive looked tight-lipped and pale, turning every knob on the projector. "I don't know how this thing works," she muttered. "And I can't even think straight, I'm so pissed off."

"Pissed off?" I stepped back. "At me?"

"Not at you!" She turned one knob with so much force, I was afraid it would snap off. "Did you hear what Mr. Murphy just said to Tim?"

I shook my head and reached over to turn on the projector.

The bulb flickered on, casting a bright, blank light onto the screen across the room.

She narrowed her eyes. "He threatened to make him wear the sissy hat during his presentation, and then he called him *limp-wristed*."

"So?"

"He's a total homophobe. He hates gay people."

"I'm sure he didn't mean anything by it," I said, glancing over to check on Levi. He was still watching me, a smile in his eyes.

Olive's eyes flashed. "Are you serious, Reyna? Didn't you hear about that sophomore who had a breakdown last year after Mr. Murphy accused him of being gay? He had to go to Silver Hills." She lowered her voice. "The *mental* hospital."

"That's probably just a rumor," I said.

"Girls, are you ready?"

Olive jumped. Mr. Murphy had materialized behind us. I reached over to plug in the connector as he tapped his watch with one finger. A moment later, the image of Genghis Khan lit up the room. I felt unusually bold as I stepped forward, Levi's eyes following me the whole way.

"We're good to go," I said.

★ ★ ★

Strictly speaking, I didn't *need* to invite Olive over that afternoon. Our project was finished. But Lucy had been spending almost every night at our house, prowling around and rearranging the furniture like Mom never existed. Night after night I was forced to listen to Dad rave about what a good cook she was, which wasn't even true—all she ever made was pasta. So when Lucy pulled into the school parking lot and told me she was cooking lasagna for dinner, I decided company would be a welcome distraction. I ran back over to the edge of the parking lot to invite Olive. She said yes in a heartbeat.

The drive home was awkward. We were mostly silent, and when Olive did talk, she was so quiet she didn't sound like herself. The few questions Lucy asked—Are you buckled? Is the air conditioning reaching you?—Olive answered with a curt, "Yes, thanks," or "No, thanks."

When we got to the house, I led her straight through the garage, down the hallway, and into my room. It was the fastest path through the house, conveniently bypassing the messy living room. "Why are you always so shy around everyone besides me?" I asked, trying to distract Olive from all the crooked family photos on the walls. "Lucy probably thought you were mute."

She just shrugged. "How long has she been screwing your dad?"

"They've been *dating* since April," I said. "At least, that's when they met." I didn't like to think about Dad screwing anyone, least of all Lucy.

Reaching my room, I dumped my backpack on the rug next to the closet as Olive followed me inside and asked, "Why do you hate her?"

I paused in my tracks. "I don't hate her."

"You *so* do," said Olive. "I'm not blind."

51

"I don't know what you're talking about."

She rolled her eyes. "The hatred is practically dripping off you, Reyna. The whole ride home it was like you were sitting in a puddle of it."

I had to laugh.

She grinned. "I rest my case."

I glanced at the door to make sure it was closed. "I mean, she's nice, but I can't believe my dad is still dating her."

"Why not?"

I sat on the bed and told her about the accident—how Lucy drove right through the intersection without stopping. How Dad's car didn't have side air bags. How she was the reason I almost became an orphan.

"Yeah, but you didn't."

"Barely," I said. "There was a slab of glass an inch away from his spine."

"But she didn't *mean* for it to happen."

"She almost killed him!" The hair on my arms prickled. "Isn't that enough of a reason to want her out of my life?"

"Not if he really cares about her—"

"Can we just change the subject?" If Olive tried to defend Lucy for another second, I thought I might scream.

"Fine, jeez." Olive looked down at her fingernails. "What did you mean before when you said I act quiet around everyone but you?"

I leaned back against the headboard, relieved to talk about anything else. "Nothing, really," I said. "Just that you take your personality and zipper it up around everyone else."

She laughed. "Most people bore me to death."

I gave her a wry smile. "I'm glad I can provide amusement."

She moved toward the bookshelves along the back of the room and pulled out one of Mom's old tennis trophies. Dust came off on her fingers. "This was your mom's, wasn't it?"

I didn't answer. It was obvious—her name was on the trophy.

"How'd she die?" Olive set it back on the shelf. "You never told me."

I stiffened, and she came over and sat on the edge of my bed. "Sorry. I know I shouldn't be so cavalier about people dying. I was just wondering."

"You don't always have to blurt out everything on your mind," I told her. "You might actually have more friends if you didn't."

Her face softened. "It just means I trust you."

"I know." I relaxed my shoulders and tried to trust her too. "A drunk driver hit my mom when I was seven. On her way home from the grocery store. In the middle of the afternoon."

"Shit." The bed creaked as Olive leaned back and rested her back against the wall. "That sucks. I'm sorry, Reyna."

I opened my mouth to say thanks, but she didn't give me a chance.

"I'm not romanticizing tragedy or anything," she said, tucking her hair behind her ear. "But that's one of the reasons you don't bore me to death, you know? That you've had to deal with shit. Do you know what I mean? We have a lot in common."

I wanted to tell her that having a dead mother was nothing

53

like having an alcoholic mother, but I bit my tongue. It wasn't worth arguing over.

"Can I see this?" She picked up an old hacky sack that was sitting on my nightstand. As I opened my mouth to tell her it belonged to my mom, there was a soft knock on the door.

"Reyna?" Lucy poked her head into the room. "Madison's on the phone. She said she tried your cell, but it was turned off."

I jumped up and took the cordless phone out of her hand. "Thanks."

"No problem." She smiled as she turned to leave, like she was proud of herself for doing me a favor. I rolled my eyes at the back of her head.

She closed the door behind her.

I brought the phone to my ear. "Hello?"

"Hey, Reyna!"

Just by Madison's voice, I could tell she was with Abby and Leah. She always sounded extra hyper when they were together.

"Hey," I said, "What's up?"

Turning my back to Olive, I crouched and pulled my cell phone out of my backpack. Then I pressed the button to turn it off silent mode. Madison began babbling on the other end of the line about our annual Halloween party as I scrolled through my missed calls from during the school day. Two were from Leah, one from Madison. I also had a text that said, *CALL US ABOUT HALLOWEEN.* Every year since third grade, Leah threw a huge party on Halloween weekend, and it was always followed by a sleepover with just the four of us.

"So anyway, is seven to ten good for the party?" Madison was asking. "Because we have to send out the invites tonight if we want to compete with the other Ridgeway parties—"

"Um, actually, I can't come until ten," I said, realizing for the first time that the Halloween plans I'd made with Olive would overlap with the party. "I'm going with someone to the Springdale haunted house from eight to nine."

"Oh!" Madison sounded shocked. "A boy?"

"Just the girl I was telling you about."

Out of the corner of my eye I saw Olive's back straighten.

"Maybe you should bring her along," said Madison. "That way we can see for ourselves what's so weird about her."

"No, that's OK." I glanced over at Olive. Her ears were perked like a dog's.

"Come on! Bring her to the sleepover."

"I don't know if that's a good idea," I said.

"What does she want?" mouthed Olive.

I lowered the phone. "She wants you to come to Leah's sleepover after the haunted house on Halloween night."

"I'd rather have a sleepover with just the two of us."

I didn't say anything. I tried Olive's trick of staring without blinking. It worked.

"Fine." She rolled her eyes and sighed dramatically. "In the name of our friendship, I'll endure the adolescent torture ritual known as the slumber party."

"OK," I told Madison. "Olive is coming, and she says thanks for inviting her."

"I say no such thing," muttered Olive.

"Awesome!" said Madison.

We hung up and I sat back down on the bed near Olive. "Maybe it'll be fun," I said, trying to reassure us both. "I'm sure they'll like you."

She cocked an eyebrow at me. "Are you delusional? Nobody likes me."

★ ★ ★

When I got to school on the morning of Halloween, Mr. Mancuzzi, the principal, was standing in the parking lot threatening detention to anyone whose costume revealed more skin than was permitted by the school dress code.

Olive and I walked straight past him. Between her overalls and my long-sleeved blouse buttoned to the collar, our costumes were so modest they couldn't possibly get us in trouble. Or so we thought until Mr. Mancuzzi spotted Olive's pitchfork.

"Whoa, there!" he called after us. "Where are you going with that pitchfork, young lady?"

"What young lady?" Olive kept walking. "I don't see any young ladies around here."

"He means you," I said.

Mr. Mancuzzi was jogging to reach us. "Girls!"

"Why would he call us girls?" Olive's face was a careful mask. "I'm an old man, and you're no spring chicken."

I stopped and waited for Mr. Mancuzzi while Olive continued her somber march toward the school.

"It's part of our costume," I tried to explain when he reached me. "Without the pitchfork, nobody will recognize what we're supposed to be."

"And just what *are* you supposed to be?" He squinted at my blouse and apron. "Farmers?"

"Sort of," I said.

Mr. Mancuzzi scratched his moustache and looked up at Olive, who was watching us from the front steps with her mouth set in a grim line, just like the man in the painting.

"At least you're dressed appropriately," he sighed. "But if I hear one word today about the misuse of a pitchfork, I'll confiscate it. Got that?"

I nodded and jogged to catch up with Olive.

It was a mark of my invisibility at school that nobody commented on my costume during the day. Olive got made fun of—people joked that she was too convincing as an old man—but nobody said anything about my outfit one way or the other. I think it was because nobody knew my name. That is, until the parade.

If you ask me, everything that happened during seventh period was the fault of Gretchen Palmer—the girl from our homeroom who teased Olive for wearing a uniform to school. The minute she saw us at the parade, she called over her posse and started poking fun. "What are you supposed to be?" she asked, eyeing Olive's overalls. "Farmers or something? You look like you're from the Depression."

"Bingo," said Olive. "What are *you* supposed to be?"

Gretchen was dressed in a skimpy nurse's uniform that showed off her cleavage. It was a miracle Mr. Mancuzzi hadn't made her change her outfit. "A nurse," she said. "Obviously."

Her friends stood behind her and adjusted their stethoscopes. They were nurses too.

"I see," said Olive. "Well, you better go—you wouldn't want those cops over there to mistake you for prostitutes." She pointed at a group of boys dressed as police officers.

"*Excuse me?*" Gretchen was clearly itching for a fight. "Put down your pitchfork, loser, and apologize for that."

Olive just laughed.

"I said *apologize*, Olive Garden."

"Olive," I said, poking her in the side. "This is stupid. Let's go."

But she ignored me. "I'm not apologizing," she told Gretchen. "*You* apologize."

Gretchen grabbed one of her friends by the arm and stepped closer. "Do you want a fight? Because we're not afraid of a couple of dykes."

Anger flashed across Olive's face. "What did you just call us?"

"You heard me—dykes. And what are you doing with that pitchfork anyway? You can't bring weapons to school."

"The better to stab you with," Olive muttered.

Suddenly, without any warning, Gretchen faked an expression of terror. "Help!" She shrieked. "Help! The farm girls just threatened me with a weapon! Help!"

In an instant, Mr. Mancuzzi materialized with an entourage of security guards. They pulled the pitchfork out of Olive's hands and demanded my brooch with its pointy edges. The parade, which had been circling the gym, dissipated, and throngs of gypsies, zombies, and disco pimps ran toward us. As a security guard demanded that I empty my pockets, Levi Siegel showed up.

"Reyna!" he called, shoving his way through the crowd. "What's going on?"

Gretchen didn't give me a chance to answer him. "These freaks were threatening me," she told Levi in full earshot of the teachers. "They should be suspended!"

Levi frowned. "Reyna threatened you?"

But before I could speak up, Mr. Mancuzzi stepped in and put a hand on Olive's shoulder. "I want you in my office," he said. "You too." I felt a cool weight settle on my back, right below my neck.

"Leave Reyna out of this," said Olive. "She had nothing to do with it."

"She did too!" Gretchen looked around at all the teachers. "They both threatened me."

Olive gave her a murderous glare. "You can accuse me of whatever you want, Gretchen, but Reyna did nothing wrong."

"It's true," Levi told a security guard. "She's an innocent bystander."

I opened my mouth to speak for myself, but there was no need—Mr. Mancuzzi let go of my shoulder. "Just Miss Barton," he said impatiently. "In my office. Now."

Olive glanced at me, then turned stoically toward him like a man on death row.

"Everybody back to the parade!" barked the security guard.

"Olive," I called. "Are you going to be—"

"I'll be fine." Gritting her teeth, she followed Mr. Mancuzzi out of the gym as Gretchen and the rest of the slutty nurses turned on their heels and marched away.

I couldn't even process what had just happened. I felt faintly dizzy and took a few steps backward, looking for a spot on the bleachers where I could sit. That was when I felt Levi's hand on my arm. "Are you OK?" he asked, leading me toward an open seat in the front row.

"I guess," I said, sitting down.

He shook his head. "That girl's been in at least one cat fight every year since kindergarten. It's crazy."

"Who?" I asked. "Olive?"

He laughed. "No, Gretchen."

"Oh." I looked across the gym. She and her friends were now clustered around the bleachers on the other side, talking among themselves.

"Olive doesn't usually talk much," said Levi. "I always thought she was shy."

I smiled. "She's not shy at all."

"But you are."

My cheeks felt warm.

"Anyway, you want to know a secret about Gretchen Palmer?" He didn't wait for me to answer. "She has eczema covering her entire stomach."

I felt my mouth open. "How—?"

"Pool party," he said. "Eighth grade."

I tried not to smile.

"You want to walk in the parade together?"

60

"Sure," I said. But before we could even stand up, a teacher began clapping her hands at the top of the bleachers and calling for order in the gymnasium.

"Line up by homeroom!" she bellowed. "The parade is over! Line up by homeroom!"

So Levi and I stood up, waved each other good-bye, and went our separate ways.

I didn't see Olive until the sleepover that night. Our plan to visit the Springdale haunted house fell through when Mr. Mancuzzi called Olive's house and told her dad what had happened at the parade. Olive got grounded for about six hours before she was able to convince her parents that she hadn't done anything wrong. Then she was allowed to go to the sleepover.

When we rang Leah's doorbell at ten minutes past ten, Olive was wearing her shy girl mask. She had put on blue jeans and a modest, gray blouse, and I watched her tuck her hands neatly into her jacket pockets as we waited on the porch. I wondered if she was nervous.

"You don't have anything to worry about," I told her. "They're really nice."

She let go of a deep breath I hadn't realized she'd been holding. "I just want to make a decent impression for once in my life," she said. "I hope you know it's all for you."

I didn't have time to answer. There was a commotion on the other side of the door, and the next thing I knew, Leah, Abby, and Madison were barging out and smothering me in hugs. They were even more hyper than usual, probably from all the candy they'd been eating. Olive stood uncomfortably in the doorway while Abby threw her arms around my neck and said, "Reyna! We've missed you so much! You should've come earlier!"

"Guys, this is Olive," I said, extricating myself from the hug.

Olive opened her mouth to say something, but Abby didn't give her a chance. She and Leah descended upon her, squeezing her around the middle and pulling her inside. "It's so nice to meet you!" Abby squealed while Madison touched her on the arm and added, "Reyna's told us so many wonderful things about you."

"Nice to meet you too." Olive stood stiff as a board, waiting for them to let go of her. When they did, she looked disgruntled, like an animal at a petting zoo.

"Here, let me take that," said Leah, grabbing the sleeping bag from under her arm. "We'll be sleeping in the play room. Come on, I'll show you." She opened the door leading to the basement and we followed her down the stairs.

The basement was bright and colorful, just like I remembered it from past Halloweens. There were streamers hanging from the walls and special black and orange confetti pieces scattered on the windowsills. I could see the leftover snacks from the party growing stale on a foldout table by the wall. "Is that stuff still fresh?" I asked Leah.

"I don't know, maybe," she said, walking over to the table and breaking one of the cookies in half. "I was going to put it upstairs in the fridge, but then I got a little distracted…" She looked over at Abby and Madison and burst out laughing.

"What?" I glanced back and forth between them. "Distracted by what?"

Madison rolled her eyes. "Before you guys got here, some people at the party decided to play Seven Minutes in Heaven. Leah went in with Drew Tubman..."

"—And came out with this!" Leah pulled aside her wild, curly blond hair to show us the biggest hickey I'd seen in my entire life.

"Wow," I said. "That's like the size of a chocolate chip cookie."

Abby laughed. "I know, right? Let's set up our sleeping bags on the floor. Then we can talk about how hormonally crazed you are, Leah."

I glanced over and saw Olive staring at the hickey. She was still clutching her overnight bag to her hip like a security blanket.

"Yeah, let's get in our pajamas too," I told Abby. "Olive and I had a long day."

At the sound of her name, Olive jerked her gaze away from Leah's neck. "Is there a bathroom where I can change?" she asked.

Leah laughed. "Why? We're all girls. Just change here."

"OK..." Olive sighed, dropping her overnight bag next to mine.

She bent over and took out some cotton shorts and a sweatshirt, while, next to her, Leah pulled off her own shirt, revealing a hot pink bra. When Olive saw it, she turned toward the wall and slid her sweatshirt over the blouse she was wearing. Then she put her arms inside, unbuttoned the shirt underneath, and pulled it out through one of the sleeves of the sweatshirt. I got into my own pajamas while she changed with lightning speed into her shorts.

"So," Madison said when we were all settled in our sleeping bags. "This wouldn't be a sleepover without Truth or Dare."

I looked over at Olive, whose face was as blank and colorless as it had been earlier that morning when she'd carried her pitchfork up the front steps into school. I wondered if she was scared. "We don't have to play," I told her. "I mean, if you don't want to."

"No, it's fine." Olive's voice sounded strained.

"That's the spirit," said Abby. "Want to go first?"

"Do I have to?"

"We won't bite!"

"Fine." She turned slowly toward Madison, who was sitting on her right. "Truth or dare?"

"Truth," said Madison.

Olive sighed. "OK. What was your first impression of me?"

Madison laughed. "That is *so* not the kind of question you're supposed to ask."

Two red splotches appeared on Olive's cheeks.

"I mean, whatever," said Madison. "I guess my first impression was that you looked shy."

"I am around some people," said Olive. "Next?"

Madison turned to Abby. "Truth or Dare?"

Abby chose dare—she always did—and Madison told her to make out with her pillow. Abby rolled her eyes and did it in a heartbeat. Then it was Leah's turn. She had to call Drew

Tubman's house and leave a message on his parents' machine saying that she was watching porn. Ten minutes later, after she and Madison recovered from their fit of hysterical laughing, it was my turn. "Reyna, truth or dare?" asked Leah.

I chose truth. I was not about to make a prank call.

"Hmmm." Leah scrunched up her face. "If someone paid you fifty bucks, would you make out with a girl?"

"Probably not," I said.

Olive looked up. "Why not?"

I shrugged. "I don't know."

"I totally would," announced Leah, but nobody paid her any attention.

"Let me guess." The expression on Olive's face was hard to read. "It's against your religion?"

"Maybe it is. Don't take it personally," I said. The truth was it had nothing to do with my religion. I just wouldn't want anyone at school to start spreading the rumor that *I* was gay. It would be impossible to live down, and Levi might lose interest in me. But I wasn't about to get into an argument with Olive, so I shrugged. "I just wouldn't want to, OK?"

She pressed her lips tightly and looked down at her fingernails.

"Anyway," said Abby, trying to smooth over the awkwardness. "Should we keep going?"

"Yeah." I looked back over at Olive without meeting her eye. "Truth or dare?"

"Truth."

I didn't know what to ask her. I would have liked to know what she saw in me—why she'd picked me out of the crowd and made me her friend on that day in the cafeteria—but it was another one of those questions you weren't supposed to ask in Truth or Dare. The game was supposed to be about crushes and boys. Who you'd kissed, who you wanted to kiss—that sort of thing. In the end, I fell back on the classic question, "How far have you gotten?"

Olive didn't answer right away. She seemed to be waiting for me to finish the question. Then she said, "...Gotten where?"

Leah, Abby, and Madison burst out laughing.

Olive narrowed her eyes. "Do you mean like sexually?"

"Obviously!" said Leah.

Olive looked down at her lap. "Does online sex count?"

The laughing stopped abruptly.

"Like with a web cam?" Leah looked shocked. "Seriously? That's *awesome*!"

"No, not like that." Olive picked at a hangnail on her thumb. "Like, just by typing out the words of what we would do..."

"Oh my God." Leah clapped her hands. "That's so kinky! I love it!"

Madison's eyebrows were raised so close to her hairline that her forehead had all but disappeared. "Who was the guy?" she asked.

"It wasn't—" Olive paused. "It was just somebody random from the Internet."

Everybody was quiet, waiting for details. I couldn't believe I'd known Olive for almost two months, and she'd never once told me about having online sex with strangers.

"Anyway, I answered the question," she said after a long silence. "I think I'm ready to go to sleep now. I'm exhausted."

Abby made a boo sound and stuck out her lower lip.

Olive fluffed her pillow. "Like Reyna said, we had a long day."

"Actually, I'm kind of tired too," said Leah. "I think my sugar high is fading."

So we all zipped ourselves into our sleeping bags and wished each other good night. I expected to hear Olive drift off first, but Leah was the first to start snoring, followed by Madison, and then Abby. Olive just kept rolling over in her sleeping bag.

"Are you OK?" I whispered after a while, turning on my side to face her.

"Just lovely," she answered.

"Are you tired?"

"No."

I pulled my sleeping bag up to my chin and stared at the ceiling. We were silent for a long time. Then she whispered, "I still can't believe I have in-school suspension for threatening Gretchen Palmer with a pitchfork."

"I know," I said.

"I'm sorry, by the way."

"For what?"

"For getting you involved."

I shrugged, but she couldn't see me. "It's fine."

"I could have protected you myself, you know." She scooted her pillow closer to mine and lowered her voice. "I wouldn't have let them suspend you. I didn't need Levi Siegel to step in like some kind of knight in shining armor. I can do that."

"I know," I said.

Olive smiled at me with her lips pressed tightly together, and then we drifted into sleep.

Let's play a game.

OK.

Say someone tells you they're going to jump into a pool with you on the count of three.

Yeah?

But say that when you jump, they don't. Say they just stand there laughing.

OK.

What would you do?

Kill myself.

Ha.

Did someone do that to you?

My mom. When I was little.

At least you know how to swim.

Ha ha.

Olive, you laugh a lot for somebody on a suicide prevention forum.

So?

Are you sure you're actually depressed?

What's that supposed to mean?

You might just be cynical.

Screw you.

I'm just saying.

Seriously. Screw you.

I wouldn't do that, by the way.

What?

The pool thing.

I know you wouldn't.

I'd jump with you.

I know.

November

5

When your mom dies, Thanksgiving is the worst holiday. I still remember what she used to cook: sweet potato pie, hot spiced cranberry cider, gooey banana bread. The year I turned seven—the year of her accident—Dad put some chicken nuggets in the oven and we toasted her memory with apple cider from the A&P. After that, we stopped celebrating Thanksgiving at our house. Sometimes we went over to Abby's and ate dinner with her family, and other times we just stayed at home and watched football on TV.

But this year, Lucy wanted to cook a bird at our house. She got the idea from a commercial—something about bringing people together—and once it calcified in her mind, there was no stopping her. I told Dad it didn't feel right to me, but he insisted. "She wants to," he said. "It'll be fun."

So when Olive called me the weekend before Thanksgiving and asked if I felt like joining her family for their annual torture-fest, I said OK. Lucy was upset—she heard me making plans on the phone and then burst out crying when I left the room—but I couldn't bring myself to feel sorry for her. She shot me irritable looks all through dinner that night, and Dad told me later he was disappointed too, but only because he wanted us to be a happy family together. Fat chance.

When I arrived at Olive's house on the night of Thanksgiving, the driveway was packed with cars. Dad didn't pull in; he rolled to a stop at the foot of the driveway and craned his neck up at the two-story house. "Looks like a party in there," he said. "Try to have fun, will you?"

"We'll see," I said, gathering my overnight bag off the floor. *Fun* and *Olive* weren't exactly two words that belonged in the same sentence. It was true we'd been growing closer since Halloween, and I was starting to trust her almost as much as Abby, Leah, and Madison. But all the same, I couldn't remember the last time we'd had *fun* together—probably the day we threw candy at each other in her bedroom.

Olive greeted me at the front door flanked by her mother and father. Her mother looked pinch-faced and angry, but her father was more handsome than I expected: tall, with a chiseled face and well-groomed eyebrows. I barely had time to notice the Ralph Lauren insignia on his shirt before he extended a hand and shook mine so hard that my elbow cracked. "Welcome," he said with a wide, artificial smile. "You're just in time for the feast."

They led me through the foyer, which was emptier and more echoey than I remembered, with tall white walls and modern art. It was a relief to step into the dining room, which was at least smaller but still looked like a museum. A heavy travertine table with a centerpiece of poufy blue hydrangeas dominated the room. Crowded around the table were all of

Olive's relatives and two empty chairs with perfectly straight backs.

Olive grabbed me by the arm and led me around the table to our seats. "You have to hear what went down between my parents this morning," she hissed, but before she could elaborate, an old woman wearing a long string of pearls looked up from the table and barked, "Posture, dear! Remember your posture." She was dabbing at the corners of her mouth with a white linen napkin, and her face had the same pinched expression as Mrs. Barton's.

"I *am* remembering," Olive muttered, straightening her shoulders. I took a seat next to her and put my napkin in my lap.

"It would be polite of you to introduce your friend," said the old woman, who I was now sitting next to. I hoped my own posture was acceptable.

Olive sighed rudely. "Nana Jane, this is my friend Reyna," she said. "Reyna, this is Nana Jane." Then she turned back to me and tapped my empty place. "Do you want white meat or dark? I'll get you some from the buffet."

"White, please," I said.

Nana Jane watched Olive leave the table; then she leaned toward me and asked me to repeat my name. Before I could answer, Mr. Barton stood up at the head of the table and tapped his spoon to his glass. I felt disoriented. It was unnerving to be plunked in the middle of someone else's family gathering, with all its politics and personalities.

"Now that we're all here..." Mr. Barton announced, clearing his throat, "I thought I'd say a few words..."

The room quieted as Olive slid back into her seat beside mine. "Here," she whispered. "If you want any gravy, help yourself during the speech. He likes to hear himself talk."

Mr. Barton began a typical Thanksgiving toast—something about coming together and the importance of family—and I zoned out, noticing that next to me, Olive was tracing a word into her mashed potatoes with her fork. At first I thought she was spelling *hell* and I felt a familiar twinge of annoyance. Thanksgiving dinner, no matter how much you hate your family, doesn't count as hell. Learning that your mom was just killed by a drunk driver—*that's* hell. But then Olive added a small swoop with her fork, and the word changed to *help*. I glanced sideways at her, but she wasn't looking at me. She was staring straight ahead at her father. And before I had time to wonder about the word, she smoothed it over with the flat edge of her fork.

Other than Olive's uncle dropping a plate of apple pie onto the carpet, dinner was uneventful. When we were finally excused after dessert, I followed Olive up to her room and set down my overnight bag on her impeccably made queen bed. "Well?" I asked. "What happened with your parents?"

"I didn't want my grandmother to hear," said Olive, kicking off her shoes in the direction of the closet. I took off my own shoes and lined them up neatly below her desk. Then I looked around, wondering whether I should sit on the floor or the bed.

"Just sit on the bed," said Olive, noticing my hesitation. "It's where we're both going to be sleeping anyway. There used to be a cot up here, but I hardly ever had sleepovers, so my dad moved it to the storage shed." She looked faintly embarrassed. "Sorry."

"It's OK," I said. Madison had a queen bed too, and sometimes we slept in it together. It was easier and more comfortable than using a sleeping bag.

"The thing about my parents—you have to keep it to yourself," Olive said, lowering her voice and making sure the door was closed.

I nodded and sat down on the bed, wondering if they were getting a divorce.

She took a seat by the desk. "My dad wants to run for public office."

I stared at her.

"District attorney," she said. "Can you believe the jerk?"

I hardly knew what to say. "Is that bad?"

"Are you serious?" She laughed. "He's a Republican."

"Oh." I looked down and busied myself with a loose thread on my shirt. I didn't want to get into politics—not with Olive.

"It's not just that," she sighed. "When you run for office, your whole life gets pushed under a microscope. Your personal life. Your *family's* personal life."

"Are you sure?" I crossed my legs and leaned back against the headboard. "It's not like he's running for president. I've never even heard of the district attorney."

"That's because you don't pay attention," she said. "It's a pretty big deal, and my mom flipped out when he told us. She threatened to tell a reporter about the time he cheated on her a couple years ago—as though *that's* the real scandal in this family."

"He cheated on her?"

"I don't know." She sighed again. "It's one of those accusations she flings around when she's drunk, only she wasn't even drunk this morning."

"Not at dinner either."

Olive blinked. "You noticed?"

"Just a guess." Mrs. Barton's pinched, angry face floated in my mind.

"It's because my dad threw out every drop of alcohol in the house this morning." She stood suddenly. "Come here. I want to show you something."

Without waiting to see if I was following, she strode out of her bedroom and led me down the hallway into another room—her father's study. When she pushed open the heavy wooden door, I heard the sound of shattered glass crunch under its arc. The room looked fancy at first glance—my eyes landed on a great oak desk and a huge, swooping reading lamp—but nothing else was as it should have been. It looked like the scene of a crime. There was shattered glass everywhere and a dozen long-stemmed white tulips scattered across the rug.

"My mom did it this morning," said Olive. "She lost control."

I felt a pang and thought of Dad after the car accident, when he received the part of the medical bill not covered by insurance. He flung his bowl of Rice Krispies onto he floor, the milk splattering all the way across the kitchen. "You

77

must've been scared," I said, staring at the scattered tulips on the floor. I thought about picking one up, putting it into a vase with fresh water, and giving it to Olive.

"Whatever," she said. "As long as I don't have to clean it, I don't care."

"It's not whatever," I told her. "It's horrible."

"I know." The corners of her mouth twitched upward in a smile. "Can't you recognize a defense mechanism when you see one?"

I stepped backward into the hallway to leave, but Olive stayed still for a few seconds. She stood there with her hand on the doorframe, taking it all in, and when she finally followed me back to her room, she took a shard of glass with her and set it on her dresser.

As we changed, I felt sorry for Olive for the first time—truly sorry. Maybe having an alcoholic mother wasn't better than having no mother at all. Her whole house had a cold, foreboding feeling—like a wax museum—and I got the creepy sensation, as I slipped out of my jeans and into my pajamas, that Mrs. Barton was standing frozen on the floor below us, waiting for a reason to come to life and light the whole house on fire.

Olive flicked the light switch by the door and the room became dark—almost pitch black, but not quite. Light was falling in a chopstick pattern through the Venetian blinds, and I saw her move toward the bed and pull down the covers. I did the same, climbing under them, and rested my head against the overstuffed pillow. Her sheets were crisp and clean.

"Reyna?"

"What?" I rolled over on my side to face her. We hadn't been whispering when the lights were on, but now that the room was dark, it seemed right.

"Thanks for coming tonight." She pulled the covers up to her shoulders.

"Thanks for inviting me," I answered. I didn't know what else to say. We lay in silence for a moment, and I rolled a certain thought around in my mind like a ball of yarn, trying to figure out where it started and stopped. Finally I blurted, "My dad destroyed a room once. Sort of like what you showed me."

She glanced over at me. "After your mom died?"

"No, this summer." I didn't remind her about the car accident—I just told her about the bowl of Rice Krispies, the shattered bowl, the overturned chair.

"I guess everybody needs to lose control every now and then," Olive said, turning on her side to face me. "Which reminds me...Do you remember how I told you my dad got rid of all the booze in the house?"

I nodded and shifted my cheek to a cool patch on the pillow.

"He didn't know about my stash—the stuff I confiscated from her months ago."

"So?"

The corner of her mouth twitched. "So I was wondering if you wanted to try some."

I stared at her.

"I've never been drunk," she told me. "And I refuse to try it for the first time by myself. That would be pathetic."

I didn't say anything. My mind was revving into high gear, suddenly nervous. I had never had anything more than a sip of wine in my life.

"I'll tell you if you're starting to get drunk." She propped herself up on one elbow. "I know how to recognize the signs. We won't get wasted, we'll just get tipsy."

"Just to test it out?" I said.

"Yeah, just to see how our systems respond." She was watching me carefully. Then she added, "I know I'm not the most fun person in the world. Not like your other friends—"

"It's not that," I said. "It's just...*now?*"

Olive raised her eyebrows. "Why not?"

She had a point. I would inevitably try my first drink at some point, and I didn't want it to be at a party—I had a brief and awful image of throwing up all over Levi Siegel's jeans. If I was going to get drunk, I preferred to test my limits in the safety of Olive's bedroom. "I guess I'll try some," I said. "I just don't want to go overboard."

She smiled and stood up, the springs on the bed creaking quietly. "I don't have any cups in here, but we can drink straight out of the bottle."

I sat up and leaned back against the headboard. It felt like a business proposition.

Olive moved through the dark room toward the filing cabinet, crouched, and pulled out the bottom drawer. It slid smoothly on its wheels until it was almost all the way open; then it made a faint screech, and we froze.

But there were no footsteps outside in the hallway—only

the sound of the TV on the floor below us. Cautiously, Olive pulled out a tall, rectangular bottle of amber liquid and left the drawer wide open as she got to her feet. "It's whiskey," she said. "My mom's favorite."

"You go first," I told her.

She climbed back onto the bed and twisted open the cap. "I hope you don't mind my cooties." Then she put it to her lips and took a swig.

The expression on her face was not a good advertisement for the whiskey. She looked like she was swallowing lighter fluid. As soon as she managed to get it all the way down her throat, she opened her mouth and gasped for air. "Ugh," she said. "That's disgusting!" But as she passed the bottle to me, she swallowed a few times and added, "My throat feels kind of nice though."

I didn't count to three or give myself any preparation. I just brought the bottle to my lips and took a small sip. It felt like liquid fire going down—and not in a good way—but Olive was right. Once swallowed, it left a pleasantly warm, tingling sensation in the throat. "Do you feel anything?" I asked her. "Are you tipsy yet?"

She laughed. "One sip isn't enough."

"Have another, then." I held out the bottle and met her eye. "And I will too."

It wasn't long before we were stretched out on her floor like beached whales. After three more sips of whiskey and two big gulps of vodka, I was more than just tipsy: I was tipped. Whenever I focused on one part of the room, it seemed fixed

81

in place, but as soon as I moved my head, everything became unhinged and floated around like objects at sea.

Olive wasn't such a lightweight. Besides whiskey and vodka, she tried four sips of coconut rum, which she claimed was supposed to taste good with vanilla ice cream. Vanilla ice cream made me think of pigging out at Abby's house when we were little, and without thinking, I sighed, "Don't you wish we went to Ridgeway?"

Suddenly Olive started groaning on the floor. I thought at first she was going to throw up from drinking too much, but then she moaned, "Why would I want to go to school with your friends? They hate me!"

"That's not true," I said. My voice sounded far away, as though my head were packed with bubble wrap. "They think you're nice." It was a lie. Madison had told me a few days after our Halloween sleepover that Olive reminded her of the kind of person who would one day "go Columbine" and shoot up a school.

She flopped over on the carpet and stared at me.

"What?" I blinked. "Why are you looking at me?"

"Promise me something," said Olive.

"What?" I sat up a little. Her cheek was pressed against the floor.

"Promise me something, and I'll promise the same to you."

"*What?*" I said again.

"Never lie to me."

I crossed my arms. "I'm not lying!"

"Suuuuure." Olive reached again for the coconut rum, only, this time she didn't sip from it; she put the bottle to her lips and chugged. There wasn't much left in the first place, but what was left, she gulped down—probably an inch or two of liquid. And then, as she let the empty bottle roll off her fingertips onto the carpet, she began to cry.

"Uh-oh." I sat up on the floor. "What's wrong?" She looked blurry just a few feet away from me, but rubbing my eyes only made them itch.

"Sometimes I just feel like you don't like me!" she burst out. "You spend all this time with me, but I get the feeling you secretly hate me."

I felt my mouth open. The edges of my lips felt crusty, but no words came out.

"Are we friends?" She stared at me. "Because I've been nothing but a friend to you, and all you ever do is mope around wishing you went to Ridgeway."

"What about the time you threw a rock at my head?"

"What?" Olive's eyes widened. "What the hell are you talking about?"

I didn't tell her it had been on the day we met, or that it had been a pebble, not a rock. All I managed to say was, "We're friends, OK? I've never told anyone else about my dad destroying the kitchen—"

"We're not friends," she said, wiping her eyes. "We're not, because if you really knew me, you would hate me. And you already hate me, so you would *really* hate me if you knew."

"Knew what?" My stomach was folding unpleasantly. I hoped I wasn't going to throw up.

"Nothing." She gulped a big breath of air. "I'm just drowning in secrets, that's all."

I had no idea what I was supposed to say. My tongue felt heavy, and I concentrated on not getting sick all over the carpet.

"Or maybe it's just my parents." She swiped at her cheeks. "Maybe that's why everything is the way it is. Do you think it's wrong of me to hate my mom?"

"Hate's a strong word," I managed to say. My speech came out slurred.

"But I do hate her." Olive was staring past me into the darkness. "I hate the way she can't control herself. The way she can't love me like she's supposed to."

The room seemed to slide in and out of focus before my eyes, and I could tell that I was either going to throw up or fall asleep on the floor, but I wasn't sure which. "I'm not in a position to judge you," I said at last.

"Of course you are," Olive sighed, turning away from me. "Everybody judges everybody else automatically. That's the whole fucking problem with the world."

It was late—or technically early—when we finally climbed back into bed. We both fell asleep on her carpet for a while, but by two a.m., we woke up and realized we were cold.

Stumbling up from the floor and onto the bed, I told Olive that my head was pounding. The room still seemed to rock slightly, as though we were sitting in a big cradle.

"You need some water," she mumbled, but neither of us stood up to get some. Instead we just wedged our feet under the covers and pulled the blankets up to our chins.

"I feel guilty," I told her. My mouth was dry and the words came out sounding scratchy.

"So?" said Olive.

I shrugged. "I shouldn't have drank anything. Dranken. Drunk?"

"Drunk."

"Leah got wasted with her older sister one time." It popped out of my mouth out of nowhere, and I began to suspect I was still drunk. "She threw up and it was gross."

"Leah..." Olive frowned. "Was she the one with the pink bra?"

"Yeah, the slutty one." I felt my hand fly to my mouth. Olive started giggling.

"I didn't mean to say that," I said. "I have a headache."

But Olive was grinning now. "Doesn't she remind you of a dog that humps everything in sight? Like she really needs to be neutered or something—"

I laughed so suddenly and unexpectedly that I actually snorted. Then Olive did too. "Shut up!" I squealed. "You're making me say bad things about my friends!" I rubbed my temples, where the headache was blaring like bad music.

"Oh—how about that hickey she had!" Olive touched her own neck. "It was like the size of a vacuum cleaner. Couldn't you see her making out with an inanimate object?"

"Not Leah, but maybe Madison," I said. "Because she's

such a prude, it would be the only way she'd ever—" I could barely finish my sentence. Olive was clapping with glee.

"You're so mean!" She was wiggling her feet under the covers. "Are you really Reyna? Reyna doesn't say mean things. Ever."

"It's your fault for getting me drunk," I said.

"More, more!" She pounded her fist against the mattress. "Tell me how great I am and how everyone else sucks."

"It's not funny," I said. "I'm growing apart from my friends."

"You don't need them." She rolled over onto her back and stretched out her arms until her knuckles grazed my pajamas.

"When we were ten, Abby touched her dog's penis," I said. Something about the buzz in my brain made the words slip out without their usual censor. "She wanted to know what it felt like."

"Oh my God!" Olive nearly snorted. "That's probably illegal in some states."

I laughed along, feeling spacey and drunk and thirsty at the same time. I also felt weirdly peaceful, as though Olive's room was exactly where I needed to be. Like all along I'd been faking our friendship, and then suddenly, to my surprise, I wasn't.

Remember that time we...online...?

That's a little vague, Olive.

You know...together...?

Refresh my memory.

Pretended to be a cop and a swimsuit model?

Oh. That.

Did you like it?

Sure. I guess.

It was a little weird, though, right?

A little.

Would you maybe want to do it again?

I don't know...

We could be something other than a cop and a model.

No, it's not that.

You pick this time—whatever you want.

I don't think so...

Why not?

I don't have room in my life right now for anything more than friendship.

Oh.

Are you OK?

I guess.

I'm just too messed up right now.

6

Thanksgiving dinner had—according to Dad—exceeded Lucy's expectations. Apparently, when they were halfway done cooking the turkey, he'd hobbled out of the dining room on his crutches and come back carrying a little blue box, which Lucy snotted all over. Inside was a diamond necklace, and once she stopped sobbing about how she was "just so happy to finally be happy," she let Dad put it around her neck like a medal of honor. She'd been flouncing around the house in her pajamas ever since then, talking about plans for a "family" vacation and collective "household" goals.

When I told Abby about it a couple days after Thanksgiving, she said exactly what I was afraid of: "Maybe it's a good thing. Your dad seems happy."

My response was, "Who ever heard of wearing a diamond necklace with pajamas?"

It was just the two of us alone in her room for once. Leah and Madison were busy with after school clubs, and even though Abby and I had different homework to do, I liked being in the same room together doing it. I missed that about middle school.

"Guess what?" she said as I flipped a page in my math book, trying to figure out how to calculate the arc-length of a partial circle.

"Let's see…" I looked up from my book. "You're transferring to Belltown because you can't live without me?"

"You wish." She laughed. "Actually, I started going out with someone."

"What?"

"Yeah…" She was watching my face to see my reaction.

"Who?"

"You don't know him." She closed her math book. "But his name is Jeremy, and we have the same taste in music. It's actually kind of creepy. Our iPods are almost identical."

"Wow." My stomach flipped over like I'd swallowed something gross.

"Are you OK?" she asked.

I stared at a random equation in my book. "Of course."

"Do you feel like you're being replaced? Madison said you might feel that way."

"You talked about this with Madison?" I knew I should be happy for Abby, but instead I felt like I was being left on a desert island and she was my boat, speeding away.

"The important thing is, you're still one of my best friends," she said.

Really? It didn't feel that way. This stung worse than Dad giving Lucy the diamond necklace. "Stop acting like a psychologist," I said after a moment, staring down at my math book. I refused to cry over something so stupid.

"I'm not acting like anything," she said. "I'm just trying to be sensitive to your situation."

"What situation? Not having a boyfriend?"

"No, going to Belltown with what's-her-name."

"Her name is Olive," I said with a stab of anger. "And she thinks you guys hate her."

"We don't hate her." Abby sighed. "She's just not our type."

Our type? What the hell was that supposed to mean?

Abby noticed the look on my face and rephrased herself. "I mean, she just seems too serious. You said it yourself when you first met her."

"Well, she's my friend now." The force in my voice surprised me. "And you're right that she's serious—that's what I like about her." I looked down at my half-finished sheet of homework and sighed. "Anyway, I have to finish this problem set. I should go home."

"Reyna, come on." She leaned over and hugged my shoulders. "Why are you being so touchy? Do you have your period?"

I almost rolled my eyes like Olive.

"Are you upset that I'm going out with someone?"

"Not at all," I lied. "I'm happy for you and Jordan."

"It's Jeremy."

"Right," I said. "You and Jeremy."

★ ★ ★

When I got home, I looked up Levi Siegel's name online and clicked on the first twenty-seven hits. Most of them were about a plastic surgeon in San Francisco, but I found a local newspaper article with a picture of Levi holding up a tennis trophy when he was nine or ten. He looked pretty much the same, only chubbier. I also found his name in a list of honor roll students at his old middle school and on the Temple Beth Shalom of Connecticut's website.

I didn't look up his screen name or send him a friend request. I wouldn't have known what to say. Instead I signed online and listened to Madison complain about Abby's boyfriend. She wasn't happy for them either but for a different reason than mine. She didn't like watching them make out every morning on the bus. We signed off after that—or rather, we both turned our statuses to invisible and sat there watching to see who else would come online—and I tried to determine whether I felt good or bad about my prospects.

This morning?

Yeah.

Without a word to anyone?

Sort of.

You just got up and walked away?

I left a suicide note.

Wow.

A decoy.

WOW.

I needed to buy myself time to think.

Where are you now?

A public library in Bridgeport.

What are you going to do?

I'm headed to New York City.

To do what?

Be free, I guess.

Wow.

I might need a place to stay for a
while.

In Connecticut?

I'm sorry to ask you.

Don't be.

I know we're basically strangers.

We're not strangers, Grace.

Yeah, I guess.

Not anymore.

December

7

There was no question when Mr. Murphy assigned a group project on ancient Greece that Olive and I would work together. I could recall dimly the period in October when I looked forward to never working with her again, but now everything before Thanksgiving felt like a different era. Thanksgiving—or rather, drinking together—had been the line of demarcation in our friendship: the point at which BC had turned into AD. I didn't even consider asking Levi to join our group because I knew Olive would hate it. Everything was finally comfortable between us, and I didn't see any point in shaking things up.

We decided to film a fake documentary about the Peloponnesian War. It was my idea this time, not hers, and our main challenge was figuring out how to produce footage of a battle between two armies when we had only two actors. In the end, we decided to use life-size cardboard cutouts and do the filming in Olive's backyard.

We met at her house on a crisp afternoon in early December to shoot the footage. We'd already written the script and decorated the cardboard soldiers in the art wing at school; now the task was to film the whole project without letting it slip into a farce. It could be funny, but not too funny—silly, but still factual.

We set up the tripod on her back porch, overlooking the yard, a small storage shed, and the train tracks off in the distance, barely visible through the trees. Olive used a rusty trowel to dig holes, and I planted the base of a cardboard cutout in each one. We arranged them in rows across the lawn to create the illusion of a crowd.

The only problem was our lack of soldiers on horseback. The cardboard slabs we took from the art wing were only two feet wide—not big enough for horses. I knew it was a corny idea, but I asked Olive whether she had any stuffed animals or My Little Ponies. "We can always zoom in on them," I told her. "You know—to make them look big?"

"As stupid as that sounds, it might actually work," she said. "I'll be right back." Then she ran up the porch steps and disappeared through a sliding glass door into the kitchen, calling, "Mom? Where's that big stuffed horse from when I was little?"

A breeze blew through the yard, and I tightened my jacket at the waist. It was windier out than I expected—windy enough to whip my hair into my eyes—and when I stopped blinking, I saw that one of the cardboard cutouts had blown over on the lawn. The base that was supposed to stay wedged in the ground had come loose, and the whole thing was scuttling along the grass in the wind. I ran over and grabbed it, trying to shove it back into the ground, but the bottom of the cardboard had become soggy, and the hole wasn't deep enough. I put a rock on the soldier's leg so he wouldn't blow away and then stood up to look for Olive's trowel.

I couldn't find it, but I did see that the door of the tool shed was slightly ajar, so I headed toward it. Even if I couldn't find another trowel, I could I always use the pitchfork from our Halloween costume—Mr. Barton was bound to keep it in the tool shed. I stepped closer, tightening my jacket again around the waist, and pushed open the door.

And then I jumped back.

In fact, I almost screamed. On a foldable cot at the front of the shed was a teenage girl lying face-up with her eyes closed, creepily dead looking. At the sound of the door opening, her eyes flickered open and snapped toward mine. She wasn't dead—just sleeping—and her face was so pale she looked like a corpse.

I tried to back away from the door, but my feet were frozen. I might have been in shock. I barely noticed that the whole shed was set up like a bedroom. Next to the cot, there was a nightstand with an old laptop resting on it, and the power cord was plugged into a surge protector in the wall. I felt my heartbeat thud in my ears. The girl had dirty-blond hair like Olive's, and I wondered for a second if they were related.

"Relax," she said. Her voice was faint and cracked, as though she hadn't used it in a couple of days. "Olive knows I'm here."

I opened my mouth, but nothing came out.

"Relax," she said again. "Are you Reyna? I'm Grace."

Something about her voice made her sound older than she

looked—like a thirteen-year-old with a sixteen-year-old's baggage. She sighed. "Look, Olive's parents don't know I'm here. I'm mooching off their wireless for a few weeks. And Olive loaned me this laptop; I didn't steal it like I can tell you're thinking. So if you could just close the door and forget about me—"

"I—I need a tool," I said.

"Oh." Her face relaxed a little. "Be my guest."

I stepped forward and reached for a trowel that was hanging off a hook on the wall. It was a different shape than the one Olive had been using before, but I took it anyway. "Thanks," I said. "I won't tell her parents."

"Bye." She held up her hand with the palm facing me, and I saw a swollen, pink scar wrapped around her wrist.

I didn't say bye in return; I just stepped backward out the door and pulled it shut it with a click. Turning around to look for Olive, I saw that the sliding glass door leading into the kitchen was open a crack. Raised voices were coming from inside.

Before I had time to digest what the argument was about, Mrs. Barton came galloping through the back door and down the steps of the porch. She had a toy horse between her legs, and she ran out into the yard shouting, "Giddyup! Giddyup, cowgirls!"

"*Mom!*" called Olive, running out after her. "*Stop!*"

I froze where I was, a few feet from the fallen cardboard soldier, and watched as Mrs. Barton bucked her hips against the big stuffed animal. "Yeee-haaaw!" she called, staggering into the flower bed by the side of the porch. "You want your horse, you better come get it!"

Olive's face was a deep shade of purple as she ran toward her mom and tackled her onto the grass. "*Stop it!*" she shouted. "*Get inside now!*" but Mrs. Barton just gave her a crazy smile and pretended to mount the horse again. I'd never seen anyone so drunk.

"Um…" I stepped forward slowly. "Can I help?"

"*No!*" Olive's hands were balled into fists.

I looked down at my feet as she began pulling her mother up the steps toward the house, and then I glanced over at the tool shed, wondering if Grace could hear what was going on. But if she was listening, she didn't come out to help. I waited by myself on the lawn as Olive pulled her mother back inside and yanked the sliding door shut behind them.

I didn't dare follow them into the kitchen. Instead I used the trowel to dig a deeper hole in the grass, and by the time Olive came back out a few minutes later, the fallen cardboard soldier was standing upright again. I dropped the trowel onto the grass as I hurried over to meet her. She had a glazed look in her eyes—a sort of dumbstruck horror.

"Are you OK?" I asked.

She didn't answer. She just plunked herself down on one of the porch steps and rested her forehead against her knees so I couldn't see her face. When I didn't say anything else, she croaked, "She must have found the stash in my room."

"What?" For a second, I thought she meant a stash of drugs.

"The alcohol. Everything we didn't finish on Thanksgiving."

"Oh." I draped my arm awkwardly over her shoulder and rubbed her back the way Dad would have done to me. "It's OK."

She was quiet for a second. Then she lifted her head off her knees and stared out into the forest behind her house. "Reyna, do you think your dad would let you sleep over tonight?"

I wasn't sure at first; it was a school night. But it reminded me of the Tuesday night Leah's parents got divorced in sixth grade, and Dad let me sleep over at her house that time.

"I can ask," I said, digging around in my pocket for my cell phone. When I found it, I dialed our home number, praying Dad would pick up, but I was out of luck. Lucy answered the phone on the second ring. "Hell-looo?" she sang. I could tell just from the tone of her voice that she was wearing the diamond necklace.

"Hi, Lucy," I said, trying to keep my voice neutral. "Is Dad there?"

"Hi, Reyna!" Her cheer was almost too much to bear. "He's in the shower. What can I do for you?"

I made up a lie on the spot. I said Olive and I needed to finish our project and that it was going to take all night. Then I told her I could get a ride to school in the morning with Mr. Barton, and she said she would call me back in a few minutes once Dad got out of the shower.

"You know, we do actually need to finish our project," sighed Olive once I hung up. "If we don't want to fail, that is."

"Yeah," I said. "Let's do it now, before dinner." But my phone buzzed as soon as I suggested it, before we even stood

99

up. It was Lucy again, saying that on second thought, I had her full permission to spend the night.

* * *

I almost forgot about the girl in the tool shed. Dinnertime with Mrs. Barton was so odd and disturbing that it took up most of my mental energy. Olive had to thwack the kitchen smoke alarm with a broom after Mrs. Barton burned a frozen pizza and accidentally left a rubber oven mitt on the hot stove. She fell into a drunken stupor by eight o'clock, and it was only later, as Olive and I got ready for bed, that I remembered about the hobo girl.

We were facing opposite sides of the room, changing into our pajamas, when I brought it up. "I meant to ask you something earlier," I said, tightening the drawstring on my sweatpants. "While you were inside looking for the toy horse, I went into your tool shed—"

Olive's head snapped up.

"And I saw your friend Grace."

She exhaled in one whooshing breath, her shoulders dropping by at least an inch. "Did she say anything?"

"Not much." I turned and headed toward the bed. "But she knew my name."

Olive nodded.

"So, what's the deal?" I climbed into bed and burrowed my feet deep beneath the blankets. "Why is a girl living in your parents' shed in the middle of the winter?"

"I put a space heater in there. It's not as if she's freezing to death."

"But how do you know her?"

"We met online." She was avoiding my eyes.

"When?"

"A couple of months ago. But she just came here last week."

"Where does she go to school?" The question popped out of my mouth before I considered the fact that she was living in a tool shed. Olive just frowned and said, "*Went* to school." Then she lay down next to me and reached over for the switch on her bedside lamp. She had to turn it three times. It got brighter first; then it grew dim; then the room simmered into darkness.

"Reyna?"

"Yeah?" I rolled over on my side to face her. The tree branches outside the window cast long, pale shadows across her half of the bed, and I could see, as my eyes adjusted, that she was watching me carefully.

"Can I tell you something that you have to promise not to repeat?"

"Sure." I wondered if Grace was some kind of fugitive running from the law. Or maybe she was Olive's long-lost sister—some kind of family secret.

She looked down at a crinkle in the blanket and smoothed it over with her thumb. "You know Tim Ferguson?"

His name caught me off guard. "From history?"

"Yeah," said Olive. "The one Mr. Murphy always picks on."

"I know who he is."

"We met online before school started."

I waited.

"On the same forum where I met Grace."

"So?"

"Did you know that he's gay?"

"I guess," I said, though I'd never thought much about it. "What does that have to do with you?"

"Isn't it obvious?"

"I guess not."

"I am too."

"Oh my God," I heard myself say. "Are you serious?"

She nodded against her pillow.

I sat up a little. "Are you—? I mean why are you—?"

"What?"

"Why are you having me sleep in your bed?"

Her eyes widened "Because my dad moved the trundle to the tool shed."

"But I'm not like that." A stalled sort of panic was setting in as I realized where I was and what people would say if they knew. "Is this why you wanted me to sleep over?" I slid my legs out of the bed and felt my toes curl into the soft carpet. "Is this why you asked me to get permission?"

"No! God, Reyna. I'm not hitting on you."

"I have to go."

I bolted for the door. The hallway outside of Olive's room was pitch dark, and I stumbled through it blindly, the floorboards sharp and cool against my feet. When I found the bathroom at the end of the hall, I fumbled for the light switch next to the door, and the florescent bulb above the sink stung my eyes as it flickered on. My face looked strange

102

and green in the harsh light. My pupils retracted into pin-points. *Gay?*

I told myself to calm down. She was still the same old Olive. But why did she have to be gay? I didn't want people at school thinking I was too, which they would if word got out about Olive. I could just imagine the rumors. *They slept together in the same bed.*

I turned on the faucet, I splashed cool water onto my face, and stepped back, letting it drip down my neck and onto my T-shirt. Why would she confess to me in the first place? Did she think I was gay too? What had I ever done to suggest a thing like that? Nothing. I shook the rest of the water off my face and hit the light switch.

When I pushed open the door to her bedroom, she was sitting up in bed, my overnight bag resting on the covers in front of her. "Take it," she said before I could say anything.

I lingered in the doorway, waiting for my eyes to adjust to the dark room. "Olive, look—" I started to say, but she pushed the bag forward.

"Take it and go sleep on the couch downstairs."

"I—"

"You're not gay. I know." She wasn't looking at me. She was staring past my head toward the open door behind me. "Get out of here."

"I'm sorry—"

"Shut up." She looked like she was trying not to blink.

"I didn't mean to react that way," I said.

"Go vomit if you have to! I don't care."

"I just don't want people thinking I'm—you know."

"Oh, that's rich." She tried to laugh, but it came out sounding strangled. "You can't even say the word."

"What word?"

"*Gay, gay, gay!*" She leaned forward, her eyes popping. "I'm *gay!* Get over it, you sanctimonious little bitch."

Her hair hung in wild tangles around her face, making her look haggard, and as I walked over to the bed, anger mushroomed inside me like a deafening white cloud. "Shut up," I told her, scooping my bag off the bed. "I'm just acting how any normal person would act."

"Get out," she said.

And I did.

HERE'S WHAT'S GOING TO HAPPEN. I'M GOING TO KILL MYSELF. I'M GOING TO GET UP AND PUT ON MY SLIPPERS. I'M GOING TO TIPTOE DOWN THE HALLWAY. I'M GOING TO STAB MYSELF IN THE EYEBALLS WITH Q-TIPS IN THE BATHROOM EXACTLY ONE FLOOR OVER THE COUCH WHERE REYNA IS SLEEPING. AND I'M GOING TO DIE. TONIGHT. WITH ZERO FAITH IN HUMANITY.

What happened?

I CAME OUT TO REYNA.

Why are you writing in all caps?

BECAUSE I FEEL LIKE SHIT.

Whatever she said, I'm sure it'll be fine.

UGH, SERIOUSLY?

Seriously what?

SERIOUSLY DON'T THROW CLICHÉS AT ME.

Sorry. I'm sure everything will suck.

THAT'S BETTER.

What's going on, Olive?

I'M A GAY, GRACE. THAT'S WHAT'S GOING ON. JUST LIKE YOU. JUST LIKE TIMOTHY "FAIRY" FERGUSON. JUST LIKE EVERYBODY ON THIS FUCKING FORUM. GAY.

Well, duh.

SHUT UP AND SAY SOMETHING SUPPORTIVE.

Like what?

ANYTHING THAT COMES TO MIND.

You're the one who always talks me off the ledge.

TELL ME NOT TO STAB MYSELF IN THE EYEBALLS. TELL ME I HAVE A REASON TO LIVE.

Stop pacing around in your window. I can see you.

I HAVE TO KEEP MOVING. IF I DON'T KEEP MOVING, I'LL ABSORB ALL THIS SHIT INTO MY SKIN AND DROP DEAD OF MELODRAMA POISONING.

Come outside, then. We can talk.

8

Big raindrops running down a windowpane eating little raindrops in their path. That's what school was like for the rest of the week. Once Gretchen Palmer found out Olive and I weren't speaking, she started passing me weird notes during math. They said things like, *Stripes or polka dots?* and *Jake Gyllenhaal or Zac Efron?* I knew it was some kind of test, but I couldn't figure out why she bothered. Meanwhile, I got word that a freshman girl had been deliberately knocked on the head with a hockey puck in gym, and it was only on Friday, when Gretchen passed me a note sealed shut with a strawberry-scented sticker, that I found out she was the one who threw the puck and the girl was Olive.

Nobody was around on Friday afternoon when I got home from school. It was snowing—the wimpy kind that doesn't stick—and the wooden floorboards on my front porch smelled like a wet dog. I unlocked the front door and wiped my sneakers against the ratty welcome mat in our foyer. That was when I noticed one of dad's crutches propped against the door of the coat closet. There was a note pinned to the squishy, band-aid colored pad at the top: *Feeling great—night on the town. See you tomorrow morning.* When I saw it, I kicked the crutch so that it clattered onto the floor, note and all. Then I sat down right there on the carpet, not even two feet into the house, and called Abby. We hadn't spoken since our awkward conversation about her new boyfriend, but I didn't care about that now. She was my best friend. I needed her.

"Hey, it's me," I said as soon as she picked up. "Are you busy right now?"

"Reyna? Hold on, I can't hear you—" There was a faint roar in the background, a sea of noise. I heard her tell someone to save her a seat.

My heart sank. "Am I interrupting something?" I should have known she'd be hanging out with James or Jackson or whatever his name was.

"No!" She sounded a little breathless. "What's up?"

"I just wanted to see if you could come over today. I have news."

"I—" she paused. "I'm at a basketball game."

"*Basketball?*"

"Hey! Stop that!" There was a squeaky noise in the background that sounded like a dog toy. "Sorry, Reyna, not you—"

"Fine, I'll just tell you now," I said. "Olive is a lesbian."

"What?"

"Olive is a—"

"Stop!" I heard the squeaky toy again. "Whoops. There's this dog running around in the bleachers—"

"Abby..." I raked my fingers through my hair. "This is actually kind of serious."

"Sorry! Can I call you back another time?"

"What?" I could barely hear her. The crowd was cheering again.
"How about we catch up later?"

"Fine," I said, knowing that *later* might as well mean *never*. It wasn't just Abby's boyfriend coming between us, it was everything—new schools, new friends, new lives. As I ended the call, my phone slipped from my hand and bounced onto the carpet. I closed my eyes and breathed in deeply through my nose. The silence in the house was a roar.

★ ★ ★

At breakfast the next morning, I saw the ring. Lucy's long, spidery fingers were draped over the back of Dad's chair. She moved her hand onto his shoulder and scratched the back of his T-shirt, the plain gold band glinting in the soft morning light. She was still wearing the diamond necklace he'd bought her only a couple of weeks earlier. That and her pajamas.
"Morning," I said from the doorway.

Lucy and Dad both jumped at the sound of my voice; then Lucy pulled her left hand down onto her lap and clasped it with her other hand so I couldn't see the ring.

"Morning, Rey," said Dad. They both smiled sheepishly, as though I'd caught them in bed. Looking closer at the table, I realized there was a tub of Ben & Jerry's ice cream sitting near Lucy with its lid open. It was empty except for two dirty spoons.

"What are you guys—five?" I turned toward the sink. "Ice cream for breakfast?"

"For dessert," said Dad. "Early morning dessert."

Gross. Feeling vaguely queasy, I took a glass from the drying rack and picked a speck of grime off its side. I wasn't going to say anything about the ring. Maybe if I ignored it, it would fall into the garbage disposal while Lucy was washing dishes. Or maybe it wasn't even an engagement ring. It didn't have a stone.

"How was last night?" he asked from the table.

"Fine," I said.

"What'd you do?"

"Watched TV."

I turned away from the sink and headed for the fridge. Dad was looking at Lucy as though waiting for her permission. Out of the corner of my eye, I saw her nod.

"Reyna?" Dad leaned forward in his chair. "We have something to tell you."

That was when all the atoms in my body got up and rearranged themselves in preparation. My face became a mask of itself. My toes tightened in my socks.

Dad looked nervous. "You know how I took Lucy to New York last night?"

I knew what was coming, and I didn't like it. I grabbed the carton of orange juice from the fridge and filled my glass.

"Well, I asked her to marry me," he said. "Right in the middle of Times Square."

"And I said yes!" Lucy held up her left hand and I saw the ring again, clearer this time. It wasn't just a plain gold band. There was a filigree trim around the edge.

"Wow," I said. Both of them were waiting—watching me. Lucy raised her hand with a nervous sort of giggle and ruffled her feathery haircut.

"Wow!" I repeated because I didn't know what else to say. I felt like the sandman, slipping apart and sliding through the cracks on the floor.

"We're going to have the wedding in May," Lucy told me, filling the awkward silence. "And you'll be my maid of honor."

"That's great," I said. Some sort of ghost had hijacked my vocal chords. The real me was disassembled in a pile on the floor, slipping through the cracks in the wood, but I couldn't let Dad see that. He looked happier than I'd seen him in years, and I wasn't about to ruin it for him.

Dad stood up and walked over to me with hardly any limp at all. His crutches were nowhere in sight. "Do I get a hug?"

I nodded and let him wrap his arms around me.

"I hope you're excited, kiddo."

"I have to go call my friends," I said, glancing over at the phone. It was the only excuse I could think of to leave the room.

"Go ahead, doll," said Lucy. And that was exactly what I felt like—a floppy doll with button eyes that couldn't cry. As politely as possible, I left the kitchen.

I didn't call anyone. I sent Abby three texts in a row, each more desperate than the last. *Can you come over today?* I wrote, nearly chewing off my lower lip. Then, *Where are you???* And finally, *If you're at another basketball game, I think I'm going to hate basketball forever.*

As it turned out, Abby was grocery shopping with her mom. By the time she called back, I must have sounded so lonely and borderline insane that her mom agreed to drop her off at my house as soon as they found some rutabagas and spiced peach jam. The whole time I waited, I stared at Mom's bookshelf and asked God to please, for the love of cinnamon buns and peppermint soap and all things holy, give me something to think about other than Dad and Lucy getting married in five months.

And it worked. When Abby arrived, the first thing she said was, "So, Olive's gay?"

"Yeah," I said, forgetting momentarily about the engagement. She must have heard me on the phone after all. Diving into the story of the sleepover, I told her about the queen bed and the weird homeless girl, Grace.

Abby wasn't surprised about Olive being gay, but she was weirded out by Grace. "Isn't anyone in her family looking for her?" she asked. "And how is she not starving to death?"

"Olive brings her food," I said. "She's connected to their Wi-Fi and everything."

"Crazy." Abby grabbed my hacky sack off the windowsill and sat down on my bed. "So they're lesbians together?"

"I don't know," I said. "Maybe."

Her face broke out in a grin. "I bet that's who she had online sex with. Remember?"

I couldn't help but laugh. Abby's smile was infectious, and I felt giddy having her all to myself for once. I didn't want to share her ever again—not with Madison or Leah, and especially not with her boyfriend. That reminded me of Dad, though. My stomach sank.

"I have more news," I said. Then I let it all roll out—the story of Dad proposing in Times Square, the gold ring, the Ben & Jerry's for breakfast.

"Oh wow," Abby said when I was finished. She tossed the hacky sack up with one hand and caught it with the other. "Are you even a *little* happy?"

I narrowed my eyes. "You know how I feel about Lucy."

"You still blame her for causing the accident?"

"Of course," I answered. "She ran the stop sign."

"Reyna, this is *obviously* not about the stop sign." Abby put on her best therapy face. "Blame the accident if you want, but it's not the real reason you don't like Lucy—"

"Don't psychoanalyze me," I said. "Please."

"Then don't freak out." She tossed me the hacky sack. "Just wait until winter break. We'll hang out every day and you can forget all about your dad and Lucy."

I caught it and kneaded it between my knuckles. "But don't you think she's taking advantage of him?"

Abby cocked an eyebrow at me. "If you say sexually, I'm going to laugh."

"Not sexually!" I threw the hacky sack back at her with a little force. It thumped her on the leg. "He's a doormat," I explained. "He lets her step all over him. She even rearranged all our furniture. It's a disaster match."

Abby arched an eyebrow at me. "Sounds like you and Olive."

"It's nothing like that," I said. But some nervous, squirming part of me wondered if she was right. All week long, Olive

113

had been creeping from thought to thought in the back of my mind like a masked assassin, moving steadily closer. Every now and then she poked her head out and fixed me with a withering stare. *You're better than this*, she whispered. And every time I looked away.

"Maybe you should join a club," suggested Abby. "Like gymnastics or something."

"What good would that do?" I opened my hand and gestured for her to throw the hacky sack back in my direction. I needed something to grind in my fist.

"For one thing, it would distract you from Lucy." Abby tossed the sack and I caught it in my palm. "For another, you need to make some new friends besides Olive. Isn't there anybody else who likes you?"

"Maybe." I told her about Gretchen Palmer's notes to me during math. "But she might just be picking on me. I can't tell. She's always quizzing me."

Abby looked thoughtful. "She probably sees potential in you. If you dressed a little better and had more confidence, you could have a lot of friends."

"Maybe." I could feel Olive moving around in the back of my mind, lurking. *Do me a favor*, she whispered. *Follow your better nature.*

"Not maybe." Abby gave me a long, hard stare. "Definitely."

★ ★ ★

In math on Monday, Gretchen passed me another note. It said, *Boxers or Briefs?* Just like last time, it was sealed with a scented sticker—this time banana—only unlike last time, she

114

didn't mention knocking Olive on the head with a hockey puck in gym.

I wrote back *Briefs.*

We were learning how to calculate the volume of a circular cone, and I kept imagining party hats filled with beer. It was one of those random images—like a kangaroo wearing a condom—that once it pops into your mind sticks there. So when Gretchen passed me the boxers-or-briefs note again—this time with the question, *Love or Marriage?*—I circled *Love* and drew three upside-down party hats with pom-poms. Then I made an arrow next to them and wrote, *The amount of beer you have to drink to understand this math equals the volume of these three cones.* It was stupid, but I passed it to her anyway.

You're hilarious!!! she wrote back a moment later, seconds before the bell. And it was only then, when I folded the note and put it my pocket, that I realized Abby was right. I had potential. A lot of potential.

By Friday, the last day of school before winter break, I'd passed fourteen notes with Gretchen. She ran out of scented stickers on Thursday and started folding the notes into intricate patterns that were difficult for me to unfold under my desk without catching the attention of Mr. Beyner, our math teacher. Karma came back to us on Friday morning in the form of a pop quiz that I almost failed. We graded it together as a class—a boy named Donald, who sat to my right, had the job of marking twelve incorrect answers on my paper—and when I saw my grade, I almost crumpled the quiz in my fist.

But I didn't. Instead I stuck it like a bookmark between the pages of my math book and took it out between every period that morning, trying to relearn the material that I'd missed over the course of the week. And that was how Olive found me during lunch, waiting in line in the cafeteria, looking over each incorrect answer.

"Sixty-two?"

I jumped. She was peering over my shoulder, just like on the day we met. At the front of the line, the lunch ladies were serving nachos, watery salsa, and corn bread.

"Geometry isn't my strong suit," I said, folding the quiz in half and shoving it into my backpack. It was the first time we'd spoken since our sleepover more than a week ago, and I felt suddenly nervous, like my fingers were made of rubber. An apology for bolting out of her room was lodged somewhere deep in my throat, but this wasn't the time to bring it up—not in front of all these people.

"Our class took the same quiz," she said pointedly. "I got an A."

Anger swelled in me, crowding out the impulse to apologize.

Olive rolled her eyes. "It was on circles. What's not to understand?"

"Shut up," I said and got out of the line. I had four dollar bills in my pocket, but I didn't even use them to buy junk from the vending machines. Instead I let my stomach growl while I wandered around the periphery of the cafeteria, scanning the room for a table where I could sit without being noticed.

That was when I heard someone calling my name. I looked around and saw Gretchen Palmer sitting at her usual table with the rest of the Slutty Nurses. They weren't actually slutty nurses, of course—I just remembered them that way from the Halloween parade. In reality, they were preppy girls who lived in North Springdale and brought fresh, organic bag lunches every day. None of them was quite prom queen material, but they would probably go on to run the student council and *choose* the prom queen. They had a comfortable place in the social hierarchy, and I decided that was reason enough to sit with them. Well, that and because Olive was still watching me with narrow eyes from the lunch line.

As I chose a seat and dropped my backpack down on the table, every one of Gretchen's friends acted as though they'd never cornered Olive and me during a parade and called us farm girls. "What's up?" said the one to my left—I was pretty sure her name was Emma.

"Not much," I answered.

"Reyna is a briefs girl," Gretchen announced. "Most of us are boxers, but now Lennie has someone to relate to."

A tall Asian girl smiled at me, and I recognized her right away from Mr. Murphy's class. "Thank God," she said. "I thought I was the only one."

I tried to act like this meant we had something in common, but the truth was I'd chosen briefs randomly. "So what middle school did you go to?" I asked.

"Glenbrook," Lennie said. "All of us did."

"We've known each other since second grade," added the girl whose name I thought was Emma. "We went to elementary school with Olive Garden too. I mean—Olive Barton."

She giggled while I looked down at my backpack, wishing I had something to eat to distract me from their scrutiny.

"We actually used to be friends with her," Lennie said. "From second to fourth grade. But she's so weird, you know? We had to break it off. Just like you did."

"I didn't—"

"The point is, we're here to rescue you." Gretchen was wearing a fuzzy lavender sweater with two pom-poms hanging off each wrist, and she flicked one of them absently as she spoke. "We're not mean people, you know. We weren't trying to get you in trouble on Halloween. We just had a bone to pick to with Olive Garden."

"Whatever," I said, ignoring the nickname. "I don't care anymore."

"We're glad."

There it was again: the plural pronoun. Eating lunch with the Slutty Nurses—I couldn't stop thinking of them that way—was like eating lunch in a beehive. There was no *I*. There was only *we*.

"Anyway, it's not your fault you got roped in with the wrong people," Gretchen said, as though Olive were some kind of drug dealer. Everyone else at the table nodded; Gretchen was obviously the queen bee. "What are you doing for winter break?"

"Not much," I said, unsure how else to respond. I felt like I was at a job interview. Even my posture was straighter than normal.

"You can come to my family's New Year's party if you want," said Gretchen. "We're all going to be there."

"Sure," I said, mainly to be nice. I was planning to spend New Year's with Abby, but the Slutty Nurses didn't need to know that. They were being polite to me, so I would be polite to them. That was the way the world worked unless your name was Olive Barton.

"Do you want some of my Sun Chips?" Lennie asked, looking over at the empty spot on the table in front of me. "You haven't eaten a thing."

"Sure," I said and opened my palm. "Thanks."

It's time to play Asshole of the Day.

Again, Olive?

I'll give you a hint: it's not Reyna this time.

Gretchen the Wretched?

That was yesterday. Pay attention.

I give up.

You're no fun. It's Mr. Murphy.

Who's that again?

My history teacher.

Oh, right. The homophobe.

You know what he said this time?

Enlighten me.

Fudge packer.

To the same guy he called
limp-wristed?

Yeah, Tim Ferguson.

I used to have a teacher like that too.

Did you ever say anything to him?

Her. No, I didn't.

Why not?

I was too busy with other things.
For example, trying to off myself
with sleeping pills.

Jesus, Grace.

It was the year I came out.

That sucks.

She had no idea how close I came
to succeeding.

She should have been fired.

So should your teacher. Maybe you
should write a letter to the principal
or something. Do what I should
have done.

And out myself in the process? No thanks.

He deserves it, though.

That's true.

The very worst.

I know.

9

I was putting on my boots to bike to Abby's house when the phone rang.

"Don't come," she said. "I'm not there."

I let go of my shoelace and watched it drop to the floor. Not there? As we spoke, Dad was in the shower singing "Lucy in the Sky with Diamonds" at the top of his lungs while Lucy made him breakfast. Literally the *only* thing stopping me from marching over and slamming his door was the fact that I was in a hurry to leave for Abby's house. We were planning to kick off winter break with an all-day '90s movie marathon.

But not anymore apparently. "I'm on my way to the airport," Abby said over the sound of traffic. "Dad surprised us last night with tickets to Puerto Rico. Awesome, right?"

Awesome? I felt my stomach drop. "You're leaving the country?"

"Technically Puerto Rico is part of—"

"Whatever!" I said. "You're leaving? Just like that?"

Abby didn't sound even remotely guilty. "It was a Hanukkah present," she said. "Mostly for Mom, since she's been so stressed lately with work—"

"You can't leave!" I burst out. "This was our week to spend

together." I felt like a baby, but it was true. Leah was going to Disney World with her gymnastics team. Madison's family was on their annual ski trip in Colorado. Abby and I were supposed to be stuck in Springdale together just like last year. It was the natural order of the universe.

"Rey, I have to go. I have to call Jeremy and the others. I called you first, of course."

Probably only because I was on my way to her house. A hard knot was forming at the base of my throat. "Didn't you hear me?" I asked. "This was supposed to be our week together."

"Actually, the reception is kind of bad right now." Abby's voice came through my phone garbled. "We're halfway through a tunnel."

Anger and disappointment swirled through me like a dust storm. "I never get to see you anymore," I said, my voice dangerously wobbly.

"Hello? Did you say something?"

"I never get to see you," I repeated. "We're practically just acquaintances now." Then I hung up before she could tell I was on the verge of crying. It was going to be a long week.

Instead of riding my bike to Abby's house, I rode to the most depressing place I could think of—the mall. I spent four hours there, wandering from booth to booth, letting pushy sales-people sell me a pair of fingerless mittens, polarized sunglasses, and exfoliating skin lotion from the Dead Sea. On Sunday I went to Mass. On Monday, I finished all my homework for the entire vacation. On Tuesday—the day before Christmas—Dad finally agreed to watch some '90s movies with me, but he fell asleep on the couch twenty minutes into *Dumb and Dumber*. I watched the entire thing, not laughing even once, and then channel-surfed for a good hour before Lucy came home from her Pilates class and flopped down on the love seat.

"Anything good on TV?" she asked.

"Nope," I said, handing her the remote. There were still six hours left before dinner, and if I checked Facebook one more time, I thought I might puke. So I followed Dad's example and snuggled into the couch, burrowing my feet under the fuzzy throw blanket I got him for Christmas in fourth grade. Then I closed my eyes and tried with all my might to sleep through the rest of vacation.

When I got so bored I thought my skull might crack, I called Gretchen.

A woman whose voice sounded like Martha Stewart answered the phone. "*The* Reyna Fey?" she asked when I said my name. "Gretchen's told me all about you, sweetheart!"

I tried not to feel creeped out as she re-invited me to the Palmer Family New Year's party on Tuesday night and gave me directions, all before wishing me a Merry Christmas and passing the phone to her daughter. By the time Gretchen picked up, there wasn't much left to say. "How's your break going?" I asked.

"Good—really good!" said Gretchen, clearly distracted. I heard laughter in the background and wondered if the Slutty Nurses were with her.

"Mine too," I lied. "I'm baking cookies with my friend Abby. Actually, I have frosting all over my hands right now—I should probably go."

"Me too!" said Gretchen. "Only, egg whites, not frosting. My mom and I are making eggnog." She laughed again. "Mom, put that down!"

So it wasn't the Slutty Nurses she was hanging out with. It was worse. I felt an ache in the pit of my stomach, wishing I could frost Christmas cookies one last time with Mom.

"Oh! I almost forgot!" said Gretchen. "You have to write a New Year's resolution on a slip of paper and bring it with you to the party. Only don't put your name on it, OK?"

"OK—"

"Ciao, Reyna!" The line went dead. As I stood there with the phone still held up to my ear, I pictured Gretchen and her mother sitting in Martha Stewart's kitchen, clinking their glasses of eggnog together. It was enough to kill my appetite for the rest of the evening.

I slept late on Christmas morning. I probably would have slept all day if Dad hadn't knocked on my door and threatened to give my presents to charity.

So I dragged myself barefoot into the living room, my hair a gnarled mess. I could see the nest of it in my peripheral vision, but I didn't bother to grab a brush. Instead I just pulled my arms into the body of my sweatshirt and hugged myself to keep warm.

"Morning, Reyna!" said Lucy, sitting cross-legged on the carpet next to the Christmas tree. She was wearing red and green pajamas with fluffy reindeer slippers. Rudolf's bulbous nose wiggled over her big toe every time she bounced her knees.

"Merry Christmas," I said with zero enthusiasm, dropping to sit on the floor. I felt like Ebenezer Scrooge, utterly devoid of cheer. I was half-debating going back to bed when Dad pulled up a chair and Lucy handed me a small yellow envelope. I pulled my hand out of the warmth of my sweatshirt to take it from her.

"This is for you," she said with a nervous glance at Dad. "From both of us."

"Thanks," I said as I slid my finger under the flap of the envelope. She wasn't about to win me over with a gift, but I did my best to smile politely. It was all I could do to stop myself from pointing out that she had used an old quilt of Mom's as a skirt for the Christmas tree.

She grinned, perfectly oblivious. "Go on. Open it."

Inside the envelope was a gift certificate to the Gramercy Concert Hall downtown, where popular bands performed. The card read:

Dear Reyna,
  Merry Christmas! This is for two tickets to a concert
of your choice.
Love, Dad and Lucy.

"Thanks!" I felt a rush of excitement followed almost immediately by a sudden drop in my stomach. There were two tickets. Who would I bring? Dad was watching me, so I mustered a smile in his direction. There was no need to ruin his Christmas with the fact that I had no friends.

"Here," I said, reaching under the tree and passing him a small rectangular box with a bow on top. "I thought these might be useful."

"Polarized sunglasses?" said Dad, tearing off the wrapping before I'd even finished my sentence. "Very nice! Thanks, Rey." He leaned over to kiss me on the head.

Lucy reached for the gift bag with her name, carefully removed the tissue paper, and pulled out a small tub of lotion barely larger than her fist. "Exfoliating cream," she read off the label. "From the Dead Sea. Cool!" She leaned over to hug me too. I stiffened at first, but relaxed when I saw Dad's expression. He flashed me a grateful smile behind her back.

We opened the rest of the presents under the tree and ate breakfast together—eggs with sausage. Dad and Lucy did most of the talking while I behaved like a perfectly polite avatar of myself. Only when I glanced down at my spoon and saw my freakishly bug-eyed reflection did I feel, for a split second, like me.

★ ★ ★

By the time New Year's Eve rolled around, I didn't know whether to dread Gretchen's party or look forward to it. On the one hand, she had been nice to invite me. On the other hand, I got the sense that if I said no, my social life would be doomed for the rest of high school.

The whole drive to her house, I pictured Dad dropping me off in front of a giant beehive with honeycomb windows.

Inside, a swarm of bees would lounge around with champagne flutes full of honey, toasting the New Year.

As it turned out, Gretchen lived in a brick house with a slew of inflatable, light-up reindeer prancing across the roof. Dad whistled at the display when he dropped me off. "Must do wonders for their electric bill," he said, shaking his head.

As I started to remind him not to pick me up until one a.m., Gretchen's front door swung open. "Reyna!" she called, popping her head out. "You're just in time!"

She must have been freezing—she was wearing a tank top—so I scooped up my purse, hurried out of the car, and waved good-bye to Dad. As soon as I got up the steps, Gretchen enveloped me in a hug like we'd been friends forever. Then she led me inside, babbling about eggnog and virgin piña coladas. Right away, I could see why none of the Slutty Nurses stood up to her on Halloween. Being on Gretchen Palmer's good side was like walking around with a giant VIP badge. For once, I actually felt wanted.

Inside, her house looked more like a preschool than it did a Martha Stewart magazine. There were wicker baskets everywhere holding board games, DVDs, and random toys. Gretchen's four younger brothers ran around playing tag in the living room while adults wandered in and out of the kitchen, carrying cocktails and little cubes of cheese on toothpicks.

Lennie King and the other Slutty Nurses were sitting in a corner around a game table, eating from a gigantic bowl of chips. There was a basket on the table next to it, and as we got closer, I realized it contained half a dozen scraps of paper.

128

"Did you bring your New Year's resolution?" Gretchen asked, leading the way.

"Yeah," I said, pulling it out of my pocket.

"Good." She snatched it from my hand and dropped it into the basket with the other pieces of paper. "Now we can get started."

"Get started with what?" I asked.

She looked at me with an evil smile. "Pick a resolution from the basket, but don't tell anyone what it is."

Reluctantly, I reached out and selected a scrap of paper. It was folded over twice, and when I opened it, I saw two words written in colored pencil: *Jamie Pollock.*

I knew that name. Jamie was a chubby girl in my math class. I didn't know much about her except that she played in the ninth grade orchestra. It was hard to miss her wandering the halls with her giant cello on wheels.

"I'll go first so you can see how it works," said Gretchen, snatching another piece of paper from the basket. When she saw what was written inside, she grinned. "Lennie, you must have written this one. I'd recognize your handwriting anywhere."

"What does it say?" asked the Slutty Nurse named Emma.

"John Quincy," said Gretchen. I knew John. He was a curly-haired soccer player in my history class—sort of a class clown.

"Date, demolish, or dump?" asked Lennie.

"You should date him," answered Gretchen. "Obviously."

I felt like I was in a foreign country. "How exactly does this work?"

"You have to guess whose resolution it is," Gretchen explained. "And then you have to say either date, demolish, or dump. Not what you'd want, but what you think the writer intended."

My cheeks grew warm as I thought of the New Year's resolution I'd written on my piece of paper. "You didn't tell me that on the phone," I said, reaching for the basket to find it. Mine was the small yellow sticky note folded over twice. I could take it out of the pile, if I could find it—

But Gretchen pulled the basket away before I had a chance to pilfer through it. "You already have one, Reyna," she said, gesturing at the paper in my hand. "What does it say?"

"Jamie Pollock," I told her. "But I have to find the resolution I brought. It's not—"

"Jamie Pollock? Gross." Gretchen ignored me. "Have you seen that cello? It's almost as fat as she is."

"Oh my God, look at this," added Lennie, pulling up a picture on her phone. She held out an unflattering photo of Jamie trying to shoot a basket in gym.

"So—date, demolish, or dump?" There was a glint in Gretchen's eyes. "Your call, Reyna."

I felt vaguely nauseated as Olive's voice echoed through my head. *Follow your better nature.* "I don't know," I said at last, looking down at my lap. "None of those, I guess."

"Come on!" said Gretchen. "Jamie's not a guy, so we can't date her. And we've never been friends, so we can't dump her. There's only one option left."

"Demolish?" All I could think was that at one point Olive had probably played this game until someone wrote her name on a piece of paper and picked *dump*.

"Bingo," said Lennie. "We resolve to demolish Jamie Pollock."

"We?" I stared at them. Apparently I was in a beehive, after all.

"Of course," said Gretchen. "There's power in numbers. Which is why we also resolve as a group that John Quincy is off limits to the rest of us so that only Lennie can date him."

The balls of my feet felt itchy. I knew if I wanted to, I could get up. I could walk away. I could call Dad. But if I did, they'd probably demolish me next.

"How can you demolish Jamie if she's not even popular to begin with?" I asked. Maybe if I pointed out the obvious, they'd drop the issue.

Gretchen's eyes narrowed. "You can demolish anyone you want. Trust me."

"My turn," said Emma, reaching for the basket. When she pulled out my yellow sticky note, I felt my heart drop straight through my stomach.

"Read more books," she read out loud. "What is this, school?"

"I didn't know—"

"It's OK, Reyna." Gretchen gave me a gentle, patronizing pat on the arm. "You'll know what to do next year."

If you haven't dumped me by then, I thought. Life inside the beehive was dangerous.

New York City?

Eventually.

But it's so noisy and crowded.

That's the way I like it.

A New Year's resolution isn't a place. It's a commitment. Like "Stop drinking when you puke." If you're my mom, I mean.

A place can be a commitment.

What would you do once you got there?

I already told you. Be free.

You're free now.

I might buy a ticket if I can find
the money.

Seriously??? Don't leave.

Don't worry. Even if I wanted to, I
wouldn't have anywhere to stay.

Let's wait for summer. We can go together.

I don't know if I'll be around that long.

Don't talk like that.

I just mean I might not be staying with
you all the way until the summer.

Oh. I thought you meant...

I know.

January

10

"So, you're Catholic?"

Levi Siegel scuttled toward me on a tiny plastic scooter, propelling himself forward against the gymnasium floor with the palms of his hands.

"Yeah," I said. "Who told you?"

"A little bird."

It was our first day back from winter break, and we were racing scooters in gym. Levi had positioned himself last in line so that he could race with me to the orange cone at the end of the track. It was far more face time than we usually had in gym. Normally he was part of the group of guys who disappeared into the weight training room while the girls played volleyball or indoor soccer. But today, scooter racing was mandatory.

"Little birds don't speak English," I said, crossing my legs on my scooter and inching forward toward the front of the line. There were four people ahead of us waiting to race.

"I have my sources," said Levi, smiling mischievously. "Are you *Catholic* Catholic?" He unfolded his legs and stretched them out in front of the scooter, almost toppling sideways as his center of gravity shifted.

"Trying to be," I said. "But not always succeeding." After all, instead of going to Mass on Christmas, I'd stayed at home feeling sorry for myself. "What are you?" I asked Levi.

He laughed. "The same as you, except Jewish. I'm trying to be *Jewish* Jewish."

I looked down at my lap and smiled. "I guess it's all the same God anyway."

"Yeah, and I owe him one." Levi rolled forward on his scooter. "For making you my scooter racing partner today."

I felt my cheeks heat up. I always *wanted* to flirt, but I never knew what to say. Fortunately, I didn't have to. There was a loud whistle as a tall redheaded girl beat her partner to the finish line.

"You're probably going to win," said Levi, eying the orange cones that made up the racetrack. "You're small. Your legs won't fall off the scooter."

"But your weight will give you momentum," I said. "I'll have to push twice as hard to go just as fast as you."

"True." He began folding his legs on his scooter as I readied myself in the crab-legged position. Then he asked, "What do I get if I win?"

"Hmmm." I thought for a second. "The satisfaction of knowing you're a really good thruster?" It was simultaneously the dumbest and most flirtatious thing I'd ever said in my life.

He laughed.

"What about me?" I hoped my face wasn't too red. "What do I get if I win?"

He didn't even blink. "Ice cream after school on Friday."

A loud whistle screeched as we rolled toward the starting line, and Mr. Graham bellowed, "On your marks...get set...*Go!*"

I propelled myself forward—shot in a straight line down the track—yanking my feet up onto the scooter so my legs wouldn't touch the ground. I was going fast enough at first to feel a breeze against my face, but it only lasted a few seconds. My momentum slowed halfway down the track as I began swooping my arms in the butterfly stroke to keep myself moving. Behind me, a few feet to my left, I heard Levi catching up, so I bent low at the waist to make myself as compact as possible. I rolled forward, tucking my arms at my side, closing in on the finish line in a diagonal path. A few people cheered as I thrust my chest forward to propel me the few extra inches toward the final orange cone. When I looked back, I saw Levi a couple of feet behind me, butt on the floor, his scooter toppled beside him. He was grinning from ear to ear.

"You win," he said.

★ ★ ★

In history class, Mr. Murphy handed back our documentary on the Peloponnesian War. It was the first time I'd been forced to make eye contact with Olive since we handed in our project before winter break. Olive had finished editing the video herself, and I never saw the final product. This time, we had to peer at a piece of paper that had a big C+ scribbled at the top in red marker. Underneath, it said: *Creative idea, sloppy execution.*

"Oh well," said Olive, crumpling the page in her fist. "It could've been an A if I'd had a little help with the editing."

"I would have helped if you'd asked," I said. "I could have posted it online like Mr. Murphy wanted."

"That's not the hard part," she snapped. "It took me two seconds to put it on YouTube."

I didn't say anything; I just turned around and stared at the front of the room as Mr. Murphy drew a Venn diagram on the blackboard labeled, *Modern Democracy vs. Plato's* Republic. Our assignment for the period was to compare and contrast the two.

John Quincy—the guy Lennie had resolved to date—spoke up from the back of the room. "Wait, what does Play-Doh have to do with anything?"

Everyone laughed except for Mr. Murphy. "You think you're funny, Quincy?"

John grinned.

"Here." Mr. Murphy crossed the room and fished the Dr. Seuss hat out of his desk. "You want to be the class clown, I have just the hat for you."

He tossed it across the room and John caught it, still smiling.

"Wipe that smile off your face," said Mr. Murphy. "And don't even think about taking off the hat until the end of the period."

As John pulled the bottom of the Dr. Seuss hat over his ears, the top flopped over and partially covered the word *Sissy*. He tried to straighten the top half, but it kept folding over, and the more attempts he made to adjust it, the more the class laughed. John seemed to love the attention, grinning as he moved the hat back and forth.

"Enough!" Mr. Murphy looked murderous. "Nobody look at Quincy!"

"But he's wearing the hat," said Levi. "Isn't that the point?"

Mr. Murphy had no answer. He just growled and told us to break into groups to do our assignment. This time I didn't even think of turning around to ask Olive if she wanted to work together. Instead, I turned around to make eye contact with Lennie King just as Levi flicked a tiny piece of eraser in my direction and called, "Hey, Reyna!"

People were getting up out of their seats to move around the room, so I flagged over Lennie and met her in front of Levi's desk. "Do you guys want to work together?" I asked.

"How about a group of four?" Lennie said, looking hopefully at John Quincy.

"Cool," said John. So we pulled our desks into a square and started working. Levi and I came up with a list of characteristics about democracy while John came up with a list of characteristics about Lennie. Then he curled a strip of paper into a circle and placed it on her head. "I crown you Miss California," he announced while she pretended to read her textbook. "The tallest state in the country for the tallest girl in the class."

Lennie laughed, her cheeks pink.

"How tall are you, Reyna?" John asked, turning to face me. "Four-foot-eleven? You're the opposite of Lennie. You can be Miss Rhode Island."

"I'm five-foot-two, thank you very much." I pushed a pencil toward him. "*Work*."

"I can't work!" he said. "This stupid hat keeps falling in my eyes."

"So take it off," said Lennie. "You should refuse to wear it. I'd like to see the expression on Murphy's face."

"Yeah right." John cracked a smile. "Like that homo last year?"

"What homo?" I asked. Only when I saw Levi's startled expression, I regretted my word choice. "I mean, who are you talking about?"

"The freak in the padded cell at Silver Hills," said John. "He refused to wear the hat, and look where he ended up."

I put down my pencil, surprised. So Olive had been right about that rumor after all.

"Everybody knows that guy was crazy to begin with," said Lennie. "Mr. Murphy just sent him over the edge."

"Guys, is anybody but me actually doing work?" asked Levi.

Feeling bad, I grabbed my pencil and leaned over our diagram. But John pulled it away before I could read anything. "Doesn't this look like a butt?" he asked, pointing at the two overlapping circles.

Levi and I exchanged an eye roll while Lennie laughed. Clearly, the assignment was going to take a while. It was only halfway through the period—when Mr. Murphy left the room to make photocopies of our homework—that I finally stole a glance behind me to see who had the misfortune of working with Olive. To my surprise, she hadn't joined a group. She was sitting alone at her desk, scribbling in her ratty, red moleskin notebook. At the corner of her desk, on a loose-leaf page, sat a finished Venn diagram.

Lennie saw where I was looking and tapped me on the arm with her pencil. "She thinks she's so smart," she whispered. "Just because she finished first."

John glanced up. "Who? Olive Garden?"

Hearing her name, Olive stopped writing at once.

"You know which state she is, right?" John said, not taking care to lower his voice. "Florida. Flat and skinny."

Olive didn't look up. She just tore out a page from her notebook and crumpled it in her fist. Then she tossed the wad of paper into her backpack, leaned over her notebook again, and started writing something else.

My group turned our attention back to the Venn diagram in Levi's notebook. Only this time I shifted my chair so I could keep an eye on Olive. She kept scribbling away, occasionally tearing out pages, crumpling them, and throwing them into the open mouth of her backpack.

Except on the fourth time, she missed. The balled-up wad of paper bounced off the backpack and rolled a couple of feet away on the floor. In an instant, Lennie swooped down, grabbed it, and threw it at my lap. I felt my eyes snap toward Olive's. She had dropped her pencil on her desk and was staring at me, her face white with rage.

Feeling spiteful, I dug my fingernails into the crumpled wad of paper and pulled it open. There, in her tidy, cramped cursive, were two sentences:

Your sadness came pawing at my door like a lost dog.
I thought we were the same.

Before I even finished reading, John Quincy snatched the page out of my hand and called loud enough for everyone to hear, "Hark! The poet speaks!"

A few people laughed as he read the two lines aloud with emphasis on the word *pawing.* When he finished, he crumpled the page and threw it back at Olive, whose hands shook as she got to her feet.

And then, right as Mr. Murphy came back with our homework—right as John took a bow and the hat fell off—she stormed out of the room.

At lunch I found out from the Slutty Nurses that Olive and John Quincy had history. Their rivalry dated back to fourth grade, when she tagged him once during a game of recess dodgeball. Later that afternoon, he and a couple of other boys crept up behind her during art class and glued three petri dishes to the butt of her jeans. When she caught on, she whipped around and punched them both three times in the face.

When Lennie told me that John had walked away from the incident with a bloody nose, I almost said, "Well, he deserved it."

But Gretchen spoke up before I could. "I was so mad! She could have broken his nose."

"I know," said Emma. "She almost did."

Olive was sitting at the far end of the cafeteria, across the table from a chubby girl with a cello—Jamie Pollock. Usually Jamie ate with the rest of the orchestra, but today she was sharing a bag of pretzels with Olive, who was leaning forward across the table, probably on a rant about something. Jamie was leaning back, eyebrows raised, as though Olive were pointing a blow-drier straight at her face.

"Guys, look at Jamie Pollock," I said, pointing across the room. "I think she's Olive Garden's new victim." It felt good to use the nickname. Weirdly good.

"Cheers to that!" said Gretchen, holding up her carton of milk. "She's doing our work for us." Lennie clinked her juice bottle with the milk carton, and everybody laughed.

★ ★ ★

It rained on Friday, the day Levi was supposed to take me out for ice cream. I worried all through seventh period that he was going to cancel on me—we were supposed to walk to TCBY, after all—but when I showed up at his locker at the end of the day, he handed me the bigger of two umbrellas and said, "Ready?"

"Ready," I told him, zipping up my jacket. If he had asked me to marry him at that very moment, I probably would have said, *Ready* to that too. How many guys even brought *one* umbrella with them to school?

On the walk to TCBY, our sneakers got soaked. It was freezing outside, and I didn't feel much like eating ice cream when we got there. But once Levi convinced me to take off my shoes and socks under our table, I started to warm up to the idea. Then he sat down across from me with two chocolate milkshakes and asked promptly, "What's wrong?"

"What do you mean?" I asked.

"You looked like you were thinking about something sad."

"I did?"

"Yeah." He grinned. "You were staring into space like your dog just got hit by a flying saucer—"

"I'm not sad!"

He laughed.

"I was just thinking about frozen yogurt." I pulled my milkshake closer to me and unwrapped the straw sitting next to it on the table. When I stuck it through the plastic lid, it made a soft screeching sound, like a badly tuned violin.

Levi was still smiling. "Why on earth would you be thinking about frozen yogurt? It's not as if we're at TCBY..."

I laughed. "My mom used to order chocolate yogurt with chocolate sprinkles every time we came here."

"Used to?"

"Yeah." I unwrapped my straw. "She died when I was seven."

His face went white.

"It's OK," I said. "You didn't know."

"We can go someplace else—"

"Don't be silly." I smiled to let him know it was fine.

"So you *were* thinking about something sad," he said. "If you were thinking about that."

"Not sad, exactly." I looked out the window, at the ribbons of rain on the street. The wind was blowing ripples across them, and it reminded me of music. "More like nostalgic."

"Nostalgia is sad."

"Not always."

"Reyna?" He leaned forward as though he wanted to tell me discreetly that I had something in my teeth. "Do you believe in God? Like a God that sits up in the clouds and watches everything we do and say?"

I'd been about to take the first sip of my milkshake, but I stopped, my lips hovering a few inches over the mouth of the straw. "What?"

Levi twirled his guitar pick necklace around his finger and looked down at the swirled pattern on the tabletop. "I'm writing a song called 'The O in God,'" he said. "And you seem like somebody to talk to about it."

I sat up straighter in my chair. "Because I believe in him?"

"So you do, then."

"Of course," I said. "Don't you?"

He thought about it for a second. "Not really."

"Oh." I tucked down my chin and took a sip from my shake. It was startling, like a cold flower bursting in my mouth.

"I mean, I did," he said. "I used to. I mean—I sometimes still do."

I couldn't quite figure out why were talking about God and not other things, like music we both liked. Not that I minded. It was just a little strange, that's all. I had a feeling Abby and Jeremy, or whatever his name was, didn't talk about God on their first date. They probably compared their iPod libraries.

"I thought you were trying to be religious," I said, recalling our conversation in gym. It was one of the things I liked about Levi.

"Yeah, *trying*." Levi sucked in his cheeks as he sipped from

144

his straw. "Besides, you don't have to believe in God to practice the traditions."

"I would," I said. "I would have to believe."

"This is going to sound stupid." Levi let go of his straw. "But do you think 'The O in God' sounds too much like *the Owen God*?"

"Maybe a little," I said.

"My little brother's name is Owen." Levi looked down again at his shake. "And the song is about how he found a bird outside our house and took it inside because it had a broken wing. Only we have a cat too, and last night she found the bird…"

I swallowed my mouthful. "Did she—?"

"Yeah. She ate it."

"That's so sad." I looked down at Levi's hands. He was spinning his milkshake between his palms, a small trail of condensation from the plastic cup leaking onto the table.

"And so I was just thinking about where it went, you know? The bird?" He stopped spinning the milkshake. "Is there such a thing as bird heaven?"

"I guess if the bird didn't sin," I said. "Then it would go to bird heaven."

"How can a bird sin?"

"I don't know," I said. "Coveting its neighbor's nest?"

Levi laughed and took another sip of his shake—straight from the cup this time, not out of the straw. Then he wiped his mouth with the back of his hand. "Sorry if that was a weird thing to bring up."

I wanted to say, *Not at all*. I wanted to keep talking as

though our thoughts mattered; as though we might discover something together, like on those rabbit hole nights with Abby and Leah and Madison. I wanted to feel like we were different, but different in the same way—different together. I didn't know how to say that, though. So I answered, "Only a little."

He took his straw out of the milkshake and set it down on his napkin. "I just want you to know that you can talk to me about dead birds anytime you want."

"Thanks," I said. And I meant it too.

It has to be dark.

Why does it matter?

The moon has to be out.

What are you, a werewolf?

Let's go now.

It's freezing.

It looks like a smudge of chalk

What does?

The moon.

Let me get this straight. You want us to walk outside in the middle of the night, while it's snowing, and lie down on the train tracks?

In a nutshell, yes.

And do what?

Read Sylvia Plath poems with a flashlight.

Olive, I take back everything I ever said about you.

What do you mean?

You *are* disturbed.

11

On Sunday morning, I went dress shopping with Lucy. Not that it was my idea—she conned me into it. When she knocked on my door at nine in the morning, I didn't want to get out of bed at all, but I gave in after she told me she needed help picking out something Dad would love. Only when we pulled up to the bridal boutique on Hope Street did I realize we were shopping for her wedding dress.

The bridal salon was empty when we walked in. Little bells chimed against the glass door, but nobody came to greet us. We walked around examining lace and satin gowns for a while before a chubby blond woman with a birthmark on her chin came out and asked which one of us was the bride.

Lucy wasn't the only the one who needed a dress though. I had to pick out a maid-of-honor gown—something in lavender, her favorite color. It had to be tea-length, chiffon, with sleeves. Those were the rules. I found three dresses that qualified and dragged them to the fitting room at the back of the store.

Lucy plucked six wedding gowns from the showroom and brought all of them with her into the fitting room next to mine. The chubby owner of the store trailed after her, lifting the trains so they wouldn't drag on the floor. Then she helped

Lucy climb into the first one while I tried on one of the lavender dresses, which I could already tell from the rack was going to be too low-cut.

Lucy pulled aside the heavy curtain a moment later, just as I was zipping up. "What do you think?" she asked, beaming at me in a soft, feathery dress that matched her haircut.

"Nice," I said.

"Not bad for the first one, right?" She did a little spin. "I don't know about yours, though—I think it's too low cut."

I could've told her that myself, but I didn't say anything. Instead we pulled the curtain shut between us and undressed.

"This is fun, isn't it?" Lucy asked through the curtain. "Everything here is so pretty."

"Mmm," I said, searching for the zipper on the side of my dress. *Fun* wasn't exactly the word I would have used for being tricked into a shopping trip with Lucy.

"Have you ever been to a wedding?"

"Not that I can remember."

She laughed. "You'd remember."

I found the hidden zipper, buried beneath a layer of lavender chiffon, but before I could extricate myself from the dress, Lucy asked something that sounded like, "Are you cited?"

"What?" I began bunching the fabric of my dress to pull it over my shoulders.

"I said, are you excited about the wedding?"

I paused with my arms halfway in the air, the dress over my head. "Oh—yeah."

"Good! I am too."

I closed my eyes and tried not to say anything sarcastic.

"Reyna?"

"Yeah?"

"You don't sound very excited."

"Well, I am," I lied.

"Would you cheer up for my sake?"

I pulled off the dress and stared at myself in the mirror—at the frown lines around my mouth. I had absolutely zero interest in cheering up for the sake of a woman who wanted to forget my mom ever existed. It popped out before I could stop it: "No thanks."

"Excuse me?"

I sighed. "Never mind."

"Is something wrong, Reyna?" Below the curtain, I could see the taut tendons in her bony feet. "I'm just trying to include you. I want us to be a happy family. I'm *trying*."

"I know," I said. "Never mind."

"If you have a problem, let's talk about it."

I stared at myself in the mirror but didn't say anything.

"Is this about the car accident?" She wouldn't let up. "Do you still think it was my fault? Is that why you're putting me through this?"

I opened my mouth to repeat, "Never mind," but what came out was: "Of course it was your fault. You ran the stop sign."

Lucy inhaled sharply. "I know, and I'm sorry! I've already apologized a million times."

I ignored her, gritting my teeth and keeping my eyes fixed carefully on my reflection in the mirror. I knew what would happen if I closed them. A hundred awful memories lurked there, and I could feel them waiting, jostling for my attention. Leah's backyard. A Sunday afternoon in August. The smell of wet cement around the lip of a swimming pool. Leah's mom, standing on the porch with a cordless phone. The look of horror on her face.

From the other side of the curtain, Lucy asked, "Have you ever stopped to consider things from my perspective, Reyna? How bad *I* felt after the accident?"

I shrugged but of course she couldn't see me.

"Your father was in a coma with a fractured skull," she went on. "And I was the one who had to break it to you. Do you know how hard that was for me?"

I let out the breath I had been holding. "It couldn't have been too hard after six hours."

"What are you talking about?" She slid off a strappy silver sandal, and I imagined her standing there half naked, the wedding gown crumpled at her waist. Hate flowered inside me, huge and grotesque.

"Six hours," I said. "That's how many hours between the time you got in the accident and the time you called me to tell me about it."

"*That's* why you hate me? Because I didn't call sooner?"

"No." I wanted to say, *I hate you because you're not my mom and you never will be.* But Abby was right. It was easier to blame her for the car accident or for not calling me sooner or for just about anything else.

"I waited to call you until he was stabilized." Lucy said. "It was for your own good, Reyna. I was thinking of *you*."

I couldn't answer. A memory was pulsing behind my eyes—*the* memory—the one buried like a coffin beneath the others. It had been a chilly spring morning in March. Not a nice day, exactly, but a crisp one. Mom had dropped me off at school in the morning and never made it home. A drunk driver clipped her on the highway. Her car flipped over just once, but that was enough. When I got home from school, I found out from our next-door neighbor. I had a little pink lunch box with a Velcro flap on top, and it was the only soft thing I could find to wipe my nose against when I started to cry.

A train of shiny, white taffeta appeared in my fitting room for a second below the curtain and then disappeared as Lucy pulled it away. My chest felt like a room clouded with smoke, with nowhere left to breathe. I dropped the lavender dress on the floor and sat down next to it wearing only my underwear. Then I gulped in a big breath of air.

"Reyna?" Lucy stopped moving. "Are you crying?" I didn't answer, so she started to pull open the curtain. "Reyna, we have to get to the bottom of this—"

"Stop!" I yelped. "I'm not dressed."

She let go as I sucked in another deep, shuddering breath. Somewhere in the corner of my mind, I wondered if I was having a panic attack.

"You know what? Let's go home." Lucy's voice came through the curtain softer than before. "I'll make you some eggs and we can talk about what's really bothering you."

"It doesn't matter how nice you are to me," I burst out. "It doesn't change the fact that you're not my mom and you never will be."

Lucy let the words hang in the air.

★ ★ ★

I couldn't explain my hatred for Lucy, but it bubbled on my skin every morning when I woke up and made me into a person I wouldn't like to be around. I knew I was being unfair—I knew she didn't *mean* to cause the accident, I knew she wasn't *trying* to replace my mom—but I couldn't let it go. Dad got sick of hearing me say I was "just tired," but I never felt like talking to him. Instead I spent my afternoons hanging out with Gretchen and the Slutty Nurses, who only made things worse. I didn't realize it then, but they wanted something from me. Every heart on this planet holds a tiny bit of hate, like a bead of mercury, beautiful and dangerous. They were out to own mine.

Olive took the brunt, of course. She made it easy. During homeroom one morning, when John Quincy grabbed the attendance clipboard and called out, "Miss California? Miss Rhode Island? Miss Florida?" Olive turned toward Gretchen and me and said, in her haughty way, "I suppose you two get a kick out of this."

"No," said Gretchen, not missing a beat. "But we get a kick out of your outfit."

Olive was wearing a dark denim skirt that looked like something the Gap might have sold before the millennium. Ignoring Gretchen's comment, she glanced pointedly at John Quincy and said, "Naming women after states is sexual harassment. I don't find it funny."

153

"What's funny?" countered Gretchen, "Your skirt?"

If Levi had been in our homeroom, he probably would have stuck up for Olive or said something funny to Gretchen about her own clothes. I would have too, if something clever had popped into my head. But the only thing I could think to say was, "Denim is very Florida."

Gretchen laughed, prompting Olive to give her the finger as Mr. Lee wrestled the attendance book out of John Quincy's grip. Once he began taking role call for real, Olive turned around in her seat and glared at the clock, waiting for the bell to ring.

Gretchen and I shared a look; then I felt my mouth open—quick and lethal, with a mind of its own. "Lesbo," I said.

Gretchen laughed again, louder than before. It didn't matter that *lesbo* was a word I hadn't heard anybody use since fifth grade. That wasn't the point. You didn't have to be funny to make Gretchen laugh. You just felt on the safe side when she did.

★ ★ ★

There was only thing stopping me from turning into a complete monster, and that thing was Levi. We saw each other exactly eight times a week—once every day in history and three times a week during gym—and I lived for our conversations. In the week since our ice cream date, we'd talked about which Harry Potter house we'd be sorted into, the best way to make Rice Krispies treats, and our favorite kinds of sushi.

When Levi showed up at my locker on Friday morning with a guitar case tucked under his arm, my first thought—absurdly enough—was that first period had been cancelled. Then, as he grabbed my hand and pulled me into the first-floor stairwell, I started to wonder if he was taking me to an assembly in the auditorium. I didn't realize until I followed him up the stairs into the empty band classroom on the second floor that we were cutting gym.

"So what's up?" he asked, stealing the words right out of my mouth as he closed the door behind us and hit a switch. The lights flickered on one by one, illuminating a big, cluttered room I'd seen only once before at freshman orientation. There were music stands and plastic chairs crowded in a semi-circle at the center of the room. Levi grabbed one and spun it around to sit with his legs on either side of the back.

"Um—what about gym?" I asked, glancing toward the door.

"We get two free absences."

"Oh." A thrill was passing through me, running like a current down the wire of my spine. I was cutting class with Levi. Everything else about my morning—the bad milk in the fridge, the strained silence in the car with Lucy—receded into the background.

"So are you friends with Gretchen Palmer now?" Levi asked, tapping his feet against the band room floor. "I saw you guys at lunch yesterday."

"I guess," I said. "I mean, she invited me to sit with her."

He frowned. "How can you be friends after what she did on Halloween?"

"I don't know." I pulled up a chair and sat down across from him. "Why?"

"She's scary."

I laughed.

"No, seriously." Levi ran a hand over his coppery hair. "It doesn't seem like you."

What would seem like me? I wanted to ask.

"I can tell you're not shallow," he said. "Your favorite book is *The Little Prince*."

I tried to smile—he must have stalked me online—but all I could muster was a faint twitch of the mouth. He was right. Every person has a best self and a worst self, and Gretchen was bringing out my worst self.

Desperate to change the subject, I glanced around for something—anything—to talk about. "Is that your guitar?"

"Yeah." He kicked the case with his toe. "Talk about old friends."

The wistful tone in his voice softened me. I relaxed into the back of my chair and imagined myself leaning in to kiss him on the lips—to let him know I belonged to him, not Gretchen. But all I could think to say was, "How long have you played?"

"As long as I can remember."

"It looks hard."

"Not really." He pulled the guitar from its case and passed it to me. "Try."

I didn't even know where to place my hands. I wrapped my right arm under the curved base and reached up for the strings.

Levi laughed.

"What?" I asked. "Not like this?"

"No." He came around and stood behind me, moving my arm over the top of the guitar so that my palm rested near the hole at the center. Then he guided my other hand over to the stem and pressed my pointer finger onto one of the strings. "Like this."

"This?"

"Yeah." He was leaning over me awkwardly, his guitar pick necklace dangling by my ear. I could feel the heat coming off his body. "Play," he instructed.

I strummed for a few seconds while holding down the chord. It sounded pretty good, but then again, I'd never heard a guitar sound bad.

"That's it," said Levi. "You're a pro."

I would have kept playing all day as long as we could stay in the band room together, alone, almost touching. But the minute he took a step back, I fumbled the chord.

"Are you doing anything for Valentine's Day?"

The question took me by surprise. I pressed my fingers onto the guitar strings to quiet them and looked up. Levi was watching me out of the corner of his eye.

"I don't know yet," I answered. "Are you?"

"Maybe." He glanced down at his sneakers and looked, for once in his life, a little nervous. "Do you want to come to a party with my Ridgeway friends?"

"You have Ridgeway friends?"

"Yeah." He grabbed a sheet of music off the floor. "But it's not their party. Just some girl they know. Can I see the guitar?"

I handed it to him and watched as he started to strum the chords of "House of the Rising Sun." It sounded twangy and full of omen and also pretty catchy.

"OK," I said, tapping my foot on the leg of my chair. "I'll be there."

I can't.

Why not?

They'd just send me back.

To your aunt's house?

To boot camp.

What?

To cure me again.

GAY boot camp?

Bingo. The only place in the world where they leave notes on your pillow like, "The opposite of homosexuality is not heterosexuality. It's holiness."

Don't tell me you believe that crap.

My dad's a minister, Olive. My mom teaches Sunday school. You may think it's crap, but I grew up believing it.

Hating yourself, you mean?

If I could change myself for them, I would.

There is nothing about you that needs to be cured.

I wish I could believe you.

February

12

My brain, as Valentine's Day approached, became as flimsy and full of holes as a paper doily. I couldn't seem to remember to floss my teeth or clean my room or study between periods at school. What I *did* remember was to make every possible excuse to hang out with Levi. I even dropped by the band room one afternoon to talk to Mr. Wilson, the music instructor and the only male teacher at Belltown High with a ponytail and earrings. He was sitting at his desk, sorting through CDs when I knocked on the door and asked whether there were any spots left in his advanced guitar elective.

"What do you play?" he asked, sizing me up. "Acoustic or electric?"

"Neither, but I'm a fast learner," I said.

He gave me a big, crinkly smile that stretched from one silver-hoop earring to the other and then pointed at his wedding ring. "Ah, the things we do for love."

I was too embarrassed to show my face in the band room after that, but I did purposefully leave my math binder in a classroom across the hall so I'd have an excuse to come back at the end of the day as Levi's class let out.

And it worked. As I lingered by room 206, Levi stepped out

of room 207 and waved at me. Waving back, I smiled and pointed at the classroom. "I forgot my binder in there."

"What a coincidence," he said. "I left my jacket in the library. Want to walk with me?"

"Sure," I said, ducking into room 206 to grab my binder. The library was on the opposite side of school. It was the perfect excuse to spend time together.

Or it would have been anyway if we hadn't run into Olive. She was walking up the stairs as we were walking down them. I looked straight ahead, intent on ignoring her, but Levi stopped in the middle of the stairwell and said, "Hey, Olive. How's it going?"

She paused with one hand on the railing, skeptical. "Fine... Why?"

"No reason," said Levi. "Just asking."

I felt my cheeks burn. Why did he have to be so nice? Anyone else would have ignored her and kept walking. "We've got to get to the library before it closes," I said, not looking at either of them. "We should probably go."

"Me too," said Olive, hurrying up the remainder of the stairs.

Levi waited until she was gone. Then he looked at me, confused. "What's the deal?"

"Nothing." I tried to smile like everything was fine, but my face was frozen in a grimace.

Levi looked unconvinced. "I thought you were friends."

"Not anymore." I forced myself to keep walking. "We got into a fight a week before winter break."

"Why?"

"She's gay," I said, lowering my voice. "Or lesbian or whatever. She likes girls."

Levi looked nonplussed. "So?"

"So," I said. "I don't."

Levi raised his eyebrows. "I didn't know you were *that* kind of Catholic."

"What kind of Catholic?"

"The intolerant kind."

I paused at the base of the stairs. The disapproval in his voice felt like someone dumping ice water on me. "I just meant—" I searched for the words. "It's not that *I* care whether she likes guys or girls—it doesn't have any effect on *me*—it just—"

Levi was watching me, waiting.

"I just wouldn't want her to get the wrong idea about our friendship," I finished with a shrug. I knew I sounded lame.

Levi pushed open the door at the base of the stairs and held it open for me. "Was she hitting on you?"

"No," I said.

"Was she asking you to change your own beliefs?"

I shook my head.

"Then what's the problem?"

"I don't know," I admitted, walking through the door.

"Well, I don't either." Levi followed me, letting the door swing shut behind him. "If you ask me, her love life is none of your business. But I guess I'm biased. I have two moms."

I stopped dead in my tracks.

"And if you have a problem with it, you better never come over my house," he said lightly. "Otherwise they'll talk your ear off."

"Levi—I'm so sorry—" I started to say. My face was burning crimson. "I didn't mean to insult your family."

"It's OK." He smiled. "I'm just saying you should think about it."

"I will," I said. And I meant it. "I'm really sorry," I told him again, wishing I could take it back. "Now you probably think I hate your family."

"Nah." He shrugged. "You're too smart to hate anyone. I think you've just never had a reason to think about any of this stuff before now."

"You think I'm smart?" The words popped out before I could stop them.

He smiled. "I think you're smarter than the people you hang around with. Actually, I *know* you're smarter than the people you hang around with."

Warmth spread from my cheeks to my fingertips. Hearing Levi say I was smart felt better than a million party invitations from Gretchen Palmer. He was right—she *was* scary.

As we reached the library, Levi slowed down, faint pink splotches forming on his cheeks. "I just remembered I left my jacket at home this morning."

"Oh." I slowed to a stop, a few feet away from the library doors.

"So it's not in there after all." He looked embarrassed. "Sorry."

"It's OK," I said, smiling as we turned and headed toward the front of the school, where the buses were lining up. Either Levi's brain was just as full of holes as mine or he was making up excuses to spend time with me. Either way, I didn't mind.

Valentine's Day arrived on the eve of Gretchen's birthday. All week long, cheap carnations and paper hearts rained down like some kind of perfect, pink storm. Valentine's Day fell on Pajama Day—or rather, Pajama Day fell on the fourteenth of February. Spirit Week was late this year because of basketball playoffs.

When I showed up at my locker on Friday morning, Gretchen was waiting for me in a pair of hot pink boxers that showed off a dark, splotchy birthmark on her inner thigh. She didn't seem to care that it resembled a wart, or that it was twenty-five degrees outside and she was probably freezing cold. In her hand was an entire ream of glittery pink stickers, and the minute I stepped up to my locker, she reached over and pinned one to my cheek.

"Happy Valentine's Day!" she said. "Why aren't you wearing pajamas?"

I *was* wearing pajamas. They just weren't cute, like hers. Mine consisted of gray athletic sweatpants and a fleece pull-over. Also—in honor of Valentine's Day—a red hair elastic. But I never got a chance to point it out to Gretchen. Before I could say anything, she stepped a little closer and whispered, "OK, important question. What are you doing tonight?"

"Going to a Ridgeway party," I answered automatically. "Why?"

"No!" she gasped. "Really?"

Immediately, I wished I hadn't said anything. All week long I'd been trying to avoid Gretchen without actually telling her outright that I didn't want to be friends. Mentioning the Valentine's party was not exactly part of my plan.

"It's just a little gathering," I amended. "Probably not very big."

She looked devastated. "But it's my birthday!"

I broke eye contact and glanced down the hallway, wishing I'd had the presence of mind to make up a better excuse—a sick relative, maybe, or some kind of family bowling tournament.

Gretchen put on her best puppy dog face. "You don't have to go, do you?"

"Sorry," I said, looking down at my shoes. "I promised someone."

"Who?" She narrowed her eyes.

To my relief, the bell rang just as I opened my mouth. I changed the *e* sound in Levi to the *i* sound in "I better go."

"Well, this royally sucks." Gretchen slung her purple back-pack over one shoulder. "If one more person can't make it, I'm going to have to push back my party."

"That's fine," I said. "I mean, that sucks. I mean, happy birthday."

"Whatever." She rolled her eyes. "At least wear a freaking sticker." Then she tore off another glittery heart and jabbed it at my shoulder.

★ ★ ★

Real, honest-to-God pajamas. That's what Olive was wearing during English. Red and green plaid flannel pants with a matching button-down top—the kind of set that goes on sale at Macy's right before Christmas. I wasn't sure what shocked me more: the sight of her in flannel or the fact that she was voluntarily participating in School Spirit Week. Still, as I passed her desk on the way to mine, I said, "Nice pj's."

"You too," she answered.

For a split second—literally half a hundredth of one—I thought maybe something had softened between us. I actually felt relieved just long enough to picture myself sitting with her after school in the parking lot, saying something like, "Sorry I overreacted to you being gay. I've been thinking about it, and maybe I was wrong." But then she looked away, and the feeling evaporated as I watched her flip open her bloodred moleskin notebook. She leaned over, scribbling something in a slant across one of the pages.

English took off to a slow start as Ms. Mahoney made us read aloud from *The House on Mango Street*. The room was warm, and my mind grew soft and spongy as I followed along in the book. I found myself wondering if Olive knew how obnoxious she looked scribbling in her journal, but then I started thinking about getting one of my own, just to annoy her. I'd write about Lucy for the most part, but also about the people at school and Levi and those dim, wispy, cotton candy thoughts I would have been embarrassed to tell anybody else. Somewhere along the line, my eyes got heavy and I let them close.

I slept for a good five minutes with my chin propped in my hand. It wasn't a deep sleep, but it was a peaceful one, and when I woke up, it took me a moment to realize that someone across the room was reading aloud from *The House on Mango Street*. There was a faint tapping on the front right side of my desk, and I blinked at it groggily, my dream and reality not yet clicked into place. It was only when I realized someone was trying to pass me a note that I woke up.

It was David Beck, my Language Arts partner from sixth grade. He was a short, skinny boy with bad skin, and even though we'd known each other forever, we didn't talk much. I couldn't think why on earth he was passing me a note now. Snatching the folded paper from his hand, I propped up *The House on Mango Street* and opened the note behind it.

> *Reyna—*
>
> *I just want you to know that I submitted a poem about you to the lit mag. Don't have an aneurysm. I changed your name. Also, I kept it to five lines, since that's all the space you deserve in my life. Good luck living with yourself, you stupid, timid bitch.*
>
> *—Olive*

At the sight of the familiar handwriting, my heart revved up like a getaway car and zoomed off, leaving me in a cloud of dust. Olive was sitting two rows ahead of me, tapping her fingernails against the desk. The sight of it infuriated me. Cramming the note into my pocket, I stared at my copy of *The House on Mango Street* and watched the words swim around on the page like fish scattering in a pond. *When I am too sad and too skinny to keep keeping, when I am a tiny thing against so many bricks, then it is I look at trees.* None of it made sense.

167

A minute later, David's hand appeared again, hovering by the side of my desk. Even though I knew better, I reached over and snatched the note.

Don't you have anything to say to me?

Yes, I wrote back. *Has anyone ever told you that you need braces?*

When David handed it to Olive, her spine shot straight up as she whipped around to stare at me. Eyes wild, knuckles red, she grabbed her pen and scrawled something else. David passed it back to me.

Let's be honest. It's not my teeth you find so odious.

If I had known what *odious* meant, I might have denied it. Instead I just folded up the note and didn't write back. At the end of the period, when David stood up to sling his backpack over one shoulder, I tapped him on the arm and said, "Thanks."

"Sure." He looked embarrassed. "Any time."

"One thing." I lowered my voice as Olive shoved a couple of binders into her backpack, followed by the tattered moleskin notebook. "Next time, just rip up the note."

History was made in fourth period history.

Five minutes into Mr. Murphy's brain-bleeding lecture on the Byzantine Empire, Tim Ferguson walked into the room carrying a hall pass, a handful of roses, and a tiny, pink teddy bear. I did a double take. He was also wearing a tutu.

Mr. Murphy dropped his jaw as soon as the door swung open. "What the hell is this?" he demanded as everyone in the room burst out laughing. Behind me, I felt Olive move her feet off the bar at the base of my chair. We hadn't made eye contact since English.

Tim did a curtsy and stepped forward. "A tutu, your majesty." He had a grin on his face like he'd been waiting forever for this moment. From the far left side of the room, John Quincy wolf whistled, and I looked around, smiling, to meet Levi's eye. He raised his eyebrows with an innocent sort of waggle as though to say, *Gosh! Whoever could those roses be for?*

I turned toward the front of the room and watched as Tim made an elaborate show of twirling on his tiptoes like a ballerina while the class laughed. Mr. Murphy was not amused. "Why don't you swish your way over to your seat?" he growled.

"Can't," Timothy answered brightly. "I'm here on behalf of the Cupid Squad." He held out a rose, daring anyone to object. Mr. Murphy muttered something underneath his breath, but he knew as well as everybody that members of the Cupid Squad were entitled up to five minutes of uninterrupted pandemonium in every class. People took the opportunity to chat among themselves while Cupid-Tim made his rounds. Lennie even got out of her seat to come over and poke me on the shoulder. "Gretchen says you're going to a party tonight," she said. "She's canceling her birthday for it. Can we come?"

I glanced over at Levi, who was watching Tim prance around the room with the rest of the roses. Then I said somewhat stupidly, "She can't cancel her birthday."

"Her birthday *party*," said Lennie, rolling her eyes. "Anyway, give us the deets at lunch. I think Timmy has a rose for me."

"I don't even know where the party is—" I started to say, but she'd already turned toward the front of the room where Tim was rifling through his roses. I looked over at Levi for the second time and saw that he was watching me.

"It's on Durham Drive," he said quietly. "Just FYI."

I was surprised to realize he'd been listening. Tucking my hair behind my ear, I almost asked how we were going to get to the party—by car or on foot—but before I had a chance to formulate the question, Tim skipped toward me from the front of the room and held out the tiny pink teddy bear wearing a miniature guitar pick necklace.

"For Reyna Fey," he announced. "The cutest-freaking-most-adorable thing *ever*."

I glanced over at Levi, who was pretending to stare at the blackboard, but before I could say anything, Mr. Murphy coughed loudly from the front of the room and called, "Ferguson! On with it!" He looked like he was trying to refrain himself from physical violence.

"I would love to," chirped Tim. "But I have one more special delivery." With that, he walked straight up to John Quincy, paused dramatically, and placed the final remaining rose on his desk. "For you," he said. "From me."

John almost toppled the books on the desk as he scrambled out of his seat. "What the hell?" He brushed the flower onto the floor. "You frickin' homo—"

"Ferguson!" barked Mr. Murphy.

Tim looked elated. There were bright pink splotches high on his cheeks. "I'm out now," he said. "In more than one sense of the word." Then he pivoted on his ballet slippers and marched out the door.

Mr. Murphy looked around at all of us, a vein throbbing near his temple. "There's a word for people like Tim," he said after a moment. "The PTA would have my neck for saying it, but I'll give you a hint. It starts with the letter F, and it ends with the letters A-G-G-O-T."

A few people laughed, but most of the class just sat there, stunned. John Quincy used his sleeve to wipe the surface of his desk like somebody had placed a warm diaper on it. As for me, I had other things on my mind. I looked over at Levi, who was watching Mr. Murphy with a deep frown. Then I picked up the stuffed bear and noticed a note tucked into its shirt. *Looking forward to tonight*, it said.

I was too.

PLEASE come?

I hate parties, Olive.

We'll say you're my cousin from out of town. Or that you live next door and you're homeschooled or something like that.

I'm not even invited.

Neither am I. That's the point of crashing.

Go on your own. I have plans.

Like what? A date with an oncoming train?

Ha, very funny.

Come on. It'll be fun. We'll show up and ruin Reyna's night.

That's your idea of fun?

That's my idea of vengeance.

13

Durham Drive was long and stick-straight. Twenty-eight driveways and twenty-eight mailboxes led to twenty-eight identical houses painted in safe shades of blue, taupe, and beige. Abby, Leah, and Madison lived side by side in numbers fourteen, sixteen, and eighteen, and I prayed, as Levi's mom turned the corner, that none of them would see me drive past their houses on my way to somebody else's party. But Abby's house was the only one on the block with all its lights on, and I felt my stomach lurch the minute I realized how many cars were parked outside. I took my phone out of my pocket and opened my messages to look for some kind of last minute text from Abby. When I scrolled to the bottom, my fingers got sweaty. There was nothing. She hadn't invited me to her own party.

Levi's mom pulled to a stop at the end of the driveway and reminded us that she'd be back at midnight to pick us up. In a hoarse voice that I could barely hear, I thanked her for the ride as last-minute excuses jostled in my head. I could say I was sick. I could say I'd forgotten my phone at home. I could say I didn't feel like going to the party after all. But Levi was already clambering out of the SUV, his sneakers crunching against the packed snow on the driveway. So I climbed out after him and stared at the house with dread in the pit of my stomach.

Abby's front door was open and the split-level foyer was packed with people. I followed Levi as he made his way up the steps and through the crowd. I knew the house so well, I could have navigated it with my eyes closed, but instead I kept them open, combing the crowd for Abby, Leah, or Madison. The party was concentrated in the living room, but down the hallway, just past the bathroom, I could see the door to the sunroom where we once played Light as a Feather, Stiff as a Board with Abby's cat.

Tonight the living room was decorated with red balloons in honor of Valentine's Day. I grabbed one by its string and held on tight as we pushed our way toward the oversized L-shaped couch in the middle of the room, where a few dozen people were hanging around, drinking out of red plastic cups. Twisting the nylon string around my fingers, I tried to choke off the awful feeling in my gut but ended up choking off my circulation instead. The tips of my fingers felt numb by the time I spotted Leah on the sofa. Her eyes widened at the sight of me.

"Levi, I know these people," I croaked as she jumped to her feet, nearly spilling her drink. There was a faint ringing in my ears. "They're my friends."

"Sweet." Levi was craning his neck around. "My friends are here too."

I didn't get a chance to say, *Nope, not sweet*, before Leah barged through the crowd and threw her arms around my neck, obviously drunk. "Reyna!" she cried. "We *totally* meant to invite you!"

Madison appeared behind her, clutching a red plastic cup. I hadn't noticed her at first, but now the sight of them both made my stomach twist into a hard knot. "Oh my God." Madison's eyes grew wide. "Who told you about this—"

She didn't get a chance to finish before Leah interrupted her. "Reyna, you have to find Abby! She's like, *so* stressed! She's going to freak out when she sees you."

"Her parents gave her permission to invite six friends over," said Madison. "That's why we didn't invite you. It was supposed to be just six Ridgeway freshmen, but then Abby's brother invited a bunch of juniors, and he's got a fake ID—"

"Do you want me to leave?" My head was spinning, and knowing the reason for not being invited didn't make the situation any less embarrassing.

"No!" Madison's eyes widened. "Of course not! It's just that Abby's freaking out. We don't even recognize half the people here."

I thought for a minute she meant Levi, but when I turned around and followed her gaze, I saw a handful of faces I knew from Belltown. John Quincy and Lennie King were strolling up the stairs with their hands in each other's butt pockets. Emma and Gretchen trailed behind them, talking on their cell phones. I had the odd impression, as they laughed simultaneously, that they were talking to each other.

"Oh my God," I whispered. "It's my fault. They found out about the party because of me."

But before Madison could say anything, Levi tapped me on the arm, and I turned around to see two semi-cute boys looking at me. One was skinny, one fat. They both had Justin Bieber hair.

"Grant and Brett, this is Reyna," said Levi. "Reyna, these are my friends from middle school." I nodded at both of them and then turned back to Madison.

"Where's Abby?" I asked, steeling myself for the worst. Half of me wanted to see her. The other half wanted to run away and hide in her bedroom.

"I think she's in the kitchen—"

"Does anyone want beer?" Abby's older brother Jason was walking around carrying a blue cooler. Both of Levi's friends dove in and grabbed a bottle just as Abby showed up looking frazzled, a cordless phone in her hand.

"Reyna," she sputtered, looking between Leah, Madison, and me. "What are you—? We were going to invite you—"

"It's OK," I said, my face heating up. "Madison told me."

"I'm *so* sorry."

"It's fine," I said. It wasn't, but I didn't want to make a scene.

Levi grabbed two beers from the cooler and handed one to me. "Hi," he said to Abby, eyeing the phone in her hand. "Are we crashing your party? I thought it was open."

"It is open, bro," said Jason. "This is my house too." He tipped back his plastic cup and took a gulp.

"I'll drink to that," said Levi, holding up his beer. "Cheers?"

"Cheers," I echoed. He helped me pop off the top of my bottle, and everything got foggy from there.

★ ★ ★

I don't know when Olive showed up. Maybe around the time Leah started throwing grapes into the air to catch in her mouth, or maybe just after the phone rang when Abby started screaming, "Shut up! Shut the whole house up!" Or it might have been right after Tim Ferguson arrived wearing jeans so skinny Gretchen Palmer almost died of envy. Nobody knew who invited Tim to the party in the first place, until he told everyone he read about it on someone's away message, and then people left him alone.

All I know is that I was two beers deep before I noticed Olive. Or rather, before I noticed Grace. She was the one I spotted first, standing by the piano looking just as bedraggled and corpse-like as she had on the day I met her. Only this time she was wearing a long purple raincoat, and Olive was close by, picking out a beer from the cooler.

When Leah's next grape missed her mouth, it bounced past me and rolled along the floor toward the base of the piano, where Grace bent down and picked it up. I thought she was going to throw it back at Leah, but instead she placed it on top of the piano and let it sit there.

"Hey," called Leah. "Pass that?" But Grace didn't say anything or even look up. "Hey, hobo girl!" Leah tried again. "Can you pass that grape?"

Grace flicked it straight onto the floor and turned around, her back toward us.

"Hey!" Leah wandered over drunkenly and touched Grace on the arm of her purple raincoat. "What's the matter with you? Aren't you having fun?"

"No, not particularly," droned Olive, materializing beside them. "Maybe we should get a hickey from a vacuum cleaner. Isn't that your idea of fun, Leah?"

"What?" Leah's eyes grew wide.

Olive looked smug. "Making out with inanimate objects. Ring a bell?"

"Ignore her, Leah," I said, stepping forward. "She's mixing you up with someone else."

Comprehension dawned in Olive's eyes. "Oh, right, that wasn't you." She turned around and spotted Madison, who was sitting cross-legged on the floor, talking to a cute boy I didn't recognize. "Hey, Madison!"

"Shut up." I stepped sideways to block her view. "Don't you dare say anything I told you in private."

"Why not? You don't respect the things I tell you in private."

"That's different," I said. "Besides, I said I was sorry for overreacting."

Something in her eyes changed. "If you're so sorry, then make it up to me."

"What?" I looked around. Levi was watching us carefully.

"You heard me," said Olive. "I'm giving you a second chance. Do you have anything to say to me? Anything to say to Grace?"

"I'm sorry," I blurted.

"Sorry for what?"

"I already told you—for overreacting to what you told me!"

"And?"

"For running out of your room?" I hated the sound of the question mark in my voice.

"Not good enough." She shook her head.

"I'm sorry!" I didn't know what else she wanted me to say.

"I needed a friend, and you gave me a coward."

Madison was making her way toward us.

"I'm really sorry," I breathed. "Please don't tell her."

But Olive turned toward Madison without hesitating. "Reyna thinks you're such a prude that making out with a vacuum cleaner is the only way you'd ever get a hickey. There. I've said it. Her words, not mine."

Madison's eyes widened "What?"

"It's not true," I muttered.

"It is." Olive addressed the entire crowd that was forming around the piano where we were standing. "She said Leah was a slut and Madison was a prude. She said it herself on Thanksgiving. Don't kill the messenger."

"You called me a slut?" Leah giggled. "Aw, thanks!"

But nobody else laughed. Abby walked up to the piano and pushed her way into our circle. "What's going on?"

"Olive is putting words in my mouth," I lied. "She's making things up."

"You're such a coward." Olive shot me a dirty look. "You won't even own up to the things you say."

"Olive, maybe you should leave," said Abby, stepping over to stand next to me. I felt my heart swell up. She may not have invited me to her party, but she was still my friend. She would stick up for me, and that was what counted.

Olive just laughed. "Wait until you hear what Reyna had to say about you, Abby."

"Reyna would never say anything bad about me," said Abby. "She's my best friend."

But Olive was grinning now. It made me sick to my stomach. "You might want to rethink that," she said. "Reyna betrayed you the worst of all."

"Shut up!" I pleaded.

She ignored me, looking straight at Abby. "Reyna told me all about your first encounter. *Sexual* encounter, I mean."

Abby's eyes widened. "What are you talking about?"

"I'm talking about Fido," answered Olive, loud enough for everyone around us to hear. "Or Sparky or Buddy or whatever your dog's name is."

"Gizmo," said Abby, her cheeks pink.

Olive exploded with a laugh that turned heads. People moved in closer around the piano. "Exactly," she said. "Exactly."

"I hate you," I whispered. My hands were shaking at my sides.

Olive raised her eyebrows in mock offense. "It's *your* story, Reyna. You're the one who told it to me. Why don't you tell it again? Tell us how Abby violated Gizmo."

A few people started laughing, and John Quincy, who didn't even know Abby, let out one of his famous wolf whistles. Abby blinked furiously and turned to walk away.

"Abby!" I called after her. "I never said that!"

"Then how would Olive know about it in the first place?" hissed Madison, getting up to follow Abby. "I can't believe you told her, Reyna."

My heart sank, and I looked over at Levi, who was watching me with a frown on his face. He'd been drinking too, and my only hope, as I opened my mouth to defend myself, was that he wouldn't remember any of this in the morning.

"I didn't say Abby violated her dog," I blurted. "I said she touched his gizmo."

As soon as the word popped out, the crowd around me burst out laughing, and I felt my face flood with color. "I mean, his...thing."

Leah was one of the only people not laughing. "You can call me a slut whenever you want, Reyna," she said. "But don't tell Abby's secrets. That's not cool."

"I know—" I started to say, but a loud clatter from the front hall interrupted me. I heard a collective gasp from the crowd. Across the piano, the color drained from Olive's face.

I turned my head just in time to see Tim Ferguson wrestling his way out of the coat closet by the front door, his hands and feet bound together with dishcloths, his mouth gagged with an old sweatshirt and duct tape. I felt—rather than saw—Olive push past me and run across the living room. Grace trailed close behind her, the purple raincoat flapping. When they reached the foyer, Olive crouched down, yanked the sweatshirt out of Tim's mouth, and untied the dishcloths to free his hands and feet. I ran with everyone else over to the top of the stairs to see what was going on. Peeling duct tape off his cheek, Tim coughed, "Assholes—wanted to put me back in the closet—"

"Who did this?" demanded Olive.

"Nobody," said Tim, but it was obvious.

"Go home, homo," John Quincy called. He was leaning

over the banister with a red plastic cup in his hand as though he meant to pour it over the ledge.

Tim ignored him, rubbing the spot on his elbow where he'd bashed through the closet door. I felt sick to my stomach for the millionth time that night. Olive probably thought I was no different than John—just as spineless and self-centered and prejudiced. Maybe she was right.

It became difficult to see anything as the people around me moved closer to gawk. That's when Levi came over and wrapped his arm around my shoulder. "Can you believe that?" he said. "What kind of jerk throws someone into a closet?"

I felt too dizzy—too drunk—too awful—to say anything, so I closed my eyes against Levi's shoulder as he led me over to the couch and sat me down. More than anything else, I wanted to go to sleep and obliterate my memory of the night.

Four other people were sitting on the couch talking drunkenly about what had just happened to Tim. "Wait, he's gay?" one girl asked. "Like Dumbledore?"

"Dumbledore is *fictional*."

Closing my eyes again against Levi's shoulder, I had just enough time to wish I'd never woken up in the morning before Olive climbed back up the steps and announced to everyone that Tim was leaving because he obviously wasn't welcome here.

Not too many people paid attention. They kept rambling, sipping from beer bottles and plastic cups. One blond boy with glasses said, "What if you had two dads and you walked in on them having sex? That would be traumatic."

"Hey, shut up," said Levi, leaning forward on the couch. "I have two moms."

Somebody wolf whistled.

"That's different," said the blond boy. "That's awesome."

"You idiot." Olive looked murderous as she marched over. "A hate crime just happened, and you have the nerve to sit here and make jokes? Do you seriously think gay marriage would be the end of the world?"

"It's unconstitutional," said the boy.

Olive folded her arms. "What about the right to life, liberty, and the pursuit of happiness?"

"It's a slippery line."

"You mean a slippery slope?" Her eyes were bright with rage. "Are you saying that Tim doesn't deserve to be happy? Just because he's gay?"

I stood up. I wanted to leave. I didn't care if Levi was still sitting on the couch, watching everything unfold like reality TV. I wanted go to the bathroom—to the porch—to the street—to anywhere but here.

Olive whipped her head around. "Where do you think you're going, Reyna?"

I sat back down like the couch was a magnet.

"Look," she continued. "I'm sorry about what I said to Abby and Madison. I really am. But if these are the kind of idiots you choose to associate with, you deserve it."

I leaned away from her, toward Levi's shoulder. "Just because we're sitting on the same couch doesn't mean I agree with him," I said, looking over at the blond boy.

"If you don't say anything against him, then you might as well agree with him," she answered. "Or did you not learn about Nazi Germany?"

"I hate to say it," said Levi, "but she has a point."

"Thank you!" Olive turned back to me. "You don't know how defend your opinions, Reyna. That's why you always avoid talking about politics. Don't deny it."

I looked over at Levi, a headache blooming behind my eyes. "You've seen me defend my opinions, right?" I asked him.

"I guess," he said. "About some things."

"Then defend them now," Olive demanded. "Do you agree or disagree with this idiot?" She pointed at the blond boy with glasses.

"Disagree," I said.

"Why?"

I thought about it for a second. "Because it would be just as traumatizing to walk in on your straight parents having sex."

"Thank you," she said.

"But that doesn't matter," said the boy, adjusting his glasses. "Marriage is between a man and a woman. If you lose that definition, people could marry goats if they wanted to. Or socks."

"Are you stupid?" Olive's eyes bulged. "Why would anyone marry a sock?"

"He doesn't mean they actually would," I said. "He's just playing the devil's advocate."

Olive clenched fists by her sides. "Well, it's a waste of time. The devil already has enough advocates." Then she turned on her heel and left, Grace following her like a shadow.

"So go marry a sock," I said to no one in particular. The living room was swimming in front of my eyes. "Honestly, I don't care anymore who anyone wants to be with. It's their own business." I half-expected everyone around me to turn around and stare, but the party kept going, breathing and pulsating like a living creature. "I don't care if she's gay," I repeated, turning to Levi. "I don't care about anything as long as you still like me."

"I do," he said. "I think."

I'm sorry I made you come with me.

I'm sorry too.

It was depressing.

I know.

I'll find a way to make it up to you.

Come with me to the tracks.

That wasn't what I had in mind.

Please?

Now?

Of course.

I just took off my shoes.

But you're not really tired, are you?

I guess not.

Then put them back on and come with me.

You're becoming obsessed, Grace.

I know.

Are you OK?

Maybe.

14

Turn the knob, Rachael Ray. The stove is hot.
Sprinkle me with sea salt. Set me on the pan.
I'll evaporate like steam. I'll disappear for you.
I'll be nothing but an empty calorie, a statistic.
Don't think straight, it'll kill you.

Nobody read the February issue of the *Breeze* except the people who were published in it—and me, of course. As literary magazines went, it was pretty slim: ten pieces of paper bound together with staples running down the left side. All the artwork was done by a sophomore with a loopy signature who specialized in wispy pencil drawings of sad-looking eyes.

On Monday, my pride still wounded from the Valentine's party, I ducked into the library after third period to grab a copy from the stack by the door. I expected to see Olive's name in the table of contents, but it was nowhere to be found, even when I flipped through the rest of the magazine. Only through process of elimination did I manage to locate her poem at all, published anonymously under the title, "Disappearing." Rachael Ray was a famous chef whose name rhymed with mine—sort of. "Don't think straight" was probably a double entendre. But other than that, I had no idea what to think. Sprinkle me with sea salt?

My detour made me late to history, but it didn't matter. We had a sub. The minute I walked through the door I saw a woman writing *Study Hall* in big letters on the blackboard while John Quincy chased Lennie around the back of the room with a fake spider.

"Hey you." Levi turned to face me as I sat down. He was wearing a threadbare yellow T-shirt with Jimi Hendrix's face plastered across the front, and I had a feeling that Olive, from her seat behind me, was watching both of us over the top of her moleskin notebook. But if Levi noticed her, he didn't let on. "All recovered from Friday?" he asked. "You must have had a monster hangover on Saturday morning."

"Yeah." I smiled and settled into my seat. "I ate an entire box of macaroni and cheese for breakfast, though. That helped."

He laughed. "I ate a burger."

As the sub tried to get John Quincy to sit in his seat, Levi straightened his face and asked, "So how's it going?"

"Pretty good," I said. "You?"

"Pretty *well*," muttered a voice behind me.

"That depends whether you're free on Friday," Levi answered, paying no attention to Olive. "If you are, I'll be good."

"Free for what?" I asked.

"Eating popcorn and wearing 3-D glasses."

I laughed as he twirled his guitar pick necklace and added, "It's the opening night for *White Heat*. I thought you might want to see it with me."

"The one about aliens causing global warming?" I asked.

From behind me, Olive let out a snort and muttered something under her breath.

"What'd you say?" Levi asked, noticing her for the first time.

"I said that movie looks stupid," she repeated. "Your taste in cinema is lamentable."

Something in me snapped. Even though Levi flashed her a grin like he couldn't care less, I felt the word *lamentable* crawl under my skin like a spider. She sounded so smug, I wanted to slap her. Instead, I turned around and whispered, "Your teeth are lamentable, Olive Garden." The minute her eyes widened, I stood up, marched to the front of the room, grabbed a bathroom pass, and headed out the door.

Ensconced in the handicapped stall of the girls' bathroom, I sat down and peed my heart out, wondering who I was becoming and why nobody was stopping me. Nobody except Levi anyway. My only hope was that he hadn't heard what I said. If he had, it was only a matter of time before he realized the truth about me. I was no better than Gretchen Palmer. I was worse.

Outside the stall, I heard the bathroom door swing open and shut. A pair of familiar sneakers shuffled in and stopped just outside my stall. I stood frozen, watching them. Then, with a deep breath, I stood up and flushed the toilet. When I stepped out, Olive was waiting for me.

"I didn't deserve that," she said right away. "Nobody deserves that."

I stepped past her toward the sink, avoiding my reflection in the mirror.

"You can't just say that kind of thing," she persisted, fidgeting with the bottom of her ugly blue sweater. "Not out of nowhere. Not randomly."

"It wasn't out of nowhere." I turned on the faucet and plunged my hands into the cold stream of water. "And it wasn't random. People call you Olive Garden because it sounds like your name, and they call you a freak because you freak them out."

I knew my words were cruel, but I couldn't help myself. Every shard of anger I'd felt all year toward Dad, Lucy, and Abby came back like a dagger pointed straight at Olive.

"*People?*" She was standing in front of the sink now without washing her hands. "What about you, Reyna?"

"I feel the same way," I answered.

"How would you feel if I shot myself in the face?"

"Yeah right." I knew she was trying to goad me, and I wasn't about to fall for it. The idea of someone as arrogant as Olive suffering from low self-esteem was laughable.

"You think I'm joking?" Her eyes widened. "I'm not the boy who cried wolf."

"And I'm not the wolf," I said.

"Maybe you're more important to me than you think."

"Well, I don't want to be." I turned off the faucet and wiped my dripping hands against the front of my jeans. "I'd prefer to be nothing to you."

She stared at me.

"I never asked for any of this," I reminded her. "And I'm sorry if that sounds harsh, but it's true. I never asked you to write that poem. I never asked you to be my friend."

I expected her nostrils to flare. I thought she might say, "Get out," or even, "You're better than this," which I knew deep down that I was. But she didn't do anything except stare at me. So I left the bathroom with the toilet still gurgling. The door closed behind me with a swish.

Four times in one week?

Five, actually.

I've created a monster.

Shut up. Are you coming?

I never thought I'd say this, but I'm actually tired of reading Sylvia Plath.

Fine, then don't come.

I have no choice.

Why?

I don't trust you there by yourself.

You think I'd kill myself?

I wouldn't put it past you.

Then come if you must.

I will. And I'm bringing you a beanie.

Olive, don't.

It's freezing.

You've already loaned me too many clothes.

The beanie is hideous. You'll love it.

Fine, just hurry up.

Where's the fire?

Nowhere. But the middle of the night is the only thing I look forward to anymore.

That's what worries me.

15

I put down the lip gloss that tasted like a Creamsicle. It was dark in my room—too dark to tell I was wearing anything on my face—so I stood up, crossed the room, and hit the light switch by the door. In the space of a heartbeat, my room glowed warm and yellow, like I was seeing it from outside on a cold night. I blinked a few times and walked back to the mirror, where I'd been sitting since before the sun went down, applying foundation to my cheeks and spraying clouds of body mist over my collarbone and throat.

When it was time to go, I called Dad and met him by the front door with the car keys in my hand. It was all part of the ritual humiliation of not having a driver's license: the necessity of asking your father to drive you to your first real date. When Dad saw me, I think he was relieved that I was wearing jeans and a black scoop neck sweater, which was pretty much the same thing I wore to school every day. What he didn't know was that I'd shaved my legs with baby oil and sprayed body mist into my armpits and the cups of my bra, which was most definitely not part of my everyday routine. I was also wearing eye shadow—turquoise, in honor of Mom.

We drove all the way to Oakwood Avenue in silence, our

thoughts hovering in separate, unknowable orbits. It was one of Dad's best qualities—the way he could be quiet without making people feel awkward. Only tonight, just this once, I would have liked a little distraction from my thoughts. I would have liked him to ask me about Levi or even about the movie we were going to see. In my nervousness, I grabbed Lucy's moisturizing cream off the dashboard and rubbed some down the inner sides of my wrists, where the skin was milky and smooth. I liked the way the veins felt underneath, sliding up and down, but I stopped when I realized how strong I smelled—like body mist and deodorant and Creamsicle and now hand lotion. If Dad noticed the cloud of aromas around me, he didn't say anything.

It was only when we were halfway to the theater that he spoke at all. He didn't ask me how I met Levi or what made *White Heat* such a popular movie. Instead, he asked about Olive. More specifically, he wanted to know why he hadn't seen her around the house in a while—had something happened?

I told him we weren't friends anymore, and then I stared ahead of me out the windshield. If silence was Dad's best quality, it was probably my worst. But he knew me too well. The longer I watched the double yellow lines disappear under our car, the more he pushed. He wanted to know whose decision it was to end the friendship—who broke up with whom—as though we'd been going out. Then he wanted to know how I felt about it, and whether I'd done anything like apologize or try to make things right. Worst of all, he wanted to know if Olive was lonely. Not me—his daughter. Olive.

"It's not as if she doesn't have other friends," I told him, although I realized, as soon as the words hung in front of me in the air, that they weren't true. Other than Grace, the only person I'd seen her hang out with was Jamie Pollock, the cello player. "She sits with someone else at lunch now," I told Dad.

"Who?" Dad turned on his blinker and made a left turn into the parking lot of the movie theater. "Anyone I know?"

I shook my head. "Just a new victim."

Dad frowned. "Friends aren't victims."

"I was," I told him. "She picked me out of the crowd like I had a target on my head. I don't even know what she saw in me."

"A smart, thoughtful person?" Dad looked troubled. "Just a guess."

I rolled my eyes, even though he couldn't see my face. We were pulling up behind a long row of cars next to the entrance to the theater, which was packed for the opening night of *White Heat*. I considered hopping out of the car right there, a hundred yards away from the entrance. Unbuckling my seat belt, I grabbed my purse and put my hand on the door.

"I mean it, Rey." Dad stopped driving even though the cars in front of us kept inching forward, leaving a gap in front of our Subaru. "Put things right."

"There's nothing I can do tonight," I said, unlatching the door. I could already smell the buttered popcorn wafting out of the theater.

"Then we'll talk about it later," answered Dad. "When I pick you up." I registered the disappointment in his voice and filed it away under Things Not to Think About.

The first thing Levi said when he saw me was: "You smell good." We were standing three feet apart. As soon as he turned his head to look for the popcorn line, I rubbed my wrists against my jeans, praying he wouldn't start sneezing once we sat down next to each other.

At the concession stand, we ordered an extra large cherry soda with one straw. Just when I was about to ask for a small bag of popcorn, Levi gestured at his bulging side pocket and whispered, "Peppermint patties." I knew right then that he intended to kiss me.

"That'll be all," I said to the girl behind the counter, fumbling with my wallet. Of course, Levi handed her a five-dollar bill before I could even find my money. "Thanks," I told him. "I'll pay you back."

"Don't be crazy," he said. "It's not like this is the twenty-first century."

I laughed. It was the first time all night. We moved from the concession stand toward the long, winding line outside the biggest theater in the Cineplex. The people at the front had already finished their popcorn. I hoped we wouldn't have to wait too long.

As though in answer to my prayer, the crowd started moving the minute we joined the end of the line. Levi kept his hand covering the bag of peppermint patties in his pocket, only lifting it once to grab two pairs of 3-D glasses—or 3-D kiss impediments, as I suddenly thought of them.

Inside the packed, dimly lit theater, finding two seats together was hard, but we managed, climbing over people's feet and squeezing past their knees. By the time I sat down and set my phone to vibrate, Levi had already opened the bag of peppermint patties and was holding out a handful for me to take. As we slipped on our glasses and waited for the previews to start, my whole body buzzed with sugar. I was nervous, and the theater was too cold for comfort. Below the seat, my toes scrunched of their own accord.

Levi put his arm around me right from the start. He didn't wait for some stupid, scary scene. For that, I was grateful; otherwise I would have had to pretend to be afraid. When I finally rested my head against the crook of his neck, I could feel his heart hammering down below in his rib cage.

The movie was stupid. Each time I bent to take a sip of our soda, Levi held the straw up to my lips and I lost track of the plot even further. The Creamsicle-flavored lip gloss I'd applied in my room had mostly rubbed off, and I wondered whether he could taste it when he sipped from the straw. Did it ruin the flavor of the soda? I had no way of knowing. Every now and then I glanced over and saw him looking at me. Once, he was even leaning toward me, but I lost my nerve and turned back toward the screen. It was midway through the movie when we worked up the courage to look at each other at the same time. Through the clunky 3-D glasses, I saw the pores on his nose up close.

Then we were kissing. His face was in my hands, and my heart was in my lap. At first, his mouth felt dry. Then he plunged his tongue against my teeth, and everything deepened. It took me a minute to discover how to breathe—in and out, separate from the kiss.

We kept going for the rest of the movie, never once moving our heads farther than a few inches apart. I think we were both too nervous that if we stopped, we'd notice the ridiculous glasses and laugh. We kept going even as the credits rolled at the end of the movie and the audience clapped. Only when the lights came on and the theater began to empty did we break apart to look at each other.

Somewhere in the woods behind her house, Olive was lying down on cold gravel, staring up at a moon that reminded her of a smudge of chalk. If Levi and I had known, what would we have done differently? Left the movie? Called the police? In everything that came after, I regretted a million things, but never once the kiss. In the cold theater, our toes came back to life. We pressed our foreheads together while Olive watched the sky swell out, opening above her like a mouth.

Saturday

I once heard a psychologist say on the radio that Seung-Hui Cho, the Virginia Tech gunman, had "suicidal ideations" for months before he killed thirty-two people and then himself with a semi-automatic handgun in the engineering hall. After that, the phrase kept rolling over in my head like a static cling sheet in the dryer, sticking to everything. *Suicidal ideations. Suicidal ideations. Suicidal ideations.* I wasn't thinking about suicide itself—just the way the words sounded. Hard and clinical, like the Latin name of a wart. I repeated them so often, I actually grew worried. If somebody had hooked me up to a lie detector and asked, "What are you thinking about?" my mouth would've opened and out would've popped the phrase *suicidal ideations*.

But on the morning after *White Heat*, I wasn't ideating anything at all. I woke up around ten to a dark, gloomy room. Through the slats of my blinds, I could see the sky outside, a deep shade of gray that looked almost purple. High above the house next door, a thundercloud was massing up, ready to burst.

I hadn't even moved yet when my phone buzzed. It was still set to vibrate from the movie, and I thought it was Levi, texting me to say good morning. I reached toward my nightstand and yanked the phone under the covers, where it cast a blue light onto my pajamas. But the text was from Abby, not Levi. It said, *OMG, check the news.*

At first I just stared at the little blinding screen, surprised. Abby and I hadn't talked since the Valentine's party. But then I thought of all the millions of possible disasters that might have transcended our fight—earthquakes, tsunamis, terrorist attacks—and climbed out of bed. The house was eerily quiet as I walked into the living room and looked for the remote, disaster scenarios playing out in my head one after the other. More than anything, I wanted noise—something to blast away the unnerving silence in the house. I couldn't call Levi because it was too soon, and I couldn't call Abby because I'd betrayed her at a party I barely even remembered, and I couldn't call Gretchen because she was the spider at the center of a big web and I was the fly.

So I dug out the remote from behind the couch and turned on the TV. It was already set to channel four, Springdale's local news station, and there was footage on the screen of a stalled train with a news ticker running below it that said: *Grisly Suicide at Talmadge Hill.*

I actually thought for a second they meant a grizzly bear. That's what gave me pause—the thought of a bear jumping in front of a train, rearing its claws at the bright headlights. I leaned toward the TV, searching for the bear in the footage. And then I remembered that *grisly* was a word on a vocab quiz I aced in eighth grade, and it meant something like gross or terrible or scary. That's when I put down the remote and stared at the wreck on the screen. There were policemen standing all around, stringing up yellow tape, and the newscaster was interviewing a conductor who stood to the side with his hat in his hand.

"A young woman," he told the reporter in a flat, stunned voice. The microphone barely caught the edges of his words. "All bundled up. Looked warm. Stepped onto the track and lay down like she was going to sleep." The camera didn't move off his face, even though he was gazing offscreen toward the train. "I've never had this happen before," he finished, the sun rising behind him in a tight, angry ball.

The screen switched to another interview—a woman on the night train who felt a bump; a policeman who said he wouldn't release the name of the minor; a janitor at the train station who claimed he saw a girl in a purple raincoat hanging around for twenty minutes outside the ticket booth, staring at the timetable, just three hours before nightfall.

I wasn't listening. My eyes were scanning the footage, searching for clues. Nobody was saying anything specific about the girl. Nothing about the color of her hair or the contents of the handwritten note they found a hundred yards away. Nobody listed any identifying features whatsoever until the cop let slip that the girl wasn't wearing her glasses at the time of the impact. *Glasses*, I thought. *Olive wears glasses*. Then the station switched over to a commercial, and I thought to myself, before I had even consciously decided to believe: *wore*.

Olive *wore* glasses.

There was always the possibility that I was being paranoid. It wouldn't have been the first time. For almost all of second grade after Mom died, I spent my bus rides imagining new and horrific ways that Dad might've died while I was at school. Every time he left me alone in the house to grab groceries from the A&P, I visualized a yellow Hummer backing out of its spot and running him over in the parking lot, his paper bags splitting as they hit the pavement, cans of beans and alphabet soup rolling every which way.

Now the paranoia was back in full swing. Reaching for my phone, I attempted to come up with a text that wouldn't give me away. Nothing as obvious as *are you alive?* because if she was I wasn't ready to give her the satisfaction of knowing that I cared. Instead, I wrote, *I have a sweater of yours. Do you want it back?*

Waiting for a response, I felt the familiar restlessness, the rush of dread, the urge to walk somewhere fast. Dad's old treadmill skulked in the corner of the living room like a hunched, forgotten monster, so I walked over to it in my pajamas and stepped onto the end of the rubber mat. The front was piled high with a stack of sweatshirts from Dad's company, so I kicked them onto the floor and turned the knob. Soon I was running in strides, sucking in gulps of air, listening to my heart thud.

I ran for three minutes—not even half a mile—when my phone buzzed. I lunged forward to turn off the treadmill and reached into my pocket. There was a new text from Abby. *Dad says it's a BHS freshman. Do u no her?*

The stitch in my side throbbed. Abby's dad was a reporter for the local news station, so he would be one of the first to know the details. I breathed in deeply and stared out the window. The thundercloud over the house next door had burst open while I was running, and now loud, fat raindrops were hammering against the street. Definitely not bike weather.

"Dad!" I called, craning my neck around. "Are you up?"

No answer.

I thought I could hear the shower running in the bathroom at the other end of the house, but the noise was faint, and it might have just been rain. "Dad!" I called again.

There was a rustle from the direction of his bedroom. I got off the treadmill and slipped one of the company sweatshirts over my pajamas. Then I hurried to the front door, where my sneakers were pushed up against the wall with their tongues wide open, waiting for my sweaty feet. "Dad!" I shouted again. "I need a ride!"

There was a creak in the hallway as Lucy rounded the corner in her bathrobe. "Morning, Reyna," she said. "Where do you need a ride to?"

"Nowhere," I answered automatically. "Where's Dad?"

"He's in the shower." She frowned at me, a faint crease between her eyebrows. "What's wrong?"

"Nothing."

I didn't want her to see my face, so I turned around and pretended to stare out the peephole in the front door. "Could you tell him I need a ride to Olive's house?"

"You can ask me, you know," she said. "I can drive."

I pressed my forehead harder against the cool door.

"If you give me a second, I'll put on my shoes—"

"No thanks," I said. "I'll wait for Dad."

I could tell even with my back to her that she was turning around to leave, and I was glad. But as soon as she was gone, I felt a shudder move through me, slow and deep, like an earthquake before a tsunami.

"Reyna?"

I startled. She had paused at the end of the hallway.

"Are you OK?"

I wasn't. It was just like my panic attacks in elementary school. I could be climbing a jungle gym or eating birthday cake, but if I even *thought* about Dad dying, I'd start shivering from head to foot, not really crying—just freaking out.

I felt Lucy come up behind me and put a tentative arm around my shoulder, which I shrugged off.

"Reyna, sweetie... What's wrong?"

"*Please* get my dad," I said.

"Tell me what's going on."

"A girl killed herself last night." My teeth were clattering so loudly in my skull, I could barely hear myself. I reached over and started to turn the knob on the front door as though I'd walk by myself to Olive's house, even though it was pouring rain and I was shivering like a hypothermia patient.

"And you think it's Olive?"

"She's not answering her phone." Another shudder moved up my spine. "I don't know what to think."

An expression of resolve settled over Lucy's features. "I'll

204

drive you," she said, removing the towel from her hair. "Let's get in the car. Now."

"No," I said again. "I'll wait for Dad."

"You need my help, Reyna. I can do this just as well as your dad."

I wanted to tell her that this wasn't some kind of convenient opportunity for her to parent me; that giving me a ride to Olive's house wasn't her chance to prove that she could replace my mom. But she was already grabbing her car keys off the console table by the door, and I realized that she intended to drive me in her slippers and bathrobe, even though the front walkway was slick with rain and it was freezing outside.

She and I both shivered as we got into the car. I could feel the wind blow through my flannel pajama pants as I pulled the door shut and held my fingers out toward the vent, waiting for the heater to start up. Lucy turned the ignition and backed out of our driveway without a word. "It's on Cedar Street," I told her, managing to breathe properly for the first time since I started panicking. "All the way at the north end."

She nodded and reached over to turn on the radio, but the story on the air was something about a peanut butter recall, not anything to do with Talmadge Hill, so I turned it off. The same questions were flopping over and over in my head: *Why are you so sure it's her? Maybe she's just sleeping late. Why are you so morbid?* Then it hit me. "The stove is hot."

"What?" Lucy glanced over at me.

"The stove is hot," I repeated.

"What does that mean?"

The realization was coming in waves, little by little, what the title meant. "She wrote me a poem," I said. "In the lit mag."

"A poem about a stove?"

"It was called 'Disappearing.'" I swallowed quickly. "It was a warning."

Lucy pressed her lips together, and I stared straight ahead through the windshield at the thin rows of birch trees that ran parallel to the road. The white tree trunks sped by in a blur, the knots in their bark fixing me like a hundred unblinking eyes.

When we got to Olive's house, Lucy didn't pull into the driveway. The garage door was open, and we could see a fancy white Lexus pulling out. I leaned forward, hoping to make out the shape of Olive sitting in the backseat, listening to a pair of headphones, staring out the window.

But she wasn't there. The backseat was empty and the only people in the car were Mr. and Mrs. Barton, sitting up front. They seemed to be fighting about something. Or rather, Mrs. Barton seemed to be yelling while Mr. Barton stared ahead through the windshield, his mouth set in a grim, straight line. They turned out of the driveway and sped down Cedar Street, the car leaving two little clouds of smoke hanging in the air where they had accelerated.

"Wait for me here," I told Lucy, unbuckling my seat belt. "I'll be back in two minutes."

"Take as long as you need," she answered.

I didn't thank her. I couldn't. Instead I ran around the back of the house and up the porch steps toward the sliding glass door where Mrs. Barton had once galloped out with a toy horse between her legs. I headed straight for the gas grill on the side of the porch and lifted up the cover to look for Olive's spare key, which I'd seen her use a few times after school.

"Olive!" I called, ramming the key into the back doorknob and twisting. It opened with a soft click. "Are you here?"

No answer.

I ran through the hallway on the first floor, checking every room. Then I bounded up the hollow wooden stairs, two at a time, shouting her name. She wasn't in the sunroom or her father's study or even the bathroom where I'd stared at myself in the mirror on the night everything had fallen apart between us. The only room left to check was hers, but she wasn't there either. The bed was perfectly made except for a faint depression near the front, as though she'd sat there not long ago, tying her shoes.

When the weight of that empty spot hit me, I knew I had to leave. The tidy room, the cold sheets, the frilly bedspread—all of it rose up in my throat. I swallowed over and over as I ran down the staircase, trying not to feel sick. Outside, it was raining hard. I almost forgot to the lock the door behind me.

When I was halfway to Lucy's car, my sneakers and sweatshirt soaked with rain, I remembered. *Grace.* Her name exploded in my head like a firework. Running toward the tool shed at the edge of the lawn, I called, "Grace! It's Reyna!" but she didn't answer, and the door was locked. I ran around the side of the shed, banging my fist against the wood. "Grace!" I shouted again. "Open up! Are you there?"

But there was no answer. I couldn't hear anything coming from inside the shed—not even a cricket. A desperate, terrible hope was pulsing in the back of my head, almost too awful to bear. *Let it be Grace*, I thought. *Let it be her they found.* I remembered her empty eyes from the Valentine's party, and the way she stared at me like she wanted to hate me but couldn't even find the energy. Maybe Olive was already at the police station, identifying the body, filing a report for the weird homeless girl she met online.

I ran back to the porch, grabbed the house key from the grill, and brought it over to the shed. My fingers were numb from the cold rain, but I managed to jam the key into the slot on the door handle. I thought at first that I was in luck. Pressing my weight into the door, I twisted the handle to the left, but nothing happened. Then I twisted it to the right. It still wouldn't budge. The key fit roughly inside the slot, but not enough to unlock the bolt.

Worried that someone would see me wrestling with the door, I returned the key to its hiding spot and ran back to Lucy's car, drenched to the bone, my hair as wet as if I'd just come out of the shower. Ducking into the passenger seat, I caught my breath as Lucy watched me, waiting for my verdict.

"Drive," I said. "She's not here."

"Reyna?"

"What?"

"I'm sure Olive is fine." She meant it to be reassuring, but I could've screamed, it was so much the opposite. "I'm sure it was someone else."

"How can you be sure?" I snapped. "Did you see her just now?"

Lucy glanced sideways at me and said something so quickly I couldn't understand it. Something like "Safari."

"What?"

"I'm sorry," she repeated. "I'm sorry I'm not your mom."

For a second, I had no idea what she was talking about. All I could think of was Olive, and whether I was ever going to get a chance to put things right between us.

But then Lucy went on, "You probably think if your mom were here, she'd know what to say. Well, I'm not her, but I'm trying the best I can."

Now? She wanted to have this conversation *now*?

"I never asked you to be my mom," I said through gritted teeth.

"I know that," said Lucy.

"Please just drive me home."

But she didn't budge. "I'm not driving anywhere until we talk."

"Fine!" I exploded. "About what?"

"About us," said Lucy, calm as ever. "And about your mom."

I could barely see straight through my rage. "You mean how you wish she never existed in the first place?"

Lucy looked stunned. "Of course I don't wish that—"

"Well, I do," I said. "Then I wouldn't have to sit around watching you treat my family like an Etch A Sketch."

"I'm not trying to erase your mom, Reyna. Or you."

"Please! You'd love it if I disappeared," I said. "You and Dad could go on your honeymoon without worrying about who's going to stay at home with me—"

"No." She gripped the steering wheel tightly, even though the car was still in park. "I'm tired of being treated like this, Reyna. I don't deserve it. In the ten months we've known each other, I've been nothing but a friend to you."

Olive's voice came back to me, echoing through my head like a whisper in a microphone. *I've been nothing but a friend to you…All you ever do is mope around wishing you went to Ridgeway…*The memory of that sleepover—how she cried, how she showed me her dad's office, how she trusted me—hit me so hard I almost reeled.

She was right. They were both right. Olive and Lucy had only tried to be my friends. So why had I looked for every possible reason to hate them? I felt the familiar prickling sensation in my cheeks that always happens when I'm about to cry.

"I'm sorry," I said. My voice came out as a squeak.

Lucy let out the breath she had been holding. "It's OK."

But it wasn't OK. There were so many things wrong, I didn't know where to start. "None of it matters," I told her. "My dad's not ready for someone else."

"He's not ready, or you're not ready?"

"Neither of us," I said.

"Well, I'm here to stay," Lucy repeated. "And I want you to know that you can turn to me whenever you need help." She turned the ignition and we rode silently back to our house, my hair still dripping wet from the rain. When we pulled into our driveway and unbuckled our seat belts, she reached over and touched me on the arm.

"I mean it," she said. "I'm here for you, whatever you need."

I didn't answer. Half of me wanted to shout at her again, and the other half wanted to reach over and hug her—to ask for her forgiveness. I did neither. I let her reach over and squeeze me around the shoulder.

Inside the house, a message was waiting for me on a purple sticky note by the kitchen phone. Dad had written: *Gretchen saw "interesting" news blurb. Call her cell.* I crushed the note in my fist and dropped it in the garbage on the way to my room. I had only one plan for the day, and that plan was to memorize the four stages of mitosis for a biology test on Monday. The test would be there whether Olive was or not, and I needed the distraction more than I needed a phone call with Gretchen. While Lucy told Dad about Olive, I shut myself in my room, lay down on the floor, opened my text-book against the carpet, and repeated the words *prophase, metaphase, anaphase,* and *telophase* over and over like lyrics to a beautiful song. It blasted everything else out of my head.

Midway through the afternoon, when it became clear that I had no interest in talking to Dad no matter how many times he knocked on my door, Lucy called me into the kitchen and practically force fed me salad and leftover pizza. The whole time I ate, I could hear the newscaster's voice on the TV in the living room saying something soft and murmury about infant car seats and the price of gas, but nothing about the incident at Talmadge Hill. Halfway through my bowl of wilted lettuce, I got up, cleared my plate, excused myself, and wandered back to my room, which smelled stuffy, like stale perfume.

I tried praying for a few minutes with Mom's rosary, but it felt strange, like something an old woman would do. Out in the living room, I could hear Dad and Lucy making inquiry calls to the Springdale police department. But if they learned anything, they didn't come into my room to tell me. For the rest of the day, I resigned myself to counting the cracks on my ceiling, thinking about cell cleavage, and wondering if there was such a thing as bird heaven or not.

Sunday

When I woke up, my mind was warm with a dream I couldn't remember. The light falling through the window slats was butterscotch, and in the hazy space between opening my eyes and gaining consciousness, I remembered nothing of Abby's text yesterday morning, nothing of the story on the news, and nothing of Olive's empty house. I remembered only the soft, papery texture of Levi's lips on Friday night, and my toes, curled and freezing in the movie theater.

I sat up slowly. Something was buzzing at the edge of my consciousness, a brief blip every few seconds that shook me out of sleep. It was my phone, vibrating intermittently from across the room, deep in the pocket of my crumpled jeans. That was when I remembered how yesterday had started, and everything that came after Abby's text. I stumbled to my feet, crossed the room, and crouched by my jeans to pull out the phone. There was another text waiting for me, this time from an unfamiliar number. *Go to the tool shed.*

I didn't panic. That was what the yesterday me would have done. The today me slid calmly into my jeans and put on my shoes, taking care to double-knot the laces. Then I grabbed my winter jacket off the back of my desk chair and slipped it on over the men's extra-large T-shirt I'd worn to bed. My eyes were still crusty with sleep, but I crept down the hallway and into the garage, where I pulled open the door and stepped outside. The driveway was still damp and full of puddles from yesterday's storm, but it wasn't raining anymore. Wheeling my bike out of a cobwebbed corner, Grace's name throbbed in my head.

The ride to Cedar Street took twenty minutes by bike—maybe longer, since the muscles in my legs took a while to wake up. When I reached Olive's house, I dropped my bike on the grass and headed straight for the tool shed, knocking quickly on the wooden door. I felt different than yesterday—calmer, but also foggier, like I was one layer deeper in a dream. No one answered, even when I knocked so hard my knuckles hurt. Yet I had the eerie sensation of being watched, as though Grace were lurking around the corner in the woods. Or maybe she was inside the house, peering out a window. I abandoned my knocking and tried twisting on the doorknob, just like yesterday.

This time it was open. The door sprang forward eagerly, with a faint creak that sounded like a seagull. Inside I could barely see anything except for the rickety trundle bed and the unplugged space heater. The sheets and blankets were rumpled to one side as though Grace had decided to roll out of bed in the morning straight onto the floor.

"Hello?" I stepped into the dark, musty space. "Is anybody here?"

Silence.

It didn't surprise me. The shed wasn't very big, and unless someone was hiding under the bed, there wasn't room for

214

another person. Just in case, I bent down and twiddled the switch of a lamp that was sitting on the floor next to the discarded blankets. Dim yellow light filled the shed, and that was when I noticed the envelope.

It was small and white—not a normal business envelope, but the kind that usually holds a greeting card. It was sitting on the rumpled bed in the center, where the mattress sagged, and a neon-green sticky note was stuck to the top with three sentences scrawled in Olive's handwriting. They made an upside-down pyramid.

> *This time I decided not to change your name.*
> *Thought I'd give you fair warning.*
> *Do you miss me now?*
> —*Olive*

My fingers felt odd and weightless as I peeled off the sticky note and tore open the envelope, which held a single piece of paper folded over four times. It was typed.

To Those Who Care:

Did you know that some high school newspapers aren't even allowed to mention suicide, just in case it would give students ideas? Shame, since the *Beacon* would have been a good place to publish this letter. How are you reporting my death anyway? Did you say it was an accident? It wasn't. And while the blame falls on many of you, there is one in particular who deserves to know exactly how he killed me.

Mr. Murphy, if you're reading this, let me explain. I'm gay. I'm everything you hate. I'm a limp-wristed fudge-packing pansy and all those other words you used in class this year—or the female equivalent anyway. No doubt if you had known that one of my "kind" was lurking in your classroom, you would have tormented me as much as you tormented T.F. But I have news for you. You didn't need to. It worked all the same.

To Reyna: I want you to know I'm not ashamed of being gay. I don't hate myself. I just can't deal anymore. I'm so tired of your cowardice and your cruelty. So tired of the way you reflect the opinions of those around you, more or less blindly, with the illusion of thought. Do me a favor and learn something from this. That would almost make it worth it.

Olive Barton

I wish I could say I biked straight to the police when I read the letter. But I didn't. That would have meant Olive was really dead. Instead I turned off the lamp, left the tool shed, and shut the door behind me, wondering why the world seemed so pixilated all of a sudden, like little pieces of my body were disassembling themselves and changing places with little pieces of the sky, the puddles, the pavement, the smell of the grass. I rode home with the wad of paper folded tightly in my fist, the streets empty and unfamiliar in the hazy morning light.

★ ★ ★

Dad was scrambling eggs when I got home. The smell wafted through the front door as soon as I stepped inside, and I almost threw up on the spot. "I'm sick," I announced before

216

either of them could ask any questions. And then I bypassed the kitchen altogether and headed for the only place in the house where I could think.

The attic was accessible by a pull-down staircase located in my closet. I kicked my shoes aside, yanked on the rope hanging from the ceiling, and leveraged my weight to lower the stairs to the ground. Then I grabbed my phone and climbed up the steps, ducking my head once I got to the top. The attic was only four feet high—not tall enough to stand—and dead bugs were in every corner along with boxes of old junk. I took Olive's letter out of my pocket, stuffed it under a pile of books where nobody would ever find it, and lay down on my back to figure things out.

The worst part wasn't that Olive was dead. That part didn't seem real to me yet. The worst part was the thought of Levi reading the letter and knowing the awful truth about me. He would look at me with those big, disappointed eyes, just like Dad. He would say, "This just doesn't sound like you."

I stared at my phone for a long time, wondering whether to call my friends. But if I told them Olive was dead, I'd have to tell them how I found out, and that would mean revealing the letter. I scrolled through my address book so long that the light from the screen stuck in my vision even when I closed my eyes. I almost called Abby about five times. I almost called Levi about ten. I even almost called Gretchen. In the end, I didn't call anyone. Dad found me.

"Reyna?" he asked from the bottom of the stairs. "Are you feeling OK?"

"Fine," I called, staring at a speck of dust on the roof that seemed to fade like a star whenever I looked at it.

"Can I come up?"

"You shouldn't," I said. "Your ankle's still bad."

He took a few cautious steps up the rickety stairs and saw me lying on the floor of the attic, still wearing my winter jacket and pajamas. "Rey, what's wrong?"

"I told you," I said. "I don't feel well."

Dad took another step up the stairs and leaned against the attic entrance. "Then what are you doing up there?"

"Trying to be alone."

Dad just stared at me hard. "Any news?"

I closed my eyes.

"Have you reached Olive?"

"No."

"The police wouldn't tell us anything when we called them yesterday. Has anybody tried calling her parents?"

I shrugged.

"I'd like to talk to them." Dad shifted his weight, and the staircase creaked beneath him. "You don't have to go through this alone, you know."

"I know."

Dad stared at me for a while longer; then he lowered himself through the door and down the stairs until I couldn't see him anymore.

"Thanks," I said to the air.

Monday

"Guess who?"

A pair of warm, soft hands reached around to cover my eyes. I could smell Levi even before he touched me. He was sweaty, but in a good way.

I cast around for a funny answer—something clever that wouldn't give me away. He obviously hadn't heard the news yet. It was only first period, and we'd just finished running a warm-up lap around the gym. "Duke Orsino," is what popped out of my mouth.

"What?" Levi took his hands away. "From Shakespeare?"

"Never mind," I said. "It's you!"

He laughed. "You're weird sometimes." I felt queasy with nerves, ready to tell him what had happened to Olive, but then he touched me on the small of my back and added, "In a good way," and I felt the heat from his fingertips radiate outward.

"How was the rest of your weekend?" I asked numbly.

"Good," he said. "How was yours?"

I should have said, "Not good. Did you see the news?" But I couldn't do it. I couldn't admit it was real. "My weekend was fine," I lied. He probably thought I was blushing because of our kiss on Friday, but that seemed so long ago now, like something that had happened to someone else.

"Want to go choose sticks?" asked Levi. It was hockey day in gym, and we both knew that if we didn't pick soon, we'd be left with the flimsy plastic sticks that bent whenever they came in contact with a solid object.

"Sure," I said, looking anywhere but at his face. We headed together toward the far side of the gym, Levi dribbling an orange puck between his sneakers like a soccer ball.

"Oh yeah"—he kicked the puck and sent it gliding all the way to the edge of the room, where it bounced off the wall—"have you heard?"

Relief and dread rushed through me at once. I opened my mouth to say, "You mean about Olive?" but he cut he me off.

"Keat's Concert Hall is giving discounts to students over Spring Break. You want to go?"

I let out the breath I had been holding. "Sure," I said. "Levi—"

But Mr. Charles chose that moment to blow his whistle. It was time to separate into hockey teams. And that was how I didn't tell him first period. Or second. Or third. Or ever.

Not too many people watched the news. That much was obvious. At first I was surprised, then relieved, then disturbed. Olive's neon green sticky note kept flashing in my mind—*thought I'd give you fair warning*—and I spent most of the morning checking around corners for some terrible surprise. Each time I opened my locker, I expected copies of

Olive's letter to come fluttering out. I closed my eyes and saw myself bending down to pick them up, sweeping the pages into my arms, crumpling them into balls. But there were hundreds—too many to collect, and they floated through the corridors, people bending down to grab them off the floor or snatch them clear out of the air like feathers.

Nothing like that happened, of course. The only copy of the letter as far as I knew was tucked safely away under a box in my attic. As for whether Mr. Murphy had a copy of his own, I wasn't sure. All through fourth period, I stared at his face while he lectured on the rise of the Ottoman Empire. He looked like a computer graphic of himself, his cheeks broad and smooth.

Nothing out of the ordinary happened until lunch. It had been easy up until that point to avoid Gretchen and the Slutty Nurses. I'd simply pretended every chance I got to be studying for my biology test. But once fourth period was over and the test was done, I was out of an excuse. As soon as Gretchen saw me in the cafeteria, she came over to the lunch line to offer me some baby carrots.

"No thanks," I told her.

"Well?" she asked. "Why didn't you call me back on Saturday?"

I shrugged.

"Do you know who it was?"

"Who?"

"You know what I mean, Reyna. Don't play dumb."

"I'm not playing dumb," I lied. Olive was right. I was a coward.

Gretchen raised her eyebrows. "A certain somebody wasn't in homeroom. Or were you studying so hard for biology, you didn't notice?"

"I have to go."

"Why?" She crossed her arms. "Where are you going?"

I glanced over her shoulder and spotted Jamie Pollock wheeling her cello through the cafeteria. Gesturing vaguely in her direction, I said, "I have to go talk to somebody."

"Fine." Gretchen rolled her eyes. "Let me know if you hear anything."

The minute she turned around and left, I felt my lungs burst open with air as though she'd been sitting on my chest. Then I ducked out of the line and carried my empty tray over to the table where Jamie was propping up her cello, getting ready to sit down.

"Hi," I said, sliding into the seat across from her. "How's it going?"

She looked at me quizzically, like I was a movie star with something in my teeth—like she couldn't figure out what to say. Maybe she thought I was popular. Either way, she didn't answer me. "I don't know if you heard," I began, "but on Friday night—"

"I know." Jamie sat down and pulled out a bag lunch from her backpack. Her voice was softer than I expected, like a child's. "Everybody in orchestra is talking about it."

I waited, just to make sure she wasn't going to tell me that Keat's Concert Hall was offering discounted tickets. Then I asked, "What are they saying exactly?"

"You know." She looked down at her hands. "That it wasn't an accident."

So I wasn't living in a bubble after all.

"Our viola player is absent today…" She didn't need to glance over at Olive's empty seat for me to fill in the rest of the sentence: *And certain other people are too.* "Why? Do you know who it was?"

I opened my mouth to tell her I was just as clueless as she was, but then I stopped. Jamie wasn't Gretchen. She wouldn't judge me.

"It was Olive," I said quietly. The words floated out so easily they almost caught me off guard. Jamie brought her hand to her mouth and sat there staring at me.

"It wasn't your fault," I added after a moment. I almost told her about the letter—specifically that she wasn't mentioned in it—but then I bit my tongue. If people knew I had a letter, they'd want to read it. All the worst parts of me would be on display for everyone to see.

Tears were shining in Jamie's eyes, and I realized with a stab of regret that I hadn't even cried yet. What kind of friend was I? Even now, my eyes remained dry.

Jamie said quietly, "I never got to say good-bye—"

"It's not your fault," I repeated, like some kind of broken record. "It's nobody's fault." But I didn't believe the second part. Not a bit. Jamie was swiping at her eyes, sniffling loudly. "I just thought you should know," I added. "Since you were her friend."

A look crossed her face that I couldn't read—confusion, maybe. She started to say, "We weren't really that close—" but then she changed her mind and looked down at her finger-nails. "Thanks for letting me know."

"You can tell the rest of the orchestra," I said. "That the viola player is fine, I mean."

She let out a small sigh of relief.

"I have to go." Out of the corner of my eye, I could see Levi getting up from the table where he always sat with his friends— a group of guys who played trumpets in the jazz ensemble. He was cool enough to fit in with the athletes and the class clowns if he wanted to, but he didn't. He preferred to sit with his jazz friends, and it was one of the things I admired most about him. Now he was headed in my direction, glancing down at his watch, so I slipped away from Jamie and headed toward the lunch line, where I lost myself in the crowd before bursting out of the cafeteria into the hallway. If Levi hadn't already learned the news, Jamie could tell him herself.

But I never found out whether she did because by the end of seventh period it was a moot point. Moments before the last bell, Mr. Duncan, the vice principal, got on the loudspeaker to ask the entire school for a moment of silence for a freshman named Olive.

That was when the whispering started—during the silence.

Tuesday

A n accident. That's how Gretchen started referring to it. An "accident with a train," as though a ten-ton chunk of steel had suddenly jumped out in front of her ex–best friend while she was out one evening on a stroll. Everybody agreed it was tragic. Worse, they wanted to talk about it. Mrs. Kushner, the school psychologist, urged the ninth grade faculty to give us time to recover collectively from the "trauma" of our loss.

People who had never spoken a word to Olive suddenly recalled stories of eating lunch with her on the playground in kindergarten or riding the bus together in middle school or working alongside each other on a project for the fourth grade science fair. She was *so* smart and *so* kind and *so* misunderstood, they said. Everybody wished they'd known her better. A cheerleader named Lizelle Bluth worked herself into a fit remembering a time when Olive drew her portrait during seventh grade. "Did you know she was good at art?" she sobbed while her friends rubbed her back and offered her a box of tissues. Even John Quincy wore a dazed expression on his face as he shuffled into Mr. Murphy's room for history that morning.

Almost everybody understood that Olive had killed herself,

but they followed Gretchen's lead in not mentioning it. We were like Puritans living in the seventeenth century, and the unmentionable scarlet letter *S* was for suicide. Because it was widely known that Olive and I were friends—or that we *had* been friends, at least—people came up to me throughout the day to ask how I was doing. I told them all the same thing: that Olive and I hadn't been speaking. Invariably, they narrowed their eyes at me like I was some kind of pariah. As for Gretchen, Lennie, and Emma, they made a point of advertising their sadness. Because I wasn't crying and they were, somebody called me the Ice Queen during second period, and I heard people whispering it throughout the morning.

By the time the fire drill happened, I was determined not to look anyone in the eye for the rest of the week, including Levi. For the first twenty minutes of history, I kept my gaze fixed carefully on my notebook, where my words swam around like fish, scrambled and nonsensical. When the fire alarm rang, I lingered at my desk so I could be the last person out the door, far behind Levi.

But our single-file line disintegrated once we stepped outside and crossed the bus lane into the parking lot. John Quincy and his posse split off to the right; Tim Ferguson and Mr. Murphy wandered to the left, arguing about something I couldn't hear. Levi came straight up to me and touched me on the sleeve. "Hey, Reyna," he said. "Are you OK?"

I almost couldn't stand it. I pulled my arm away and looked down at the cracked asphalt beneath my feet. I wanted to say, *I don't deserve you.*

"Don't beat yourself up," he said after a moment, as though reading my mind. "What happened to Olive wasn't anybody's fault."

"It was," I whispered.

Didn't he realize that while we were making out in front of a stupid movie about aliens, Olive was alone in the woods, removing her glasses, lying down on the train track like she meant to take a nap? I bit down and tasted metal.

Levi looked like he wanted to say something, but Mr. Mancuzzi was walking by with a whistle in his mouth, ushering everyone downstream. We shuffled to the teachers' parking lot, which wrapped in an L-shape around the cafeteria. There were still a few small puddles scattered on the pavement, reflecting the sky in bright blotches.

As Levi and I moved wordlessly with the stream, we caught up alongside Tim and Mr. Murphy, who were still arguing. "Half the class got As for plagiarizing Wikipedia," Tim was saying. "Yet I actually worked hard on my poster—"

"Give me a break." Mr. Murphy's lip curled. "You worked hard on the bubble letters."

"I worked hard on the whole thing!"

"Coming from someone like you, I would have expected glitter."

Tim's face was a deep shade of red. "Someone like me?"

Olive's memory taunted me: *What are you going to about it? What are you going to say?* But she knew the answer as well as I did. Nothing. Slowing my pace, I let the crowd swallow me up, praying that Levi would loose sight of me and keep walking. But he didn't. He kept slowing down to wait for me. I couldn't stand myself.

To my relief, the fire drill didn't last long. After a few minutes, Mr. Mancuzzi blew his whistle and called out, "False alarm! Back inside!" A gust of wind blew through the parking lot, ushering us back toward the school.

"You go ahead," I told Levi when we were a few yards from the building. The fire escape doors were propped open, and I'd just noticed a tall, willowy teacher off to the side, asking a group of girls if they'd seen anybody run past with an unzipped backpack. What I found strange were the items she was holding up: a handful of mechanical pencils, a crumpled napkin, a Snickers wrapper, and a small, tattered moleskin notebook the color of blood. "Does anybody know whom this belongs to?" she was asking the girls.

"It's mine," I said, pushing my way through the crowd. I would have recognized the notebook anywhere. "Sorry. I must have dropped it."

She looked over at me, surprised. "Just now?"

"No, earlier." I said, trying to ignore the stares of the group of girls.

"What's your name?"

"Reyna."

"Reyna, will you follow me?"

Heart hammering, I trailed after her through the fire escape doors, down an unfamiliar hallway, and into the cafeteria where the upperclassmen ate. When we finally stepped inside, the teacher stopped. At first, I didn't understand where she was taking me, but then I looked behind her at the wall, and it clicked. We were standing in front of a fire alarm, its clear plastic casing open. Somebody had pulled it.

"We believe the owner of this notebook is the person who pulled the fire alarm," she said. "This is a very serious offense, Reyna."

I tried to look like I had no idea what she was talking about.

"Two custodians saw a girl pull it," she said. "Her backpack was open, and these items fell out as she ran away from them. Tell me—if this notebook belongs to you, what was it doing in the backpack of our culprit?"

"I don't know," I said. "I have no idea how it got there." Had Olive left it with Grace? Was Grace here now, lurking somewhere on the school grounds?

"What's in this notebook?" asked the teacher. "If it's yours, you should know."

"Poems," I said without thinking. And then, when I noticed several folded pieces of paper stuffed at the back of the journal, I added, "And homework."

She flipped to a random page near the middle, and I saw her eyes scan it from top to bottom. Then she handed it to me. "What's this?"

There was only one sentence on the page. It said: *Perhaps when we find ourselves wanting everything, it is because we are dangerously close to wanting nothing.*

"Just something I was thinking about," I said.

The teacher frowned. "It's a quote by Sylvia Plath."

"I've been missing the notebook for a while," I lied, thinking

229

fast. "Somebody stole it. They must have had it in their back-pack when they pulled the alarm."

"Who would have stolen it from you?"

"I have no idea," I said. "It's been missing for months."

Triumph flickered in her eyes. "Flip to the last page, please."

I did and immediately felt my stomach sink. There was a date on top: February 21. The day I saw *White Heat* with Levi. Olive's last day in the world.

"Excuse me while I page Mr. Mancuzzi to discuss this." She turned and spoke into her walkie-talkie, which important members of the faculty carried on their belts in case of emergencies. The minute she was facing away from me, I slipped the folded pages out of the notebook and shoved them into the pocket of my sweatshirt, linking my hands together inside the pocket to cover the bulge. No sooner had I pressed the wad of folded paper closer to my stomach than the teacher turned back to face me, her mouth set in a grim line.

"Mr. Mancuzzi is busy," she said. "I'm to confiscate the journal and send you back to class. If we determine that *is* your journal—which I doubt—then you're in serious trouble, Reyna. In the meantime, I'd urge you never to lie to an administrator just to get your hands on someone else's private journal." She looked immensely pleased with herself.

"Sorry," I said, handing over the journal with one hand and holding the papers inside my sweatshirt pocket with the other. "I won't do it again."

"You're dismissed," she answered, slipping the journal into a binder.

I left without looking back, stopping only after I rounded the corner to duck into the girls' bathroom by the stairs. It smelled like cigarette smoke in there, but I locked myself in the handicapped stall anyway and pulled out my cell phone. I knew it was a long shot, but I had an idea. *Did you pull the fire alarm?* I typed carefully. Then I found the number that had texted me on Sunday and hit Send.

I didn't expect an answer right away, so when the phone vibrated in my hand a moment later, I nearly jumped. The text was short: *Who is this?*

Rachael Ray, I typed. *Who are u?* If Grace was as close to Olive as I was beginning to suspect, then she would get the hint. But this time the phone was silent for a while, and I began to wonder if my clue was too obtuse. Finally, just as I moved my thumb over the keypad to close the screen, a reply rolled in: *The cookbook gal?*

My heart rose and sank in quick succession, first because she'd replied at all, and then because Grace would never have used the word *gal*. It probably wasn't even her phone in the first place. She'd probably stolen it from some old man, and now I'd sent him a text. I could have pinched myself. Of course Grace wouldn't have her own phone number. She was a runaway.

There were five minutes left before the end of the period, and I had to get back to history to grab my backpack. But the folded wad of paper in my sweatshirt pocket stopped me. I knew it was probably just a bunch of old homework, but still—I had to know. Pacing back and forth inside the handicapped stall, I pulled it out of my pocket and unfolded the pages one by one.

It wasn't a bunch of homework. It was a series of conversations—twenty or thirty in total—some printed from g-chat, others from a forum called LGBTeen. The two people writing called themselves JarOfBells and KamikazePigeon. As I flipped through the pages, my eyes darted over the words. There was something about jumping into a pool on the count of three. Something about gay boot camp. Something about reading Sylvia Plath poems under a full moon. JarOfBells was obviously Olive.

The bell rang, but I didn't move. Feet frozen, I put the pages in order by date. Then I read them from beginning to end. A handful of the conversations revolved around me. Olive had dubbed me "Asshole of the Day" six times and referred to me once as "feckless." But most of the time, she spoke about me with a mild, wistful sort of regret, as though I was part of a pattern of sadness in her life that she couldn't figure out.

At a certain point, maybe two-thirds of the way through the conversations, the skunky smell of the bathroom ceased to bother me. I grew vaguely aware of the sneakers coming and going outside my stall as I read, the second bell ringing in the hallway, the pipes creaking in the walls. I don't know how long I stayed there.

I didn't expect Grace to be waiting for me at the Talmadge Hill train station like some kind of lost child swinging her legs on a bench, looking for a ride home. But I did hope—maybe

232

foolishly—that she was trying to make contact with me, just like I was trying to make contact with her. After all, who was bringing her food now that Olive was gone? Maybe she wanted to text me again, but she couldn't find a phone.

But when I got to the train station, it was empty. Talmadge Hill was a commuter neighborhood, and the station serviced the local businessmen and women who left for Grand Central every morning around eight o'clock and returned at night in time for dinner. At three in the afternoon, it was practically a ghost town. Only one ticket window was open for business, and there was a tall, clean-shaven man sitting behind it, reading a book.

I walked up to him and cleared my throat.

"Where to?" he asked, barely glancing up from his book. He was younger than he looked from across the room.

"Nowhere," I said. "I just have a question."

He looked up this time and put down his book.

"Would it be possible to talk to someone who was here on Friday?" I asked. "One of the people who was on the news, I mean?" I recalled two interviewees—a conductor and a janitor. The janitor had a potbelly and a white moustache.

"After the suicide?"

I nodded.

"Sure," he said. "That would be our janitor, Joe."

I set my backpack down on the floor next to my feet and gathered my courage. I was here to look for Grace, after all— or at least find out if anybody had seen her around. As for me, the last time I'd seen her was at the Valentine's party, where she'd been wearing the long purple raincoat.

"I'm here because of the interview Joe gave on TV," I told the man behind the counter. "He mentioned a girl who came around here on Friday a few hours before the suicide. He said she was wearing a purple raincoat."

"Sure," said the man without missing a beat. "I sold her a ticket."

I felt my mouth drop open.

"To Grand Central," he added. "One-way. Paid in cash."

It took a minute to sink in. So Grace wasn't living in the Bartons' tool shed after all or even sleeping like a hobo at the Talmadge Hill train station. She was in New York.

"Joe!" The man behind the counter called over my shoulder. "Joe, come here!"

I felt my arms prickle as I turned around. Sure enough, the janitor with the bright white handlebar moustache was standing across the room holding a mop. He'd just come out of the men's bathroom and was moving a yellow caution cone away from the entrance. When he looked up, I noticed that one of his ears was missing.

"Joe, this girl's been looking for you," said the man behind the counter. "She wants to know about what happened here on Friday."

"Is she a reporter?" called Joe. "I'm done talking to reporters."

I shook my head.

Sighing a little, he picked up his mop and rolled the bucket across the room. I walked toward him, and we met in the middle.

"I'm sorry to bother you," I began as politely as possible.

His missing ear was creepy, like something that belonged on a serial killer or Vincent Van Gogh. "I was just wondering about the girl you saw here on Friday," I said. "The one in the purple raincoat."

He squinted at me.

"Do you remember anything about her?" I asked. "Like whether she was carrying any bags? Or maybe a suitcase?"

"No bags," said Joe. "A hat. Gloves. What's it to you?"

"I know her."

"Knew her." His mouth twitched.

"No, *know* her," I said. "The girl in the purple raincoat was a girl named Grace. She wasn't the one who died."

"That's not what the conductor said." Joe was standing in front of me with his arms crossed now, his potbelly a whole foot in front of his body. "He said the train split her face right down the middle but the mother recognized the purple jacket. That's how they knew it was their daughter."

I felt a wave of nausea.

"I'm just saying," he said.

But it didn't make sense. Why would Olive's mother recognize a rain jacket that belonged to Grace, a girl she'd never met? Then it hit me: the jacket probably didn't belong to Grace at all. Olive had probably loaned it to her on the night of the Valentine's party. Everything clicked into place with a sickening clarity: Olive, dead, her purple jacket torn to pieces on the train track. Without that jacket, Grace would be even harder to track down—just an anonymous girl of medium height and shoulder-length blond hair.

There was still something I didn't understand. "Did the girl say anything about getting a ticket to New York?" I asked.

Joe looked at me like I was delusional. "The only ticket she got was to someplace else, if you know what I mean."

"But did she say anything about it?"

"Look." He shifted his weight to his other hip. "She just sat there in front of the schedule for a long time. Then I had to go clean downstairs, and when I came back she was gone. A few hours later, everybody was saying there was a body on the tracks. Was it the same girl? I don't know. All I know is what the conductor said."

"Thanks, that helps," I said, even though it didn't. All it meant was that Olive—not Grace—must have purchased the ticket to Grand Central Station. Why, I had no idea.

"Good." He grabbed his mop. "'Cause you just put me behind schedule."

"Thanks for your time," I said, but he didn't seem to hear me. He just lifted his mop and sloshed it back and forth over the tile floor. I left without saying good-bye, just like Grace.

Wednesday

REMEMBERING OLIVE BARTON
By Emily Benz, Managing Editor

Freshman Olivia Francesca Barton, known to most as Olive, passed away on Friday night outside her home in Springdale, Connecticut, at the age of 14. She is survived by her parents, Bill and Melissa Barton.

"She was such a light in everyone's lives," said Freshman Lizelle Bluth, Barton's friend from middle school. "I'm going to miss her more than words can express." Bluth went on to describe Barton as a kind, quiet, sensitive soul who loved to draw and write.

"She was always writing poems in her notebook," said Freshman John Quincy, another close friend of Barton's. "I used to tease her about it, but she was actually really good. I wish I could tell her that now."

Barton, an honors student who played the piano and tutored elementary school students in math, was loved by peers and teachers alike. "She was an excellent student and a fine thinker," said history teacher Mike Murphy. "She'll be missed."

Barton's family plans to hold a private funeral service at their home in Springdale. Students wishing to send condolences may do so via the Guidance Office in room 204. Principal Mancuzzi is expected to announce a memorial service for the freshman class by the end of the week. We'll miss you, Olive!

I spent most of first period wandering around the basement of the school with an old hall pass. I had gym first period, but gym meant facing Levi, and that I couldn't do. Everybody had already seen the obituary. Copies of the *Beacon* were stacked next to the main entrance of the school, and people tended to grab them first thing in the morning when they walked inside. At this rate, they were probably all gone. Too many people like Gretchen Palmer were using them as snot rags to wipe up their tears while they made an exaggerated show of grief. Never mind that the real Olive Barton hadn't played the piano or tutored math since seventh grade; nobody questioned Emily Benz's obituary. In her half-baked effort to fill the article with the requisite diversity of quotes—one from a boy, one from a girl, and one from a teacher—she'd destroyed any resemblance to the truth. The real Olive Barton was tough as nails, full of rage, and eerily self-possessed. But who would dare speak out against the sweet, sad girl Emily Benz had immortalized?

As I wandered through the bowels of the school, past the art wing and the photo darkrooms, I stared absently at the newspaper in my hands. There was a photo on the front page of a mouse skirting past the leg of a chair, alongside a headline that read, *Poll Finds 47% of Students Have Seen Mice at Belltown.* Nothing newsworthy. But even as I read the article below the picture, my mind kept wandering back to the grainy photo of Olive Barton on page four, playing the piano when she was eight years old. She had a look of grim determination on her face, as though she wanted to prove something to herself.

I pushed open a door at the end of the art wing and stepped outside onto the paved path that wound around the perimeter of the school. It was cold out, and the air smelled like soggy grass. Hoping I wouldn't run into any teachers, I headed down the sloping lawn toward the parking lot outside the cafeteria, where I'd spotted the teacher holding Olive's journal the day before. There were dumpsters lining the brick wall, and they continued around the corner to an alcove with a couple of exhaust fans. Bags of trash had tumbled over the sides of the dumpsters and scuttled around on the ground with nowhere to blow. Heaps of old clothes and soggy textbooks and packets of paper sat staring at the sky, rippling in the path of the fans, waiting for someone to remember them.

It was only when I traced the path from the fire escape door to the hole in the fence beside the alcove that I wondered whether Grace had been running this way when her bag split open and Olive's notebook fell out. Where was Grace hiding? Why was she still hanging around now that Olive was gone? Maybe she still had business to take care of—business with me. My mind spun around and around like a rim on a tire, going nowhere. And that was when I saw the stack.

Not a stack—a ream. A ream of printed paper straight from a photocopy machine. The print was small and crisp, and as soon as I got closer, I recognized the careful, loopy signature at the bottom of each page. It was Olive's letter. A hundred—no, two hundred—copies of it. The top few sheets had scattered off and blown around the alcove with the other trash.

Grace had been here. I felt a chill pass through my body. She'd run this way—out the door, around the dumpsters, and through the hole in the fence. Whatever she'd been trying to achieve by pulling the fire alarm, she'd failed. The teachers had noticed her too soon. She'd fled the school grounds and dropped Olive's notebook on the way out. And then the stack of letters. Or was this what the sticky note meant by *fair warning*?

There were no answers to be found in the alcove, only more questions, on and on like a train with too many cars to count. Gathering up the scattered pages, I added them to their original stack and then shoved the whole pile in my backpack, behind my math book. I would take it home and put it in the attic. And then I would decide what to do.

★ ★ ★

When my phone vibrated during lunch, I almost missed it. I was sitting in the handicapped stall in the bathroom munching on Cheez Doodles, and the girl in the stall next to me had just flushed. I heard the phone buzz as she unlocked her door and stepped out in front of the sinks, where I could see her through the crack. I watched her watch herself in the mirror, cocking her head to the side and frowning at a zit on her chin.

I knew the text was most likely from Lucy, wondering why the phone had been ringing off the hook all morning with automated messages from the attendance office. I took my time flipping open the phone, wondering how I was going to explain four consecutive absences in a row. But when the message loaded, it wasn't from Lucy. It was from the same phone number that had texted me on Sunday, telling me to go to the tool shed. This time it said, *Where is the funeral?*

I stared at it for a long time with my thumb hovering over the keypad. On Monday, the exact same number had texted asking if I was Rachael Ray, *the cookbook gal*—clearly not from someone our age. Was it possible Grace was borrowing someone else's phone and then erasing her messages? With unsteady fingers, I typed back, *I don't know. Where can we meet?*

Her reply came back almost instantly. *At the funeral.*

But the obituary hadn't mentioned a date or location— only the fact that the family would be hosting a private affair. *When is it?* I wrote.

Five seconds later: *I don't know. Don't you?*

My fingers felt sweaty and kept missing the keys as I typed back, *I'll try 2 find out and text u soon.*

Ten seconds later: *You can't. This isn't my phone.*

Where r u? I typed. *How can I reach u?*

G2G. I imagined her sitting in the food court of a mall, typing as fast as she could, just fast enough to slip the borrowed phone back into somebody's briefcase before he noticed it was missing. But no—that couldn't be. It was the same number as last time—the same number she'd written from on Sunday. It couldn't belong to somebody random.

I almost got up right then to run a reverse phone number search at the library, but as soon as I stood up, crumpling the empty bag of Cheez Doodles in my fist, the bathroom door

241

swung open and Lennie King burst in with two girls whose voices I didn't recognize. None of them had come to use the bathroom. Instead, they touched up their makeup in front of the mirror and laughed about a joke I couldn't hear the beginning of—something about a butt the size of a bulldozer.

I thought of all the inside jokes I might have been part of if I'd latched onto their group earlier in the year instead of making friends with a girl I could barely stand to be around. Who would I have been in that alternate universe, and what would have become of Olive? Would she be alive now, sitting in this bathroom stall instead of me, watching us apply lip gloss through a crack in the door? That's where every firing synapse in my brain led me that afternoon. To a complex series of circumstances I could never untangle, even if I tried.

Mr. Duncan got on the PA a few minutes before the last bell. His voice had a grainy, crackling quality, like Neil Armstrong landing on the moon.

"It has come to our attention," he said with every drop of gravitas he could muster, "that, in light of our recent loss, a non-denominational memorial service might allow our student body some closure regarding the incident over the weekend." He was careful not to use the word *suicide*. "Those who knew Ms. Barton are invited to an assembly to be held in the auditorium this Friday during fourth period. If you'd like to speak at the service, please submit your name to the guidance office." His voice trailed off for a second, and I wondered whether this was hard for him—whether

242

he'd ever had to make this kind of announcement before. "Until then, please proceed as normal," he finished gruffly. "If Olive were here, she'd want us to keep our spirits up." Then the PA crackled off, and the bathroom was silent.

I decided it was time to leave the bathroom. My legs felt stiff, and the light outside my stall seemed oddly bright, like sunlight. I gazed at myself in the mirror for a moment; then I turned and left the bathroom. I knew exactly where I was going.

★ ★ ★

Crossing the train tracks this time on the way to Olive's house, the world seemed to freeze. The sound of cars whipping past me in both directions faded to a pinpoint, and the crunch of my sneakers against the gravel filled my head like I was chewing on glass. When I was right at the center, in between the rails, I paused. The stillness stretched forever in both directions.

Without a phone number to text Grace, the tool shed was my only chance of reaching her. If she wasn't there when I stopped by, I'd have to write the date and time of the memorial service on a piece of paper and slide it under the door. It was my only hope of getting her the information.

But I didn't get a chance. When I showed up at Olive's house, Mrs. Barton was standing on the front lawn, beating the dust out of an old rug with the stick of a broom. I'd almost forgotten that she lived there at all. The house seemed like an empty shell now that Olive was gone. "Rachael!" she called when she saw me, staggering backward into a bush. "Rachael Ray!"

The pavement seemed to drop out from below my feet, and

I paused at the foot of the driveway to stare at her. Had I heard right?

"What are you doing here?" she called. Her voice was haggard. "Are you looking for Olive? She's gone, you know. Dead."

"I'm sorry," I blurted, stepping forward onto the grassy lawn. "I came to say—I mean—I'm sorry for your loss." I grimaced as I heard the words so many people had said to me after Mom died. Olive wasn't a missing sock. She was dead.

"Go away." Mrs. Barton leaned oddly to the left. "You're not wanted here."

I opened my mouth, but no words came out.

"So much work to do," she continued, swaying a little. "So much to get the house in order—the carpets—"

"I'm so sorry," I whispered. I couldn't tell if she was confused or just drunk.

"Who are you anyway?"

I stared at her.

"Who are you?" she repeated.

"I'm Rachael Ray," I sputtered. "I mean, Reyna Fey—"

"Listen…" She gestured at me to come closer and then stuck one hand into the baggy pocket of her sweatpants. The piece of paper she pulled out was small and off-white, and I recognized it right away as a page torn from the red moleskin notebook. "You're all over this note," she said. "Fourteen years, and this was all she gave us. Can you believe the nerve of that girl?"

I took the note from her and glanced at it. There were only three short sentences, scrawled in large, wobbly letters as though they'd been written on the surface of a rock.

I'm sorry. I couldn't take it anymore. Tell my parents good-bye.

It was Olive's handwriting; there was no doubt about that. But it was so different from the carefully composed letter she'd left for me in the tool shed. Confusion washed over me in waves. "What do you mean I'm all over this note?" I asked. "I'm not anywhere on here."

"Turn it over," she said.

I did, and then I almost dropped it. There was my name, written in script, over and over on each line, crammed upside down and sideways to fill every last centimeter of the page except for an inch in the middle where a one-word question was underlined and circled twice: *Friends?*

"I'm sorry," I whispered. "I didn't know."

Mrs. Barton yanked the page out of my hand and stuffed it back into the loose pocket of her sweatpants. "Sorry doesn't change a thing," she snapped. "Sorry doesn't change a phone call from the police. Sorry doesn't change the drive to the coroner's office to claim the body."

"I know," I whispered, but she didn't seem to hear me.

"Do you have any idea what it was like?" Her eyes were gleaming now, her fists clenched. "Do you know what I saw when they unzipped the bag?"

I felt a wave of nausea as she staggered to the left and grabbed at the porch railing for balance. "My husband threw up, but I didn't. I'm not squeamish."

"Mrs. Barton, please—"

"At first I thought it wasn't her," she continued, steadying herself against the porch. "Skull was smashed, of course. Couldn't recognize her face. But then I saw the raincoat. I'd recognize that coat anywhere. I bought it for her, you know. A gift for her birthday—"

With that, Mrs. Barton lost her balance and fell onto the front steps of the porch. I stepped forward to offer her a hand, but she didn't take it. She just sat where she was, yanked a small silver flask out of her sweatpants pocket, and took a swig.

With a shiver, I glanced over at the tool shed and reminded myself why I'd come. Sliding my message for Grace under the door of the shed was out of the picture, but maybe if she was inside…Maybe if she was listening…

"They're holding a memorial service at school," I said loudly, craning my neck in the direction of the tool shed. "It's on Friday during fourth period."

Mrs. Barton put down her flask. "Memorial service?"

"I just thought you should know," I said quickly. "In case you wanted to come." I felt awful taking advantage of her, this woman whose daughter had just died, who couldn't even process the sadness because she was too drunk.

"We're having our own funeral on Saturday, just for family." Mrs. Barton grabbed hold of the porch railing and raised herself to her unsteady feet. "Thanks for stopping by though. Now that you feel better about yourself, you can go home."

I felt shame swallow me whole. It was exactly the kind of thing Olive would have said—caustic, bitter, absolutely true. I didn't say anything as I turned to leave. I just glanced once more at the tool shed and hoped Grace was listening.

Hello?

Hi.

Is this Tim?

Who is this?

You might not know me.

Try me.

It's Reyna.

From history?

Yeah.

Of course I know you.

Sorry to bother you out of the blue.

What's up?

Can I ask you something?

Go right ahead.

Do you like Mr. Murphy?

Thursday

Tim showed up by my locker after homeroom wearing a pale pink T-shirt that belonged to his sister. Across the chest was a white unicorn with sparkly hooves, and underneath the hooves it said, *My other horse is a unicorn.* The T-shirt was part of our plan, but that was about as far as we'd gotten. That, and the digital voice recorder in my pocket.

Tim followed me wordlessly up the stairs toward the second floor, where we were planning to cut first period. Other than the girl's bathroom, the band room was the only hideout I knew, so that was where I led him—praying the entire time that nobody held practice there first period on Thursdays. The minute we stepped in and shut the door behind us, I felt my stomach unclench. The room was empty. A jumble of music stands and plastic chairs crowded each other at the center of the room as though in a football huddle.

"Now what?" asked Tim, dumping his backpack on the floor and looking around expectantly. Through the threadbare cotton of his T-shirt, I could see all the bones of his rib cage.

"Now we plot," I said, taking out the recorder I'd borrowed from Dad. He hadn't even asked me why I needed it—that's how nice he'd been to me ever since he got off the phone with Mr. Barton on Sunday night. Learning that Olive was really dead had pretty much stunned him into letting me off the hook all week. Even when Lucy told him at dinner how times the attendance office had called to report my absences, he just told her to "let it be" for a few more days.

"Murphy's not just going to call me a faggot out of nowhere," said Tim, tapping his foot against the floor as though an invisible band were playing all around us. "Not unless I seriously get under his skin."

"That's why we're here." I said. "To think of something."

I was glad that Tim had agreed to help—I knew Olive would have approved—but I wondered if he was just looking for an excuse to pull another stunt like he had on Valentine's Day. As though reading my mind, he added, "It's going to be hard to top the tutu shtick."

"Why don't we start by bringing up politics?" I suggested. "I could raise my hand and ask some kind of question about liberal people in ancient Rome."

Tim shook his head. "Better yet—gay people in ancient Rome. Have you seen the frescos of nude men feeding each other grapes? They're all over our textbook."

I smiled. "True."

"Only it would sound weird coming from you. Out of character, you know?"

I knew what he meant—it would sound out of character for me to raise my hand and ask *anything*. I looked around the band room, trying to visualize each of the faces in our class. I knew someone who would be perfect for the job, but I'd been avoiding him all week.

"Why don't I just do it myself?" suggested Tim. "I'll ask about all the frescos."

"No," I said. "It can't be you." In order to catch Mr. Murphy with his guard down, the argument needed to unfold organically. It needed to seem, as much as possible, like a normal class discussion. If it looked like a deliberate provocation, he'd never fall for it.

"We should get Levi," I said, reaching a conclusion I already half-regretted. "He would do it if we asked him."

"Levi Siegel?" Tim yanked on the bottom of his too-short T-shirt. "Why him?"

"He would be good at it," I said. "Plus, Murphy likes him. So he wouldn't realize he was being set up."

"Fine by me," said Tim. "You want to go pull him out of class?"

It dawned on me only then that I was volunteering to talk to Levi for the first time in days. Suddenly I felt jittery.

"I have a signed hall pass," said Tim. "We can pretend it's from the guidance office."

There was no denying the fact that three people were better equipped to hijack a class discussion than two. "I guess," I said. "If you think it would work."

"It will." He reached into his pocket and handed me a crisp yellow hall pass, the date and time filled in with pencil. "Here."

"But it's signed with your own name," I said, glancing down at the signature.

Tim grinned. "They always think I'm some new teacher they've never met."

"You're crazy," I said.

He just laughed.

★ ★ ★

Levi sat in the fourth row of his health-ed class behind a girl with a long, braided ponytail. When I stepped through the door of the classroom, her head snapped up and the ponytail grazed the top of his homework. "Hi," I croaked, acutely aware of all the eyes on me.

"May I help you?" asked Mr. Hugo, the health-ed teacher. He looked surprisingly glad to see me. Only when I stepped forward, clutching my fake hall pass, did I realize he was smiling sarcastically, with an undercurrent of deep annoyance.

"I'm supposed to bring Levi Siegel to the guidance office," I said, glancing down at the pass as though reading his name off the paper for the first time.

Mr. Hugo crossed the front of the room and took the slip out of my hand, glancing down at it before he thrust it back at me. "Tell Mr. Ferguson that if my students come crying to me with questions about material they missed in class, I'm going to send them his way for answers."

"I'll tell him," I lied.

Levi stood up and grabbed his backpack off the floor. He looked glad to see me—or maybe just relieved to get out of class—but he didn't meet my eye until both of us were safely out the door of the classroom, standing in the hallway next to a water fountain jammed with gum. Then he touched me on the arm and said, "What's up?"

"Nothing," I answered. "I just want to talk to you about something." Only I couldn't look at his face without thinking about the texture of his lips and the screech of the train.

"About what?" He frowned. "Did I mess something up?"

"No," I said. "Of course not."

"You've been avoiding me all week."

It was so ironic. Now that we were finally together, I couldn't bear to look at him because he reminded me of Olive. Instead of answering his question, I walked in the direction of the band room, hoping Tim would be able to explain some of the thoughts that were lodged in my throat. Levi followed, taking one long stride for every two steps of mine.

"It's about Olive, isn't it?" he asked. "Do you know something I don't know?"

"A lot," I whispered.

He looked taken aback. "Like what?"

"I'll tell you in a few minutes."

"Hey." He slowed his pace. "I know what you're thinking, but just because we went to a movie on the same night doesn't make it our fault. We couldn't possibly have known."

My throat swelled again. *He* couldn't possibly have known.

"Are you sure you're OK?"

I blinked a few times, wondering if I was going to cry. In a way, I wanted to. It would have shown us both that my heart wasn't made of stone. But I couldn't. As we reached the band room and I opened the door, my fingers looked pale and bloodless against the brass knob. I felt cold to the core. Tim was inside, drumming out a rhythm onto an empty plastic chair.

"Come inside," I told Levi. "I'll try to explain."

★ ★ ★

Three periods later, as we filed into history, Mr. Murphy stood at the front of the classroom with his hands on his hips like an army lieutenant. His face, as always, was as tan and smooth as a slab of wax.

On the blackboard was a page number: *206.* I flipped there as soon as I sat down, sliding my left hand into my pocket to turn on Dad's recorder. As I flipped from 205 to 206, I saw it. On the lower left-hand corner of the page was a reproduced fresco of a Roman orgy, complete with half a dozen naked men and two bare-breasted women lounging among platters of grapes. We couldn't have asked for a more perfect page if we'd hunted through the book ourselves.

I glanced over to meet Levi's eye, but he and Tim were already looking at each other like Christmas had come early. As the second bell rang, they yanked their eyes away and turned to the front of the room, where Mr. Murphy was announcing that we needed to skip backward to ancient Rome to review the chapter about oligarchy versus aristocracy, since it was obvious from the homework last week that nobody under-stood the distinction. It was then that Levi raised his hand.

Mr. Murphy looked annoyed. "Questions *already?*"

"Sorry, sir," said Levi. "It's just the painting in our book." A few people in the class glanced down at page 206 and laughed.

Mr. Murphy squared his shoulders. "Think you're funny, Siegel?"

"No, sir," said Levi, "But the painting is."

More laughter. I felt my own cheeks stretch in a smile.

"I'm serious." Levi was trying hard to keep a straight face. "What exactly are they *doing*?"

"Wouldn't you like to know," hooted John Quincy from the far side of the room.

"No, really. Was this considered mainstream?" Levi leaned forward in his chair. "Naked guys feeding each other grapes?"

As Mr. Murphy let out a long sigh, I reached into my pocket and pulled out the recorder halfway to catch it.

"I'm serious," Levi repeated. It was, more or less, the same conversation we'd rehearsed in the band room. "Did they have a word for gay back then? Or was this normal?"

Mr. Murphy was clearly not in the mood to entertain a question that was meant to amuse the class. Fortunately, he didn't seem to realize Levi was trying to provoke *him*.

"Don't even get me started, Siegel," he said. "I don't want to talk about that."

"But it's a valid question." Levi glanced again at the painting in the book. "Is this a depiction of a fringe community, or were these people rich and powerful?"

Mr. Murphy shoved his hands in his pockets. "What do you think?"

"Rich," said Levi.

"Why?"

"Their house is swank."

The class laughed, and Mr. Murphy rose to the bait. "Nobody's questioning their interior decorating skills."

"So they were?" asked Levi.

"What?"

"Rich."

"Why do you want to know?"

The class erupted again, but Levi didn't blink. "I don't understand how they could be a fringe community if they were also rich and powerful."

The corner of Mr. Murphy's mouth twitched. "Just look at Hollywood."

On cue, Tim spoke up from the second row. "Are you saying gay people in this country are rich and powerful?" he asked, "Because I'm gay, and I have no power whatsoever."

"Give me a break, sweetheart." Mr. Murphy's voice dripped with sarcasm. "You're fourteen years old. You don't even have a driver's license."

The class laughed again—not with menace, but with expectancy. They had no allegiances to Tim or anyone else; they simply wanted to be entertained.

"And I'll tell you something else," Mr. Murphy added, shooting him a pointed look. "You don't become rich and powerful wearing a shirt like that."

I was impressed by the red splotches that appeared on Tim's cheeks. If they were part of his act, they were pretty convincing. "I like this shirt," he said.

"I wonder why," deadpanned Mr. Murphy.

Carefully, ready to bring phase three of our plan into effect, I raised my hand. I made it look tentative, as though I wasn't sure whether I wanted to be called on. Mr. Murphy must have forgotten my name, because he just looked at me blankly and said, "Yes, Miss…?"

"Fey," I answered in a small voice. It took all my courage just to look him in the eye. "I was wondering if it was normal for women to be with each other too. At these…" I trailed off. I couldn't bring myself to say *orgies*.

A few boys across the room wolf whistled at my question. Levi looked over at me admiringly, and I felt a stab of pride for the first time all week.

"Lennie, let's do our next project on that," John called across the room. Lennie just tossed back her long hair and smiled serenely.

"Enough!" barked Mr. Murphy. "Between you and Twinkle Toes over here, we'll be at this all day." Tim's cheeks flushed again, whether from humiliation or satisfaction, I couldn't tell.

"Let's get serious," said Mr. Murphy. "Who would like to read aloud?"

But "Twinkle Toes" wasn't quite enough to get a teacher fired, so I pulled the recorder another inch out of my pocket and raised my hand again.

"Thank you, Miss Fey." He turned his attention to me. "Starting from the top of 206."

"No, I have another question," I said, ignoring every instinct of self-preservation in my body. This tangent wasn't even remotely part of our plan. "Did they have polygamy in ancient Rome?"

"Polygamy?" Mr. Murphy's eyes widened. "What kind of question is that?"

"I was just wondering," I said.

"Look"—he ran a hand over his close-cropped hair—"I'm only going to say this once, and if you don't like it, you can take it up with the author of a certain book." He walked over to his desk, opened the top right drawer, and lifted a copy of the Bible. Then he cleared his throat. "A family starts with one man and one woman," he said. "Not two men. Not two women. Not one man and three women. *One* man and *one* woman."

"My mom grew up in a polygamous family," I lied. "She was Mormon." A few people started whispering, and I had to look straight ahead so I wouldn't lose my nerve.

"I'm not insulting anyone's religion," said Mr. Murphy, though he was actually doing just that. "I'm telling you what *I* know to be true."

I didn't let my gaze waver. "How can you know?"

"The same way he knows he hates me," spoke up Tim. "Categorically."

In an instant, Mr. Murphy grabbed the sissy hat off his desk, crossed the room, and leaned menacingly over Tim. "What's that, Ferguson? You think I hate you?"

Tim didn't say anything.

"Wear this."

"No way." Tim swept the hat off his desk and onto the floor.

Mr. Murphy's face turned a deep shade of purple as he bent over and picked it up. Then he shoved it onto Tim's head. "It was an order, not a request."

Tim pulled it off. "You can't make me wear it just because you hate me."

"I've got news for you, Ferguson. I don't hate faggots."

The class was so quiet I could hear the desk creak when Mr. Murphy leaned in farther, one of his big tanned wrists resting on the surface. "I hate it when they interrupt my class."

The room erupted in whispers as two splotches of deep, angry pink exploded onto Tim's cheeks. I could feel the recorder hot in my hand, capturing every moment, but in place of the satisfaction I expected to feel was a sadness that flared suddenly like the tip of a match. For me, it was mission accomplished. For Tim, it was life.

It didn't take long—about half of lunch—to transfer the audio file onto my laptop and fix the volume levels. The hardest part was editing out the extraneous beginning so that the conversation started with Levi asking, "Did they have a word for gay back then?"

Tim did most of the work, since he was the one who knew how to use the editing software that came with my computer. Levi and I just leaned over his shoulder and watched him click away, our elbows touching occasionally. We were in the no-talking corner of the library, but we whispered every so often about what to do next. Tim thought we should create a fake email account and send the file to everyone in the school. Levi wanted to send it exclusively to Mr. Murphy, to see if he would apologize first. I had a better idea, but I didn't voice it right away. It was still taking shape in the back of my mind, mushrooming out like a nuclear blast, like the last split second of life as I knew it.

I hadn't told anyone yet about Olive's letter. Even when I spilled my soul to Tim over g-chat, I'd omitted that part of the story. But the longer I kept it to myself, the more of a coward I knew I was. There was only one right thing to do, and it involved the stack of letters I'd found tossed near the dumpsters, where Grace had run after pulling the fire alarm. I was pretty sure she'd meant to plaster the row of bulletin boards outside the cafeteria—before she got caught anyway.

"Are you guys worried about getting suspended?" I asked as Tim emailed each of us a copy of the file. It was the least of my concerns, but I needed to gauge how committed they were.

"Come on," said Levi. "Do you think Olive would have worried about that?"

"Of course not," I answered. "But are *you* worried?"

"You can't get suspended for sending an email unless it contains a virus."

"Or porn," said Tim.

"What if we're not just going to send an email?" I pressed my hands against my lap. They were shaking. "What if we're going to break into the school?"

"What?" A sloppy grin spread across Levi's face. He thought I was joking.

I reached into my backpack, behind my math book, and pulled out the photocopied stack of letters. "What if we get here early tomorrow, before anyone else, and hang these up?"

"Whoa, what?" said Tim.

I shoved the pile toward him.

"Is that a letter?" Levi reached over and grabbed a copy. "Holy crap."

I waited while they read the page from beginning to end; then the three of us sat there in silence. After a long time, I forced myself to look over at Levi, but his face was blank. "Wow," he said at last. "I had no idea."

"Something's weird about this," said Tim, looking over the letter. "She sounds angry, not depressed. And why would she blame Murphy more than anyone else? No offense."

I felt my skin prickle.

"Come on," said Levi. "She hated Murphy."

"But he definitely didn't have that kind of power over her."

"How do you know?"

"Because she wasn't ashamed of being gay."

"Of course she was." Levi frowned. "She was in the closet. If she was proud of being gay, she would have come out, like you did."

Tim shrugged. "Not necessarily."

I felt annoyance coupled with gnawing shame. "Are you saying I'm worse than Mr. Murphy?" I asked. "Because maybe I am, but I don't think—"

"Don't take it personally." Tim cut me off. "You guys remember the Valentine's party, right? How I got stuffed in the closet? Well, Olive and I talked for a minute while she helped me untie the tape. We talked about all the assholes in this school, Mr. Murphy included."

"So?"

"She seemed pissed, not depressed. She had a fight in her."

"Maybe this was it," I said. "A really messed-up way to make a point."

Tim sighed. "Maybe."

"Either way, Murphy deserves to fry." Levi flicked the digital recorder that was sitting in front of us on the library table. It spun around twice and pointed at me.

"Yeah." I closed my eyes to stop the world from spinning. "No question about that."

Once we shut down my computer, Tim and Levi headed to the cafeteria to scarf down lunch while I set off on a mission to visit Ms. Mahoney, my English teacher. Room 108 was on the ground floor of the school in the back wing. It overlooked the senior parking lot—a sight I knew well after spending so many hours staring out the window during class. And it was that same window—the one we propped open with a book back in September—that I needed now.

Ms. Mahoney was alone when I arrived, eating lunch at her desk. Resting on a rumpled brown bag was a half-eaten peanut butter and jelly sandwich, a green apple, and a bottle of water—not too different from the stuff Dad used to pack me in elementary school. Only in Ms. Mahoney's case, it seemed like sort of a pathetic excuse for lunch. With a deep breath, I stepped into the room and prepared myself to lie straight to her face.

"Hi, Reyna," Ms. Mahoney said, looking up from her

papers as I approached her desk. "How can I help you? Are you here to talk about your *House on Mango Street* essay?"

"I think I left my bracelet in here," I said, gesturing toward the back wall of the classroom. "During second period. I was over by the window—I think the clasp might have broken."

"Say no more." Ms. Mahoney rose to her feet. "I'll help you look for it."

"No!" I said quickly. "Don't get up—you're eating."

I headed toward the windowsill, where books were stacked on top of one another, but Ms. Mahoney persisted. "It's really no trouble," she said, wiping sandwich crumbs against her skirt as she crossed the room to join me. "What kind of bracelet is it? Silver?"

"Yeah, with charms," I lied. "There's a ballet charm and a little soccer ball and a tennis racket. It's really important to me. My best friend from another school gave it to me." I knew I was rambling, but I needed to distract her long enough to get to the window.

"Goodness," she said. "How long have you had the bracelet?"

"Since I was ten," I said, stepping up to the windowsill and pretending to look through the stacks of books. There were a bunch of Shakespeare plays, some Toni Morrison novels, a dozen copies of *Fahrenheit 451*, and a few other titles I didn't recognize. As Ms. Mahoney moved one of the stacks to look for my bracelet, my eyes landed on the window latch. If I could just unlock it—if I could just open the window a crack and slide one of the paperback novels under it, then Tim, Levi, and I would have a way into the building without a key.

262

But Ms. Mahoney was the one rambling now—telling me about a charm bracelet her little sister bought for her when they were kids, and how she lost it one day on a field trip to the zoo. I couldn't just lean over and flip open the latch. Instead, I reached out and knocked over the tallest pile of books on the windowsill. Two dozen copies of *Fahrenheit 451* toppled over and scattered onto the floor. Startled, Ms. Mahoney jumped backward, squeaking, "Oh!"

"I'm so sorry!" I said, bending over immediately to gather the fallen books. "I'm so clumsy. It's just that I don't know what I'll do if I can't find the bracelet—"

"It's OK," said Ms. Mahoney. "I understand."

As soon as she bent toward the floor, I reached behind the remaining books and unlatched the window. Ms. Mahoney lifted up a handful of books, set them on the windowsill, and bent over again. The minute she looked away, I leaned forward, grabbed the bottom of the window, and leveraged all my weight to pull it open. Too much. A draft blew through and made me shiver. Ms. Mahoney reached up to set a few books on the windowsill. I held my breath as she stayed crouched, reaching for a book that had slid all the way under a desk. I grabbed a copy of *The House on Mango Street*, shoved it under the open window, and pulled down—just in time. Ms. Mahoney stood up, a pile of *Fahrenheit 451* stacked in her arms. "Here we go," she said, setting them back on the windowsill. "No harm done."

I looked at my handiwork. The window was open just barely a crack, the faint draft blocked by the stacks of books in front of it. It wasn't the ideal way to break into the school, but it would have to do.

"I'm such an idiot!" I burst out. This part of the plan was Levi's—his idea of a good excuse to leave the room. The more I thought about it, the more I felt he had lied to me on purpose when he told me he left his jacket in the library. "I just remembered I took off the bracelet to use the pottery wheel this morning," I explained to Ms. Mahoney, my cheeks burning red. "I must have left it in art. I'm so sorry for disturbing your lunch."

"It's no problem at all, Reyna," she said, wiping dust off her knees. "I hope you find it. I never did find my sister's bracelet all those years ago. Such a shame…"

I nodded while she rambled more about her sister and the bracelet she lost at the zoo. I didn't think it was possible, but I'd finally found someone at Belltown High more desperate than I for a lunchtime companion. Unfortunately for Ms. Mahoney, I had something more important to do.

Friday, 5:01 a.m.

I knocked three times.

Lucy answered in her bathrobe, not a shred of makeup on her face. Through the doorway, I could see Dad sitting up in bed, unshaven and scruffy. The alarm clock was playing quietly on the nightstand as though trying to coax them out of bed.

"Can somebody drive me to school?" I asked. No preamble. If I'd wanted to give them time to think about it, I would have asked them the night before.

Lucy and Dad turned simultaneously toward the clock, as though they'd overslept or missed daylight savings. But they hadn't. It was five o'clock in the morning, and the sky outside the window was dark.

"Now?" Lucy said.

"In a few minutes." I adjusted the weight of my backpack. "Whenever you're ready."

They both stared at me. Finally Dad asked, "Why? What's going on?"

"History project," I answered vaguely.

"But we just woke up," Lucy said, turning to Dad. "I haven't even showered yet."

"Dad?" I said. "Can you?" I preferred his company anyway. Even though Lucy and I had reached a truce on the car ride home from Olive's house, she still tiptoed around me like I might suddenly bite off her head.

"Reyna…" He sighed and swung his legs over the side of the bed. I could see his bare feet, little tufts of black hair on the toes. "You need to tell us about this kind of thing ahead of time."

"I didn't know until now," I lied. "My group just texted me, and they said we have to finish our filming while the teachers' parking lot is still empty."

"I would drive her if I could," whispered Lucy, facing Dad. "But I need to get in the shower if I'm to drive to the reception site by eight."

"What reception site?" I asked just as Dad said, "I'll drive her then."

"The wedding reception," answered Lucy. She looked uncomfortable, like she didn't want to discuss the details in my presence. "It's all the way in New York, and I have an appointment this morning with the florist."

Mom would never have approved of a flashy wedding in New York City—her wedding with Dad was a simple affair with a small reception at the local church. But I didn't feel up for a fight this early in the morning, so I forced my face into a neutral mask and said, "oh."

Dad got to his feet. "Come on. Both of you."

Neither of us said anything. Lucy looked like she wanted to cry.

"Sorry," I said, when the silence got awkward. "I'll let you get dressed." It bothered me how easily I could lie to Dad. He always said Mom was a terrible liar, and I would have rather inherited that trait than not.

"I'll meet you in the car," said Dad. "Give us a minute alone."

I left and shut the door behind me, heading straight for the garage. Sitting by myself in the car with my backpack at my feet, waiting, I wondered why Olive had picked a train to kill her. Why not a car in a closed garage? Why not pills? Why the pain?

When Dad came out, he barely limped at all coming down the two steps that led into the garage. He hadn't worn his neck brace in weeks, and the bruises on his face were gone. Even the right side of his mouth, which had looked lopsided for months from the twenty-two stitches, had healed beautifully. There were almost no traces left of the accident, and for some reason, that bothered me. I should have been glad. But I wasn't.

As he turned the ignition and backed out of the garage, Dad rubbed the long creases between his eyebrows and sighed. It was drizzling outside and I kept my eyes focused on the driveway. At the edges of my vision, blurry hexagons of color crowded each other.

"Rey," he said as he turned out of the driveway, moving his right hand from the steering wheel to my shoulder. I shrugged it off, and we sat in silence all the way down Hickory Ridge Road. On the dark, oil-slicked street, the traffic lights reflected red, green, and white. "I hope you'll forgive me," he said at last. "For marrying her."

He looked so sad from the side. His eyes were droopy, his shoulders stooped, and suddenly I remembered how, back in elementary school, he used to wear the same expression whenever I told him I missed Mom. I wondered if that was how I looked sometimes too; if Olive had taken pity on me that day in the cafeteria and spoken to me more out of kindness than curiosity. Maybe the world was backward and nothing was what I thought; or maybe I was the backward one.

"Dad, it's OK." I wished I hadn't shrugged away the hand he'd placed on my shoulder. "I'm not mad at you."

"I know she's not your mom," he said quickly. "And she never will be—"

"It's OK," I repeated. "I know."

"I want you to be happy," said Dad. "I am."

That was the problem. I was left behind. But I didn't say anything. Ever since Mom died, the bond I shared with Dad was a sadness so deep it transcended love or laughter or fun. I thought he felt the same way; I thought that sadness would tie us together for the rest of our lives, soothing us even while it made us lonely. But now he was moving on.

"It's OK," I said, trying to comfort myself as much as him. "I don't hate Lucy as much as you think. Or as much as she thinks."

"You don't?" Dad glanced at me. "Since when?"

"Since Saturday," I said. "When she drove me to Olive's house." I didn't know whether I was lying or telling the truth. I wanted it to be the truth, but I wasn't sure.

Dad looked surprised. "She told me you were still mad at her about the accident."

"I guess it was never really the accident I was mad about." I looked down at my fingernails, which was easier than looking Dad in the eye. "I guess I was mad that you were ready to move on from Mom."

"Reyna—"

"No, it's OK." I forced myself to face him. Abby and Olive had been right—there was no reason to begrudge Lucy a car accident she didn't mean to cause, especially when Dad was OK. And there was no reason to think anyone could replace my mom just by moving around a few pieces of furniture. "I'm happy for you," I said, trying as hard as I could to feel it, not just say it. "Lucy is a nice person, and she deserves someone as nice as you."

Dad's face broke out in a huge smile. "Reyna, I'm so glad you feel that way."

"Me too," I said, smiling a little. "You can tell her I said so."

"How about you tell her yourself?" Dad gestured at his cell phone sitting in the cup holder between our seats. "She probably hasn't gotten in the shower yet."

I glanced over at him, ready to shake my head no, but then I saw the line of his shoulders, straighter than before, and love thundered through me like a stampede. It flattened me to the back of my seat and took my breath away. It squeezed the air out of my lungs and the voice out of my throat. It crushed like shattered glass every hurtful thing I might have said.

"Are you OK?" asked Dad, still smiling. "What is it?"

I reached for the phone.

"You don't have to call her if you don't want," he said. "I don't want to make you do anything you wouldn't want to do."

I dialed.

"Reyna, did you hear me?"

I brought the phone to my ear.

Friday, 5:22 a.m.

Tim and Levi were waiting for me under the overhang by the main entrance when Dad dropped me off. The sun was coming up over the parking lot, and the sky was a deep, fleecy shade of gray. It was still drizzling, but just barely. There were puddles on the ground, showing the clouds what they looked like.

Before we could sneak around to the back of the school, before we could pry open the window to room 108, before I could even say hello to Levi and Tim, I noticed the door. Dead center, Protestant Reformation style, hung a single piece of paper rippling in the wind. Olive's letter. "Did you guys do that?" I called, running up to them as Dad pulled away. "Why didn't you wait for me?"

"We didn't do it," said Levi. "Somebody beat us to it."

"What?" I stared at him.

"It was there when we got here." He glanced over at Tim. "But nobody's around. We checked all over."

"Grace," I breathed.

"What's going on?" Tim folded his arms. "What haven't you told us?"

"Nothing," I said automatically. "I told you everything." But

270

of course, that wasn't true. I hadn't told them about Grace. I hadn't even begun to describe the weirdness surrounding her.

"Something's not right," said Tim. "You're lying."

"Look." I began leading them around the side of the building, toward the senior parking lot. "The only thing I might have forgotten to mention is that someone else knows about the letter."

"You *might* have forgotten to mention it?"

"Her name is Grace," I said. "You met her at the Valentine's party."

Comprehension dawned in Tim's eyes.

"I think Olive gave her a mission to hang the letter all over school," I told him as we crossed the senior parking lot and headed for Ms. Mahoney's window. "That's why she pulled the fire alarm on Tuesday, only she got caught before she could tape anything up."

"The shy girl pulled the fire alarm?" asked Levi.

"Yeah, that makes sense," said Tim. For a second I thought he was being sarcastic, but then he added, "She could have been trying to fulfill Olive's dying wish."

"Exactly." When we reached the back edge of the building, we stared at a row of windows. There were easily a dozen, and they were all identical.

"Which one's room 108?" asked Levi, stepping up to the closest window and pressing his forehead against the glass. "I can't see anything inside. It's too dark."

"I don't know," I said, moving closer. "Which one is open a crack?"

"This one," said Tim, farther along in the row. "At least I think so." He stepped forward, slid his fingers under the narrow opening, and pulled up. The window barely budged.

"Let me try," I said. Positioning myself in front of the window, I wrapped my fingers around the bottom of the glass and heaved my whole weight upward. It worked—just barely. I did it again and again, until finally the opening was wide enough to slide through. Levi hoisted me up and I slid through on my belly, bruising my shoulders against the window frame. Inside, the books stacked along the windowsill tumbled over and scattered onto the floor.

I headed toward the door to search for a light switch while Tim shimmied in next, followed by Levi. When we were all safely inside, we closed the window, restacked the books, and hurried out of the room through the dark hallway. None of us knew what time the principal or janitors would get to school, but our plan was to hang the fliers as quickly as possible and then hide out until 6:45, when the doors would officially open.

"So are you telling me we came here today to finish some homeless girl's job?" Levi asked, rounding the corner as we reached the school's lobby. Stopping suddenly, he looked from side to side as though expecting to see Grace standing by the front door.

"I don't think she's here," I said. "If she found a way inside, she would have put up fliers everywhere, not just on the front door."

"I'm not looking for her. I'm looking for the lights."

"Over here." Tim flicked a switch, and bright florescent

lights popped on one by one, illuminating the lobby. I could see the banner saying *Welcome, Belltown!* and the lame student mural over the stairs and an entire case of trophies from the National Merit Scholarship.

"Let's go." Tim pulled three rolls of tape from his pocket and stuck his fist through one of them like a bracelet. "First the foyer, then the hallways, then the cafeteria."

"I'll put some in the principal's office," I said.

"Divide and conquer?" Levi was looking back and forth between us, waiting for direction and his own roll of tape.

Tim nodded, tossing him one. "See you guys in twenty minutes."

We split up and I made my way to the principal's office, taping up a dozen letters on the way. Mr. Mancuzzi's door was locked, but the lobby with the faculty mailboxes was open, so I slid a copy of Olive's letter into a few choice boxes, including Mr. Murphy's. Then I got out my cell phone and dialed Abby's house.

It wasn't Abby I wanted to speak to, but her father. He exercised every morning before his commute to work, and with any luck, I'd catch him just before his morning run. But, of course, Abby answered on the third ring, a little groggy. "Hello? Reyna?"

I knew what I wanted to say: "Is your dad home?" But panic seized me. "Um, sorry," I said. "I must have dialed the wrong number."

"Fine." I could tell she was about to hang up. "I'll talk to you later."

"Wait." The word lurched itself out of my mouth.

"What is it?"

"Abby, I'm sorry."

"Whatever." She probably thought I meant dialing the wrong number.

"No." I swallowed, working up the courage to say what I should have said on the night of the Valentine's party. "I mean I'm sorry that I told Olive about you and Gizmo. I never thought she would repeat it. I never thought she would even remember it."

"*Now* you want to talk, Reyna? I just woke up."

"Wait," I said. "Listen—"

"My alarm clock hasn't even gone off yet."

"You know Olive is dead, right?"

There was a crackling silence.

"Abby?"

"Yeah."

"Did you hear how?"

When she finally answered, it came out like a croak. "Yeah."

"I need—" A sob rose up into my throat. I tried to swallow it down but it wouldn't budge. "I need you guys—"

"Well, we wanted to call you." I heard a chair scrape against the floor on the other end of the line and wondered whether Abby was sitting down. "Or Leah and I did anyway as soon as we heard the news. But Madison said we should wait for you to apologize first, for the Gizmo thing."

"I'm apologizing now." I slid to the floor and sat there with my back against the wall of mailboxes. The guilt I felt on the night of the party—the guilt I'd felt every day since then—welled up inside me. "I'm sorry."

"I know," she sighed. "I am too."

"I never should have said those things—"

"Shut up. I forgive you."

I let out an animal sound that embarrassed me. Crying on the phone was awful.

"I guess I should get out of bed now."

"Sorry." My voice broke again. "I didn't mean to wake you up."

"It's OK." She shifted her phone from one ear to the other so it made a swishing noise. "Why'd you call my house anyway? Why not my cell? I know it wasn't a wrong number."

Suddenly I remembered the roll of tape in my hand and the stack of papers on the floor next to me. A sense of purpose filled me, and I swallowed the lump in my throat.

"I was calling to talk to your dad," I said. "Did he leave yet for his morning run?"

"My dad?"

"I have a tip for Channel Four."

"That's nice of you, Reyna, but I don't think—"

"Trust me," I said. "It's a good story."

She paused, the silence in the phone full of crackly static, and in that space there was so much uncertainty between us, I could hardly stand it. Then she said, "He probably hasn't left yet. I'll put him on," and I knew we'd be OK.

Friday, 11:15 a.m.

The janitors tore down every letter in the school by second period, but it didn't matter. All morning long, I saw people passing around copies like some kind of cheat sheet for a test everyone was worried about. Mr. Murphy, meanwhile, was nowhere to be found. I heard a rumor he was in the principal's office, fighting for his job.

For the second time that week, nobody got any work done as talk of Olive Barton hijacked the school. English teachers repurposed essay prompts about bigotry; government teachers lectured on Don't Ask Don't Tell; math teachers worried about falling behind in their material. As for me, I had other things on my mind. The closer we got to fourth period, the more I started worrying about Grace, and whether she was going to show up for Olive's memorial service. The final phase of our plan involved Tim getting up on stage to give a eulogy, where he would invite people to visit his blog and download a memorial tribute to Olive. Really, it was our audio file that was available for download, and I wanted Grace to see it—to know we were trying our best to make things right.

The brilliant thing, of course, was that nobody suspected me of plastering the hallways with copies of the letter. Why would they? It condemned me as much as Mr. Murphy. Sure, people gave me weird looks. They stared at me as though they couldn't figure out whether to pity me or hate me. But they didn't suspect me.

By the time fourth period rolled around, I felt oddly close to Grace. It seemed like we were the two invisible heroes of the day, working behind the scenes to bring justice to Olive Barton, to make her death mean something. Of course, as soon as I thought of myself as a hero, I felt sick to my stomach. I had no business feeling proud of anything. Maybe Grace did, but not me.

As the freshman class filed into the auditorium during fourth period, I saw that the stage had been decorated with a few flowers, and a big picture of Olive from the yearbook sat framed on the grand piano that was used during talent shows. I hadn't submitted my name to the guidance office to give a eulogy, and I wondered with a jolt of panic whether anybody besides Tim had, or whether Olive's memorial service would be as much of a travesty as her obituary.

To my relief, Jamie Pollock, the chubby cello player, was standing to the side of the stage. As a handful of teachers corralled people into their seats, Vice Principal Duncan stood at the podium and announced that Jamie would give the first eulogy.

But when she took the microphone, I saw that she looked pale and nervous. "I didn't really know Olive all that well," was the first thing she said. "Not as well as I would have liked." I wasn't sure whether to feel relieved by her honesty or ashamed by the fact that she was speaking instead of me. Naturally I didn't *want* to speak in front of the entire school. I would have rather put a spider in my mouth. But I also knew it was the right thing to do. If I didn't speak, I was a coward, plain and simple.

And a coward I was. I sat frozen in my seat as Jamie finished her brief eulogy and invited Lizelle Bluth onto the stage to speak next, followed by Tim Ferguson, John Quincy, and Gretchen Palmer. These were the people who had submitted their names to the guidance office ahead of time: those who barely knew her and those who felt guiltiest about her death—minus me. I sunk low into my seat as Lizelle took the podium and began reciting a terrible poem about the one time Olive drew her portrait in the seventh grade. I couldn't stand it.

Levi, who was seated at the front of the auditorium, kept glancing around to find my face in the crowd, as though he wanted to give me a hand squeeze. I appreciated it, but it didn't do much to help. The more I thought about getting up and speaking, the more I dreaded his face in the audience, staring back at me.

On the stage, Lizelle was finishing her awful singsong poem. "*She was good at piano and English and art. We'll miss her so much, now that we're apart...*"

Suddenly a scream pierced the room.

I couldn't tell at first where it had come from. Like everyone else, I whipped around in both directions, but nobody seemed to know where to look. Half the audience was glancing over at the teachers; the rest craned their necks around, lost. Finally, the girl sitting in front of me gestured at the stage and I saw Gretchen Palmer pointing toward the emergency exit, her face colorless. "Ghost!" she shrieked. "Ghost!" I followed her pointer finger toward a narrow shaft of daylight falling through the door, and that was when I saw a silhouette—skinny, medium height, shoulders stooped. As my eyes adjusted, I recognized the halo of stringy blond hair.

With a loud clatter, Lizelle dropped the microphone onto the stage and utter pandemonium broke loose. The crowd erupted as people began screaming, pointing at Olive as though she were wielding a gun. Security guards clamored forward from every corner and surrounded her, fumbling with their walkie-talkies, shouting things I couldn't hear.

Mr. Duncan scrambled onto the stage and grabbed the microphone from where Lizelle had dropped it. "Settle down!" he shouted. "Ninth graders! Settle down!"

I sat frozen and pinned to my seat as people all around me ignored him, jumping to their feet and shouting, blocking my view of Olive. I kept seeing little flashes of her in between all the bodies around me. Her face looked pale and sweaty, her hair a mess.

"Obviously Ms. Barton is alive!" shouted Mr. Duncan over the roar. "We'll be taking her into custody. Settle down!"

Olive was struggling against the grip of a security guard, attempting to make her way toward the stage. "Let me speak," she was saying. I could see her lips move.

The tornado in the pit of my stomach gathered speed, swirling around like a perfect storm of confusion, anger, and relief. All I could think was, *She lied to me?* Olive never lied. There had to be a reason.

"Let her speak," I said in a hoarse whisper that no one around me noticed. So I turned to the girl next to me, someone I'd never met before. "They should let her speak," I repeated, but she just looked at me like I was crazy. "*Let her speak!*" I said again, and this time she caught on. Both of us chanted the words at the same time, and then a few people around us picked it up. "Let her speak!" we shouted together in one booming voice until our whole row was doing it, and then our entire side of the auditorium. The security guard with a grip on Olive looked around at the teachers, waiting for direction.

"Settle down!" shouted Mr. Duncan for the millionth time. "No one may speak!"

Olive looked desperate. She was pushing hard against the security guard's beefy arm, cursing at a teacher who was trying to calm her down.

I stood up then and pushed my way out of my row, stepping on toes and knocking knees in the process. Dashing down the aisle toward the front of the auditorium, I felt a hundred eyes crawling over me like terrible, itching ants. But I kept running, bounding up the steps and onto the stage, headed for the podium. In the split second before I grabbed the microphone out of Mr. Duncan's fist, I saw his eyes widen and the color drain from his face.

"Let her speak," I said breathlessly into the mic. I could hear my voice all around me, bouncing off the walls, echoing in my head. I needed to know what had happened.

Olive was looking at me from halfway down the aisle, eyes wide and scared. "Let her speak," I said again, louder. Words came into my head that I barely had time to consider. "Give her a second chance."

The crowd was uproarious. I couldn't tell how many people were chanting for Olive to speak and how many were booing me, but it didn't matter. Before anyone could make sense of the chaos, the auditorium doors burst open with a bang, and Mr. Murphy came bounding down the center aisle. "*What the hell is going on here!*" he shouted, his waxy face glistening with sweat. A hush fell over the auditorium. Only one sound could be heard, and it was Olive. She was crying.

"Let her speak," I said one last time into the microphone as Mr. Duncan grabbed it out of my fist. In the quiet room, my voice reverberated even louder than before. Tears were streaming down Olive's face.

With a nod from one of the teachers, the security guards released her and she burst forward, up the steps, onto the stage. "I'm sorry," she cried, grabbing the mic from Mr. Duncan. But she wasn't looking at him or even at the audience. She was looking at Mr. Murphy. "I'm sorry I lied about you killing me."

"Did you write this?" he demanded, holding up a photocopy of her letter.

"Yes."

"Were you trying to get me fired?"

She gave a small nod.

"Then the charges against me are baseless!"

"No." She swiped at her cheek. "They're not."

A vein bulged on the side of Mr. Murphy's neck. "Excuse me?"

"I'm not dead," said Olive lifting up her chin. "But you're still a bigot."

The room erupted again.

"*Enough!*" barked Mr. Duncan. He had a walkie-talkie pressed against his ear, and he was pointing madly with his other hand toward the door. "Mr. Mancuzzi's office! Now!"

Olive protested, but her words were drowned out as two security guards approached her from behind, linked their arms through hers, and ushered her away. "Someone call this girl's parents," I heard Mr. Duncan mutter as she disappeared through the door. "Get them on the phone right away."

I was next. I felt a hand clamp down on my shoulder and push me forward so quickly I almost tripped. Before I could turn around to see who the hand belonged to, two more security guards materialized, grabbed me by the elbows, and led me through he door after Olive.

Alive, was all I could think. She's alive. The words sounded like a foreign language in my head. I couldn't see Olive's face, but I could see the back of her hair, snarled and matted like it hadn't been washed in a week. She was limping slightly, the tongue on her right sneaker pulled up a few inches, as though her foot was too swollen to fit inside.

Giddy excitement and dread washed over me in waves as we made our way down a hallway behind the auditorium. Olive glanced over at me a few times from behind the gnarled curtain of her hair, but I couldn't read her expression. It wasn't until we got all the way to the principal's wing that I realized my fingernails were digging into my palms. The security guards led us into an office with wood paneled walls, where Mr. Mancuzzi was leaning back in a chair that had little tufts of foam coming out of it.

The guard with his hand on my shoulder lingered by the door, as though he wasn't sure what to do with me. "Have her wait outside," Mr. Mancuzzi told him, not even looking at me. I opened my mouth to protest, but nothing came out and the hand on my shoulder guided me toward the door.

That was when Olive turned around for the first time. Her eyes were red and swollen. "Please don't leave," she whispered. I froze in my step.

"Outside. Wait your turn—" Mr. Mancuzzi started to say, but I found my voice before he could finish.

"No," I said. "I'm staying with Olive." I still didn't know whether to be angry or not, but one thing was certain: I had another chance. I wasn't about to blow it.

Mr. Mancuzzi did a double take as though noticing me for the first time. "All right," he said. "Sit down, then, and don't be a nuisance."

Behind him, through a window, I could see a News Channel Four van pulling into the parking lot. There were two police cars parked up front, and one cop was standing in front of both of them, speaking into a walkie-talkie.

"Olive Barton," said Mr. Mancuzzi, standing up and pacing by his desk. "An hour ago, everyone in this school thought you were dead."

Olive didn't say anything.

"I thought you were dead."

She pressed her lips tightly together.

"Did you plan this?"

I could tell she wanted to answer him but something was stopping her. Whether it was fear or rage, I couldn't tell.

He kept at it, pacing around with one hand on his walkie-talkie as though it were a holster. "Care to explain why you crashed your own memorial service?"

"Not my service," she said at last, looking down at her lap. "Grace's."

"Who?"

"My friend." I could see the muscles in her jaw moving up and down as she swallowed. "She was the one who killed herself on Friday."

I felt something drop in my stomach. Grace. Gone.

"A Belltown student?" asked Mr. Mancuzzi.

"No," answered Olive. "I met her online."

Mr. Mancuzzi looked confused. "And you mean to tell me you switched places with her?"

"It's what she wanted." Olive closed her eyes. "At least, I think it was."

Mr. Mancuzzi was growing impatient. "You may as well start explaining yourself unless you want me to call in the police."

Her eyes flew open. "Police?"

"Faking your own death is against the law." He crossed his beefy arms across his chest. "Were you with this other girl when she stepped in front of the train?"

Olive nodded, her face pale. "We were lying on the tracks together, reading with flashlights. It's what we did for fun."

"*Fun?*"

Olive began picking at a hangnail. "She kept saying she wasn't going to get up when the train came. I thought she was joking. She told me she didn't have a fight left in her, and I said she was just being dramatic. She told me I had to fight for her because she couldn't fight for herself anymore. Then she said this weird thing. She said, 'I'm doing this for you, Olive. If they think you're dead, they'll listen to you.' That was when we heard the train, and I realized she was serious. I told her I wasn't getting up unless she did. She gave in. We both got up. I started running. But when I turned back, she was still there. The light was coming. I couldn't—" Olive's voice broke as she peeled back the skin along her hangnail. "There wasn't enough time—"

The silence in the room seemed to crackle as Mr. Mancuzzi and I digested the image of Grace standing on the track—the light of the train gliding toward her—while Olive watched. The cyclone in my stomach was gone. All I could feel was numb horror.

"What did you do next?" I asked.

Olive shivered. "I ran."

"In the woods?"

She nodded. "I was screaming at first, but nobody heard me because the train was still going. Once it stopped, I realized I should hide. I didn't want anyone to see me. I was crying pretty hard."

She was crying now too. Thick tears crept from the corners of her eyes and clung to her cheekbones before darting down her face. "I could see my purple jacket hanging off the edge of the track," she went on. "And I knew they would think it was me because both of us were blond and the same height. That's when I got the idea to write the suicide note."

"But the note was typed," said Mr. Mancuzzi, holding up a copy of the letter I'd plastered all over school.

"There was another note." Olive swiped at her cheeks. "A handwritten one."

The image of Mrs. Barton floated into my mind, and I recalled the crumpled note she'd shown me at her house—the one that looked like it was written in a hurry on the bumpy surface of a rock. The one with my name scrawled all over the back.

"I tore a page out of my notebook and wrote something on the back," said Olive, cringing at the memory. "I couldn't even see what I was writing. It was too dark. I took off my glasses and put them on a rock with the note pinned underneath, so the police would find it. And then I went home."

"Home?" Mr. Mancuzzi's eyebrows were furrowed. "But how—"

"The tool shed," I whispered, a puzzle piece clicking into place. "That's where you went, wasn't it?"

She nodded.

Mr. Mancuzzi shot me a look as though to say, *Stay out of this*. Then he turned back to Olive. "You've been hiding out all week in a tool shed?"

"Mostly." She glanced over at me, but neither of us

286

mentioned that she had sneaked into the school and pulled the fire alarm.

"If you were living in a tool shed, how did you type this note?" He held up the photocopied suicide letter again.

"By sneaking into my parents' house," she said. "I had to get my other pair of glasses. And food, obviously. And send a few texts. I used my dad's phone while he was in the shower."

Suddenly it hit me. The cookbook gal. Olive's father had written that.

But Mr. Mancuzzi still looked baffled. "I just don't understand," he said. "Why would you fake your own death? It doesn't make any sense."

"Because that's what Grace wanted." There was a note of desperation in Olive's voice. "I think that's what she meant when she said she was doing it for me. That people would listen if they thought I was dead."

"Listen to what?"

Olive opened her mouth to answer, but she didn't have to. I knew what she was going to say. And to my surprise, I understood completely.

"To the truth about why Grace was depressed," I said. "To the reason she gave up."

The hard lines on Olive's face softened. Then she reached over and plucked the typed suicide note straight out of Mr. Mancuzzi's hands. "In a way, this letter was true," she said. "Only for Grace, not me."

"She had a teacher like Mr. Murphy," I added, recalling the printed-out conversations I'd pored over in the bathroom.

287

Olive nodded. "Total homophobe. Made fun of gay kids just so her students would think she was funny. Grace tried to kill herself twice that year."

"That's what this is all about?" Something seemed to click into place for Mr. Mancuzzi. "Revenge on Mr. Murphy?"

Olive looked up and met his eye. "As long as teachers are allowed to say whatever they want, people like Grace are going to kill themselves."

They stared at each other for a moment. Then Mr. Mancuzzi sighed and looked again at the letter. "I'm afraid your word won't hold much weight now that you're alive."

Olive's cheeks flushed. "So I have to get killed to matter? That's not fair."

"Nobody killed anybody," said Mr. Mancuzzi. "Let's just be clear about that. The only murder here is self-murder."

"You're murdering me," she whispered. "As we speak."

Mr. Mancuzzi pressed his fingertips together. "You would need cold, hard evidence to back up an accusation like this against a teacher. A prank isn't enough."

"Prank." Olive stared at him. "You think this was a prank?"

"What do you call that?" He gestured at the photocopied letter in Olive's hand. "Sneaking into the school? Postering the walls? It's a prank if I've ever seen one."

Olive's nostrils flared.

"How'd you break in?" Mr. Mancuzzi leaned forward. "Did you steal a key?"

"No."

"Were you acting alone?"

"I thought I was."

"You thought?"

Olive glanced over and locked eyes with me. "Now I know I had help."

At the periphery of my vision, a security guard was crossing the room, moving past me like a shadow. He reached Mr. Mancuzzi's desk and handed him a slip of paper.

"I'm sorry," Olive croaked at me. Her face looked small and pinched.

"I am too," I whispered.

"Are you angry with me?"

I shook my head, coming to a decision. I was done being angry. Done hating Lucy. Done blaming the world for taking my mom. And most of all, done being a coward. "I deserved it," I told her. "I deserved everything you wrote. I'm sorry."

Suddenly Mr. Mancuzzi rose to his feet and crumpled the piece of paper in his fist. "Not in my school, they won't," he told the security guard. "No press allowed."

"Press?" Olive's eyes narrowed.

"Abby's dad," I mouthed.

"Don't go anywhere—either of you." Mr. Mancuzzi turned and grabbed his jacket off the back of his chair. "I'll be right back." The security guard trailed after him out the door, and it clicked shut behind them, leaving us alone.

I didn't waste any time.

"Olive, we have evidence," I said. "We have cold, hard proof. We got Murphy on tape. I used my dad's recorder. He called Tim a—" I paused.

Olive didn't look impressed. She got up and walked to the window, where a tree branch was brushing against the glass. In a few minutes, the fifth period bell would ring and dozens of students would flood through the front door onto the paved path beyond that tree, heading to their next class. How many of them would notice the news van in the parking lot?

"Olive," I repeated. "We have an audio file. It's already online. We just didn't have a chance to give everybody the link. Tim was supposed to—"

"It doesn't matter," she said. "I never should have written that letter."

"What?" I stared at her. "Why?"

"I got carried away."

"The press is here," I said. "This is our chance to prove you right. If we could just get everyone to download the file—"

"Give it up, Reyna."

I stood and approached her from behind.

"Hey," I said.

She didn't answer.

"Hey," I repeated. "You're alive."

"I wish I wasn't."

I wanted to say, "Don't say that." I wanted to apologize again. I wanted touch her arm to make sure she was really there. But she was standing so stiff that all I could bring myself to do was stare at the back of her head and say, "It's not your fault."

Olive looked at me then, her eyes red. "She never got to see New York City," she whispered. "That's where she was headed when she ran away from home. She was only supposed to stay with me for a few days."

"It's not your fault," I repeated.

Olive looked out the window. "She talked about New York like it was heaven. Like it was the only place where she could be herself. I asked her to wait until school was over so I could go with her. I asked her to wait for the summer."

I could see the weight of the confession tugging at the lines on her face. Every nagging thought is a pound of guilt you have to carry around when someone dies, and it takes a long time to lose that weight.

"Wait a minute," I said as something clicked into place. "Grace was the one wearing the jacket, so she must have been the one to buy that ticket. Right?"

Olive frowned, and I realized she had no idea what I meant.

"The ticket to Grand Central," I said. "A few hours before she died. She paid in cash. I thought you knew."

Olive shook her head mutely.

I made up my mind right then. "I'm getting on the computer."

She gave me a skeptical look.

"Keep watch," I said. "If you see Mancuzzi coming back, tell me." Fingers thrumming, I crossed to the other side of his desk, wiggled the mouse, and double-clicked on the Internet icon on his desktop.

"What are you doing?" Olive stared at me. "Are you crazy?"

"Maybe," I answered.

"He's going to be back any minute."

I pulled up the audio file and clicked to start the download.

A blue bar popped up on the screen and began to fill slowly. "Just listen," I said. "It'll only take a minute."

But the file was slow to open, and I kept glancing out the window while it loaded, watching Mr. Mancuzzi argue in the parking lot with the driver of the News Channel Four van. I couldn't see if it was Abby's dad or not.

"Whatever that is, why didn't you just put it on YouTube?" Olive asked, watching the slow progress on the screen. "It would've been faster."

"It's not a video," I started to say, but Levi's voice interrupted me from the speakers on Mr. Mancuzzi's desk, and I saw Olive's back straighten as she heard him ask whether the ancient Romans had a word for gay. Listening to the audio footage was strange after having lived it in person. I cringed at the part when I raised my hand to ask about polygamy, but Olive didn't even raise an eyebrow. She was standing absolutely still, listening to every word. When we got to the part when Mr. Murphy said, "I don't hate faggots. I hate it when they interrupt my class," she stepped forward and leaned over the computer. I thought at first she was going to close the media player, and I bolted straight out of my chair, assuming Mr. Mancuzzi was coming back. But Olive only sat down in my place and leaned in close to the screen. I glanced out the window. Mr. Mancuzzi was still arguing with the driver of the van.

"We have to put it on YouTube," she said, all business. "Nobody's going to download a file we email to the whole school. They'll think it's a virus."

I didn't mean to smile like an idiot, but it was hard not to. "So you agree? It's solid proof?"

"It's good enough."

"Everybody will think I'm Mormon, but I can live with that." I glanced out the window and felt my jaw snap shut. Mr. Mancuzzi was gone. "Never mind," I said. "Olive, get up. He's coming back." The door of the Channel Four van was wide open, and Abby's dad was climbing out. This time, nobody was there to stop him.

Olive looked up, her hand hovering over the mouse. "Are you sure?"

"I think so," I said. "He's not outside."

"I'm almost done converting the file." Her fingers flew over the keyboard. "I just want to overlay some text. And a photo of Grace."

"We don't have time." I moved closer to the window and pressed my forehead to the glass, straining to see left and right beyond the periphery of the window, but it was impossible.

"I want to explain things. I want everybody to know what happened."

"There isn't any time," I said. "Just email it to yourself and we'll do it later."

"Lock the door." Olive glanced up. "It'll buy us a minute."

"Are you crazy?"

"Lock it."

I stood up and twisted the dead bolt, even though it was pointless. I was sure Mr. Mancuzzi carried a key to his own office.

"Should I use this photo, or this one?" Olive asked, tilting her head at the screen. I crossed the room and leaned over the desk to see two pictures of Grace on the screen.

"The smiling one," I said.

"I agree." Olive right clicked it and saved it to the desktop.

"Hurry," I told her. "We're already in trouble as it is."

"I'm hurrying." Olive leaned over and began to type furiously. "Do you think it's fair to say that Grace's last wish was to see justice brought to homophobic teachers?"

"How should I know?"

"You're right." She frowned. "Her last wish was to stare at the sky. I was the one trying to make her talk to me."

I could practically see it—the two of them bundled up in jackets and mittens, lying with their heads against the cold, damp planks of wood along the tracks between the rails. I could see Grace's blank eyes, gazing up at the moon. I could see Olive, full of steam, railing on about Mr. Murphy and me and all the bigots and phonies and cowards in the world. I could see the white light of the train in the distance, barely bigger than a flashlight. And then, suddenly, bigger than the moon.

"Just stick to the facts," I said. "Say she had a teacher like Mr. Murphy. Say she was depressed. Say that a little tolerance goes a long way."

Olive nodded and began to type.

"Say that there are millions of people in her shoes. Say that she—" I didn't get a chance to finish. All at once, the door handle rattled behind me, and I whipped around.

"Girls?" called Mr. Mancuzzi. "Did you lock the door?"

"Quick!" I hissed. "Save the file."

"It's almost finished," she said. "I just have to export it and then upload it."

"It must be jammed, Mr. Mancuzzi!" I called through the door. "We didn't lock it." There was a rattling noise as he stuck a key into the door and twisted the handle. The knob turned freely, but the door didn't open.

"Open the dead bolt!" he called, banging his fist against the wood.

"Stall," said Olive.

"What dead bolt?" I called out. "I don't see a dead bolt."

"Don't get smart with me," he answered through the door. "They have the spare key at the front desk. Are you going to make me go get it?"

"I don't see a dead bolt to unlock," I said again. "Sorry!"

"Shit." Olive was drumming on Mr. Mancuzzi's desk with the pads of her fingers. "I can't remember my YouTube password."

I groaned.

"Do you have an account?"

"My name with three sevens at the end," I said. "Password: bunny."

Olive looked at me and rolled her eyes.

"Hurry up!" I dropped down on all fours and peered underneath the door. There was no sign of Mr. Mancuzzi's feet. "He went to get the key," I said.

"Well, it's uploading." Olive stood up. "I've closed all the windows except for YouTube, which I minimized. We need to make it look like we've been doing something else so he doesn't check the computer."

"The filing cabinet," I said. "We could have been snooping."
I ran over to the big gray wall of cabinets, opened one of the drawers, and began pulling manila folders at random, scattering them on the floor like a careless burglar. When I was halfway through, Mr. Mancuzzi twisted the dead bolt and swung open his office door. I straightened at once like a puppet, an invisible hand yanking on a string connected to my spine.

"What in God's name is going on?" He stared at the papers strewn around the floor.

"I made her do it," said Olive, stepping forward from the desk. "I wanted to see my academic record."

"No she didn't," I said. "It was me. I wanted to see mine."

Mr. Mancuzzi yanked the walkie-talkie from his belt and called security.

"I take full responsibility for this," said Olive, inching her way toward the door. "It was all my idea." At first I thought she was going to make a run for the hallway, but then I realized she was moving toward me with something in her hand. Her smartphone. When she got close, I stepped sideways and positioned my hand to take it from her behind her back.

"I'm all yours, Mancuzzi," she announced as soon as I had a firm grasp on it. She raised both her arms in the air like a criminal. "I surrender." Her posture was straighter and more confident than I'd ever seen it as she glanced back and met my eye. I gave her the tiniest of nods.

Mr. Mancuzzi turned to me. "I don't understand your role here," he said. "But I don't like it."

"I was just looking for my file," I lied again, shoving the

phone into my pocket and following him to the receptionist's desk in the lobby.

"Wait for me here," he said. "Mrs. Latimer will be watching your every move."

I nodded and sat down on the bench while Mrs. Latimer, an old Hispanic woman with a ruffled yellow blouse, pursed her lips at me in disapproval. The minute Mr. Mancuzzi left the lobby, I tapped on the phone and connected to the Internet, which was allowed at Belltown High outside of the class-rooms. My fingers felt slow and clunky as I found the YouTube app and signed in. The upload Olive had started was visible in my account, but it wasn't yet complete so I opened a separate tab, signed into my email, and composed a new message to community@bhs.com.

It took exactly four more minutes for the video to upload. As soon as it did, I copied the URL and pasted it into the email. All that was left to do was choose a subject heading. I typed *WATCH THIS*, and hit Send as the fifth period bell rang.

A funny thing happened. Nobody went to fifth period. Through the big glass wall in the principal's wing, I watched a classroom door open and a couple dozen sophomores wander out. But instead of heading to their next class, they hung around in the hallway. Everyone with a smartphone pulled up the video, and everyone else leaned over their shoul-ders, jostling for a better view. I pulled up the video again on Olive's phone and watched it from start to finish, reading her words as they scrolled in white text over the photo of Grace.

By the time it finished playing, more students and teachers had wandered into the hallway. Mrs. Latimer glanced at the commotion beyond the glass and frowned.

I didn't see Levi come through the glass doors until they swung shut behind him. Then I looked up. He was carrying a hall pass and my backpack, which I'd left on the floor of the auditorium by my abandoned seat.

"Hey," he said, flashing the pass at Mrs. Latimer. "I brought you something."

"Thanks." I stood up to take it from him and our fingers brushed. Immediately, my entire hand felt like someone lit fire to it. But this wasn't the time for romance. Feeling guilty, I pulled my hand away and did my best to ignore the tingling in my fingers.

"Where's Olive?" asked Levi, pulling his own hand away a little too fast.

"With Mr. Mancuzzi." Sitting back down on the bench, I pulled out her phone again and refreshed the video. "Can you believe this?"

"That she's alive?" Levi sat down beside me. "Not really."

"No, this," I said, holding out the phone. "We just posted it to YouTube."

Levi's eyes grew wide as the video began to play. Meanwhile, through the glass wall, I could see a crowd gathering outside the principal's wing. Teachers and students were standing around with their backs toward us, looking at something in the lobby just out of my sight. When the crowd shifted, I realized what it was. Abby's dad was standing in the main entrance, a microphone in his hand, his film crew just behind him. Someone with a camera the size of gallon of milk was stepping into the lobby, panning left and right to capture the chaos. Abby's dad was speaking into the microphone, a deep crease between his eyebrows.

"How many hits has this gotten so far?" asked Levi, looking up from the video and following my gaze toward the lobby.

I took the phone back and scrolled down just below the video. "About a hundred," I told him. "And I only sent it five minutes ago."

"That's crazy."

"No wait." I hit refresh. "Almost two hundred now."

The second bell rang for fifth period, but nobody seemed to pay it any mind. The crowd in the lobby only grew more bloated. And then, without a word, Levi stood up.

"Hey, Mrs. Latimer?"

I watched him approach the reception desk, hands tucked neatly in his pockets. Mrs. Latimer looked up and put down her ballpoint pen. "I was just wondering," said Levi. "Would it be possible to check online to see if Channel Four is streaming the news? They're filming in the lobby."

Mrs. Latimer looked tempted. She peered at the commotion outside and nodded her head. "Go ahead and check."

Levi crossed to the other side of her desk, clicked around for a minute, and found the news channel's website. And there it was. Abby's dad, broadcasting live on the local news.

I looked back and forth between the fuzzy footage on the monitor and the scene unfolding in the lobby beyond the glass wall. Tim Ferguson had pushed his way to the front of the crowd, and Abby's dad was holding out a microphone, interviewing him about homophobia at Belltown High. Tim looked the camera straight in the eye and said, "If you have a soul, watch this video." Then he held up a notebook on which he had scrawled a long URL in permanent marker. "I challenge you," he said. "I challenge all of you to watch this." As the cameraman zoomed in on the notebook, I heard a clamor in real life and turned to see Mr. Murphy burst through the glass doors into the principal's wing.

"Where's Mancuzzi?" he demanded, marching straight up to Mrs. Latimer.

"You'll have to take a seat," she told him, barely glancing up from the monitor. "The principal is occupied."

"Well, I have a letter for him." He slammed a typewritten piece of paper onto her desk. "Please see that it gets delivered."

But she didn't have time to deliver anything. The News Channel Four crew had spotted Mr. Murphy through the glass and was rushing toward the principal's office like a tsunami, six dozen students riding the wave. I had the odd sensation, as the cameramen pushed their way through the doors, of seeing a flash of myself on the news before Mr. Murphy's face filled the frame.

There was a bead of sweat that rolled all the way from his forehead to the edge of his chin. When it disappeared past his collar, he resigned.

Friday, 3:06 p.m.

People looked at me differently in the parking lot that afternoon. I sat by myself on the stone wall while I waited for Lucy to pick me up. Levi had just left to catch his bus, and I could still feel the warm tingle on my lips where he'd kissed me good-bye—right there in the parking lot for everyone to see. When we broke apart, I flipped his guitar pick necklace around so it was right side up, and he gave me one of his floppy, gentle smiles and said, "See you tomorrow." Now I was alone, and most of the freshmen hanging around were people I only vaguely recognized.

But they recognized me. I heard whispering each time they passed and felt their eyes move over me from head to foot, as though in slow motion. At first I thought they must be calling me "that girl on the stage," but then I realized they were saying my name. As for Gretchen and Lennie, they walked straight past me, whispering under their breaths as they crossed the parking lot. Either they didn't see me, or they'd decided to dump me. The funny thing was, I didn't care.

Lucy pulled into the driveway a moment later in her little red Jetta. She rolled up next to me in the fire lane, and I hopped off the wall wondering whether she and Dad already knew about Olive—whether they'd watched Channel Four during the day. "Hi," I said, pulling open the door and dumping my backpack inside.

"Hi," Lucy answered. There was something skittish about the way her eyes darted over to me and then back toward the windshield. At first I thought she was acting weird because she'd heard the news about Olive, but then I remembered how I called her from Dad's car in the morning to make amends. She was probably just nervous around me.

I sat down and pulled the door shut. "How did your appointment go?"

She glanced sideways at me. "My hair appointment?"

"No," I said. "The florist appointment."

"Oh!" Her shoulders relaxed. "It was good."

"Are you going to have violets in your bouquet?"

"Violets?"

"They're purple."

A slow smile spread across Lucy's face. "Purple is my favorite color."

"I know," I said. "That's why I asked." Out beyond the parking lot, beyond the town of Springdale itself, the clouds shuffled in the sky to make room for pale blue patches the color of hope. I turned and looked at Lucy. "Guess what just happened."

acknowledgments

Endless thanks to my dream team of agents, Sarah Burnes and Logan Garrison, for seeing something in me, and to my editor, Kelly Barrales-Saylor, for making this book a reality, and to the entire team at Albert Whitman, especially Kristin Zelazko and Michelle Bayuk, for all the editorial and marketing love.

To my friends and first readers, Jessie Ellner and Ilana Shydlo, for their insight, encouragement, and tact. To my teachers, Mr. D., Anne Fadiman, Michele Stepto, Amy Bloom, Chuck Wachtel, and Darin Strauss, for being more than teachers.

To the writers who gave me a home in Austin: Bethany Hegedus, Vanessa Lee, Kari Anne Roy, Amy Rose Capetta, Cynthia Leitich Smith, Jennifer Ziegler, Lindsey Scheibe, and the rest of the AAW clan, for being more than awesome.

And for their support in innumerable ways: my mother and father; my brother, Michael; my daughter, Naomi; and my husband, Chris, who makes me the most me I could possibly be.

about the author

Sara Kocek knew she was destined to write fiction when she unearthed her childhood diary and discovered it was full of details that never happened. A graduate of Yale University, she also holds an MFA in Creative Writing from New York University. She lives in Austin, Texas, with her husband and daughter. This is her debut novel.